# A COMPLIANCE OF THORNS

## Prologue

The woman suppressed a shud  walking over her grave. The source of her unease was set out in front of her, on the beautifully polished surface of an antique maple writing desk; in the shape of three, circular, fired, black clay tablets, and a fourth in an ugly, dark, mustard yellow. Their surfaces were embossed with sinister looking designs, which looked quite alien; she was familiar with their appearance, from illustrated texts; though these were the first she had ever seen physically. She understood their origin and something of their nature, and no good had ever come from the purposing of them. They were about the size of the palm of her hand and maybe two centimetres high; each of them rested like a sort of bizarre paperweight, where she had laid it, on top of the piece of yellowed parchment that had accompanied it; in the form of a miniature scroll. Fascinated the woman had carefully unfurled each of them, her eyes flickering uneasily over the script, written on them in a muddy coloured ink, and replicating the alien characters on the tablets. They had been given to her in four pouches, made of black felt, which she had set to one side. She glanced at these, tempted to put the tablets, and scrolls back inside them, and then away inside a drawer of her desk. She resisted, determined not to show any sign of weakness or fear to her companion; the man who had delivered them to her, and who occupied a beautiful baroque chair, which was the twin of her own, opposite her.

'I suppose it's too much to hope that Bernadette O'Hare created these?' she asked; her voice was precise; educated but not posh.

The man chuckled. 'Would that make a difference?' His tone was close to disparaging.

'Oddly, yes; bad enough, but...' Her voice trailed away. When she had held the tablets, she had felt an energy crawling inside them; it had felt somehow unclean, echoing the nature of the personality of their maker.

'Bernadette didn't construct them,' the man confirmed.

'I know that.' She admitted. She had known the maker was not Bernadette; Bernadette was a piece of work, but not on the same level as who or what had constructed and charged the four tablets. She drew a prolonged breath and released it with equal deliberation; she felt a slight tremor of anxiety run through it.

'You're being paid a lot of money to do this.' He reminded her, his strange, pale blue eyes studied her, calculatingly.

'I know, and I'll do what I have to do,' She pursed her lips and peered at him a little peevishly. 'But I don't have to like it. I don't have skin in the game like you Nathan.'

He shrugged. 'You're not in the position to be judgemental.'

'No, just perfectly placed to do this dark little errand for you. I must say it came as a surprise to find you and Bernadette teamed up! What bizarre circumstance brought that about?'

'Needs must when the devil drives.'

'And in your case...'

He showed perfect, clenched teeth, in response to her unfinished sentence, in a typically mocking smile, though she thought that she detected an ingredient of self-mockery too. 'There could be the devil to pay if it goes badly.' He remarked. He watched as she picked up each tablet and parchment in turn between her pale fingers; these were slim, the nails unpainted; he knew they were strong, dexterous. She returned the tablets and parchments carefully to their felt pouches. The energy in them seemed to writhe through her fingers as if it was reaching out, poking at her, searching; she shuddered again.

'Place one inside the house, and three outside.' He told her. 'The yellow tablet is by far the most vital. Conceal it where there's plenty of space; with all that will be going on there, their presence won't be felt; Initiate each tablet with intent, set light to its parchment and burn it out on its surface. Make sure you are gone by...'

'I've changed my mind,' the woman announced unexpectedly, when the four felt pouches and their contents, lay in a neat row on the desk.

'You can't, for fucks sake!' He protested; he threw her a look of pure alarm. 'It's too late in the day!'

The woman laughed and shook her head, amused. 'So easy,' she remarked. 'Earlier, I said you weren't invited to spend the night. I've changed my mind. I've decided that I don't want to sleep alone tonight; not with these things in the house.'

He relaxed into his chair, relieved, as he watched her place the four pouches in the drawer in front of her. 'I didn't think you meant it anyway,' he said.

# One

The bodies fell still eventually; voices became silent; no more lust forthcoming; all orgasmed out. Saskia remained still, allowing fatigue to grip her companions; she preferred to avoid unnecessary connection on theses occasions; no longer requiring intimacy. The blinds and curtains were closed, but the subdued light from a Scandinavian design wall light ensured that she would not have to feel around in the dark. She drifted and elsewhere took her, for a time. She shook herself out of it. She pushed a muscular black arm from where it lay stretched out across her breasts and moved her torso from beneath it; he had been the most enduring of the two men. She had manoeuvred her body to the outside, to enable her to exit the bed more fluently; that at least had been the intention. His knee had become inserted between her legs, presumably whilst in her elsewhere state, and she had to wrench her inner leg free, no longer attempting stealth; he remained asleep; he was called Vincent and the apartment belonged to him; he was pleased with its streamlined, expensive look; he believed it impressed; Saskia had feigned admiration; it was too conventionally male for her taste. Free to move, she swung her nude body from the bed and stood up. She eased first one shoulder then the other and heard the left one click. She massaged her lower back as she felt some strain in the muscles; Vincent had tested her flexibility. She regarded the men in the bed dispassionately, black limbs in a tangle of covers.

Saskia glanced at the digital clock. It was three-twenty-two. They had fallen on her like a pair of hungry wolves, as she drank alone at the bar; there had been half a dozen failed attempts to pick her up before then. They drank together for a while and Saskia had pretended to laugh at their jokes. At first, they had indulged in some testosterone fuelled rivalry over the right to be the one to bed her; amused, Saskia had put an end to it.

'You don't need to compete for me?' she had told them in her smoky voice.

Saskia made her way to the bathroom; she took her bag with her. She needed to cleanse; to use her fresh wipes. They had used condoms until the other man, Milo, had dropped out. With mutual intensity she and Vincent had continued for another hour; without. She peed and then cleansed. She opened her phone and called her cab. She returned to the bedroom, to her clothing, which she had left on a chair. A pair of Gucci stiletto heeled sandals, in merlot and a strappy, slightly ruched mini dress in matching merlot, and a little black bolero jacket. She could not locate her flimsy lace panties; she had been wearing them when they took her to bed; she decided to write them off. She was aware that Milo, the other man in the bed was awake; he watched her in silence as she slid into her dress and fastened her sandals; she rested their soles in turn on the seat of the chair, always a risk for the heel of the first shoe, she thought, as she concentrated on balance. She ignored Milo, not wanting to engage; she smoothed down her dress, shouldered her bag, and left.

'Stevie!' It was her middle name. Stevie; not short for anything. She used it when it was convenient, when she needed impersonal sex to distract; when Ayesha was with Khalid and occasionally, when she was not.

Milo had followed her outside; he had hurriedly pulled on jeans and trainers. He was tall, well-muscled, thirtyish. He hunched in the frigid air. Saskia did not appear to feel it. Milo was the easier of the two, more amiable; Vincent his companion was bigger, more powerful, meaner.

'Can I see you again?'

'Not by design.'

'Can I have your number?'

'Not happening.' She had obtained Vincent's number when Milo was absent from the room. It was now on her phone, just in case.

'C'mon, it was good, you're different.'

'It was just okay. I'm not up for grabs. I have someone incredibly special.'

'Then why are you doing this?'

'You wouldn't understand.' A sardonic edge entered her voice.

'Try me.'

'Here's my taxi. Thanks for the sex.'

'Try me, c'mon, I need a reason.' He was persistent.

Saskia looked over her shoulder before climbing into her taxi; she looked him up and down, revealing moderate sympathy.

'It keeps me sane,' she said.

She got the cab driver to let her out at the end of Culverin Road, her usual drop off. On these occasions she needed some head space before she returned to the apartment, which was ten minutes' walk away. She welcomed the cold as it penetrated her underdressed body, sharpening her like a knife. She retrieved her iPod from her bag as she walked and inserted her headphones. She walked with a jaunty elegance as she listened to Abba's *Take a Chance on Me*. She searched the shadows for the ghost, Docker John, along Quayside Walk, as she habitually did, when she returned home from a casual hook-up. There was no sign of him; it was several weeks since she had encountered him, on the night Nathan Xavier and members of the Kadman order had tried to take her, with Docker John's help. He was becoming entity, maybe he had moved on, she thought. She was prepared to wait. She sang sotto voce to *Super Trooper* as she approached the apartment block. In the lift she turned off her iPod and removed her headphones, to listen to the sound of the mechanism.

She let herself into the apartment and saw that Ayesha had also returned home; her coat was hanging on the rack. She had left at seven, looking incredibly beautiful, when Khalid's driver had arrived in his Bentley to collect her. Saskia peered into the living room and then the kitchen, but Ayesha was in neither. She had left a dimmed light switched on in both rooms, presumably for her; she knew that Saskia always returned home before dawn. Empty food wrappers lay discarded on the work surface, Ayesha was often hungry after indulging in a night of sex and alchemically intensified pain. She had devoured a savoury roll from the fridge. And a Twix. Saskia deposited the wrappers in the waste bin, then poured a glass of ice water from the fridge dispenser and turned off the lights. She paused on the way to her room to listen at Ayesha's door. She thought that she could hear the shower in the on suite. That was her next intended destination, in her own room.

She had drunk vodka and slimline coke, but not enough to make her hungover. She never required alcohol to turn off inhibition; she was not made that way. She discarded her 'slut' dress and sandals and examined her body for bruising; she peered at herself in the wall of glass in her on suite, with calm appraising eyes. They perceived a lithe, smooth, professionally waxed Saskia, her only hair the messy, edgy balayage pixie on her head, and her dark, long eyebrows. Her aspiration was toned physicality; engineering without muscularity; through Pilates and Callanetics; a Saskia more familiar with fashion and personal style, who was totally at ease in her own skin. A curated Saskia, on her way to knowing who and how she wanted to be.

She removed the makeup from her face, then entered the large walk-in shower and began to cleanse the last seven hours of Stevie Challoner from her body. Not that it was the sex that Saskia had issues with, or the men and the women with whom she chose to perform it; they meant nothing to her; sex with them was enjoyable theatre and the novelty of having and being had by strangers. On rare occasions though a boundary was breached, and a darker personality entered, and the deviant in her considered a deeper connection with them. That had been the case with Vincent; in that last hour Milo had been in the way. She decided to let it distil for a few days; she had Vincent's number if she decided to reconnect without Milo. She did not like Vincent, but she did like the feeling of menace she got from him. She saw him as a potential counterbalance to Khalid if he met the criteria, and that was of real importance to Saskia; because Stevie Challoner represented her desire to hurt Ayesha, to punish her, for her obsession with Khalid; the other person in their relationship. And she knew that hurt was a toxic little draft, a slow poison and very real. The sex was not the issue. The timing was the issue; the cruelty of like for like. The punishment had to end. Or eventually she would lose the only person she had ever loved. She luxuriated as the air jets blew her skin dry. She chose from a selection of toiletries and moistened and sprayed her body. She emerged from the on suite into the bedroom. Only a dimmed light diffused the darkness. Ayesha had come into the room and lay curled on her side in the bed, a cover drawn up to her hip; she had her back to her, her dark hair concealed the side of her face. Saskia climbed into the bed and very carefully put her arms around her, aware that she would be tender for a few hours yet. She drew in her subtle scents, enjoyed the contact with her skin; she felt the firm rear tuck into her.

'Hello my Ayesha.' She spoke softly into her hair; it tickled her face.

'Hello little Mantis,' Ayesha whispered. She raised her elbow so that Saskia could slide her arm beneath and around her, she let her forearm rest along the top of hers, cupping the back of Saskia's hand on her midriff, with her own.

'Tell me what you have to tell me then.'

They were enthusiastic lovers, and they habitually shared a bed. They were drawn to each other to talk and then sleep even after they had spent the night taking pleasure in someone else. Ayesha had informed Saskia that she intended to continue to remain one of Khalid's mistresses, on the night they became sexually involved and Saskia had accepted that. Ayesha had known in her heart though that Saskia might need time to come to terms with their understanding, after the reality of it sank in. She had not been wrong.

'Not tonight,' Saskia whispered, surprising her. 'Not any night. I've finished being cruel.' She kissed Ayesha's hair.

Progress? Ayesha wondered.

Before Saskia happened, Ayesha's liaisons with Khalid had occurred almost every week. In deference to Saskia, she had negotiated that down to every ten days, or more. Khalid had been unenthusiastic, and Ayesha was the recipient of angst from both quarters. The first time that she had gone to Khalid after she and Saskia had become lovers, had proved to be a nightmare, with Saskia distraught by the time she returned; but on the second occasion it was taken to a higher level. Saskia had been quite relaxed when she came through the door. She had waited up for her and worked on her journals, though as always Ayesha had requested her not to stay up. She had greeted her quietly, with a slightly wan smile. It had been amiable; they had talked for a few minutes; Ayesha had been about to shower. Saskia's expression had hardened, and a coldness had entered her eyes as she studied Ayesha's appearance.

'You didn't use the goad tonight.' The voice had an edge to it. Ayesha had been only tired, not exhausted, as she was after experiencing the alchemically induced pain of the compliance of thorns. There had been no inflammation limning her tattoo.

'We don't always employ it,' Ayesha had responded, defensively. She had sensed the change of atmosphere; it had been far from subtle.

'So, it was simply about sex then?'

'Yes, it was about sex. Khalid and I have sex.'

'It's not just about the compliance of thorns?'

'No, it isn't just about the compliance of thorns. I thought that I made that clear.'

'I see. I don't think that you did.'

'But you know we have sex.'

'I know. But I thought it was the pain you went to him for, and the sex was incidental.'

'Well now you know differently.' Ayesha had been tired, and the words had been spoken more sharply than she had intended.

'Did you know when you arranged to see him that you were just going for sex?'

'Can we talk about this later?'

'We don't have to talk about it later, if you answer my question.'

'Okay. The answer is yes.'

Saskia had said nothing after that; she had bestowed a look of pure dislike on Ayesha and stalked off to her bedroom. That had been the last time they had not occupied a bed together, during any part of a twenty-four-hour period since the start of their relationship. Saskia had appeared at midday, looking sulky, and had proved uncommunicative.

'I'm out tonight,' she had announced casually at around five p.m.

'Okay,' Ayesha had responded, outwardly impassive, but inwardly dismayed. She had not wanted Saskia to go, but it was after all her choice; she had the protection of a mortal covenant too; she could hardly have forbidden it, and she did have a point.

The taxi had collected Saskia at seven-thirty, she had gone out dressed in a tight off the shoulder top, naked sandals, and a black leather mini skirt, which Ayesha had commented was okay, if it was matched correctly with other clothing. Ayesha had decided that she looked like a hooker but had declined to comment.

'Don't wait up for me,' Saskia had said, as she drew on a leather biker jacket. She had waited up for her though, drinking tea and Chardonnay, and reading William Hope Hodgson. Saskia had got back at three-thirty-three looking shattered. Ayesha had been tempted to tell her that she looked well used.

'I told you not to wait up.'

'Well, I did, it's what you do, after all darling. I was worried about you. Leeds hasn't the worst reputation, but it hasn't the best either.'

'I can take care of myself. I'm going to have a shower. Do you want me to join you tonight? I'll understand if you don't.' At least she had reached out, perhaps even had some regrets. She had been tempted to say not to bother, but she had held her tongue.

'If you want to.'

'Do you want me to? You know what I've been doing, you're not naive.'

'You know where my bed is.'

Half an hour later Saskia had slipped into bed next to her. Ayesha had seen her in the dim light of a moon in its last quarter, filtered through the white drapes. She had dressed in a loose shirt, fastened by a single button. She had lain on her back and peered at the ceiling.

'Do you want to know?'

'Not really.'

'I picked up a man, we had sex, but he didn't live up to expectation. So, I picked up another one; he was a bit rough. We had sex in his house on some grotty estate. He was much more capable.'

'What do you expect me to say?' Ayesha's body had tensed as Saskia had related her experiences. Jealousy had entered her solar plexus, like the long blade of a knife. To her surprise she had felt no anger; she was not sure that she had a right to any.

'You don't have to say anything; I'm perfectly capable of saying it all to myself.'

'Let's get some sleep. Will you hold me little mantis?'

'Of course,' Saskia had spoken in barely a whisper.

'You buy a mobile phone when we go into town. You can take it with you. I won't ring you don't worry. It'll be in case you need me for anything.'

Saskia awoke to Ayesha sitting astride her, her pliant mouth pressed down on hers. Saskia blinked at the exquisite face as it peered anxiously down. She had stirred a few minutes earlier, and missed Ayesha's presence in the bed, but then fell back into an easy sleep.

'I've brought us tea. We are okay, aren't we?' Ayesha sat back, her body upright. Saskia's hips were between her ankles. Ayesha was in her black silk dressing gown, it was open, revealing her nakedness; the inflammation caused by use of the compliance of thorns was barely visible now on the skin around her tattoo; her hair, full, dark, and lustrous fell to her shoulders. Ayesha dismounted allowing Saskia to sit and draw up her knees. She offered her a mug of strong tea.

'When you said you were finished being cruel, I thought afterwards that it might imply something else.'

'We're more than okay I promise.' Saskia sipped her tea. 'But there are things we need to talk about.'

'But not today, yes?'

'Not today. It's not that urgent. My god its after one o'clock! How long have you been awake?'

'Almost an hour. Are you hungry?'

'I'm starving.'

'How about an oven Pizza?'

'It works for me. I'll go and put some clothes on. I'll see you in the kitchen.'

'Okay little mantis,' Ayesha smiled, she cast an admiring gaze over Saskia's supple body as she exited the bed.

'You are stunning,' she could not help remarking.

Saskia glanced back over her shoulder; her familiar tight smile formed on her lips before she turned away again; even the mystery in her green eyes seemed to have deepened in the weeks since they had met, Ayesha decided.

'Envying my rear again? I promise you, yours shades it by a whisker,' Saskia responded, and meant it.

Ayesha grinned appreciating the compliment. 'You're toning up, don't go over the top and turn into one of those bodybuilder types, will you?'

'Not a chance. Date, kitchen, five minutes.'

'Date.'


'Claire's party.' Said Ayesha, she sank her white teeth into the pointed end of a slice of double pepperoni pizza.

'What about it?' Saskia asked grimly, in mid chew; she felt butterflies take off inside her abdomen. She had been dreading the event for three weeks since it had been announced and she and Ayesha had received their VIP invitation.

'We must be there in just over five hours. We need to set off at six.'

'Fine, I know what I'm wearing.'

'We've got to sort your makeup. I'm not giving you a free hand with it.'

'Thanks.'

'Don't look at me like that; you are improving but it's my one artform until I take up sculpting in my fifties. You sit at four o'clock in front of my mirror, which gives us plenty of time. Then I can do my own.'

'You'll be worn out,' Saskia joked.

'No, I won't silly! anyway you're driving us up there.'

'You want to travel up in my Jeep? A wrangler isn't the sort of vehicle you want to arrive in surely?'

'No, you can drive us up there in my car. You are down on my insurance.'

'Are you sure about this?' Saskia had passed her driving test a few weeks previously after a harrowing two-week intensive course.

'Why? How fast do you intend to drive?'

'Not very.'

'Exactly.

'Okay then, that's cool.' Saskia looked pleased by the idea of doing the driving in Ayesha's BMW.

'Have you decided what you are going to play?' Ayesha asked, her eyes lit by enthusiasm. Saskia had reluctantly agreed to play a set on the Lute during the evening; Claire was persuasive; and she recognised that she owed her; she had welcomed her, to her house for several weekends and let Saskia practise entering Location, in her own Place. Magic, Saskia had discovered, was not a prerequisite to accessing Place. She recalled her excitement when she had first achieved it, with embarrassment.

As though reading her mind, Ayesha folded her arms and compressed her lips into mock sternness.

'You're not going to hide in Claire's Place, are you? Now you've attained the skill.'

'I must come across as ungrateful.'

'Yes. This party is about you, you know.'

'That's what worries me Ayesha, I'm scared that I might get stage fright.'

'But you're used to playing in public.'

'Busking. It's not the same. You mostly get ignored.'

'Are you really scared little mantis?'

'Don't worry, I won't bottle it. Oh, and makeup isn't your only artform.'


'Will snuggles be okay on his own until tomorrow?'

'I was in Italy for two weeks last year. It was perfectly okay roaming about the apartment on its own.'

'I hope he's not lonely.' Saskia frowned.

'You're serious aren't you. I promise you it exists in the moment; it has one purpose. You know, I honestly don't know when you're winding me up.'

Saskia grinned and opened the BMW's door for Ayesha to get in, surprising her.

Ayesha was in a short, sleeveless dress, in Persian red with matching stiletto heels; She climbed into the passenger seat with easy elegance, the skirt riding her thighs to midway, over her shiny silk stockings, helped by a six-inch slit at her left knee. This would be the first occasion that she had been a passenger in her own car.

'Thank you,' she said softly, smiling in pleasure.

Saskia was wearing a short, black skirt and a fitted, black jacquard jacket, its red threading portraying frogs, and dragonflies; under it, was a pretty, white lace camisole, the top three buttons undone; it showed off a stunning Antique necklace. She was going to drive in her moccasins, but she had brought kitten heels in black suede with round toes to change into. She put these on the back seat together with her lute and their overnight case and slid into the driving seat. She breathed in the smell of still present newness of the soft black Nappa upholstery; she took enjoyment in the presence of the beautiful young woman in the passenger seat. She engaged with the interior workings of Ayesha's car; she had studied Ayesha's fluent driving skills closely and she was familiar with the instrumentation of the BMW's dashboard. Driving was still a new and pleasurable experience to her. She started the hungry engine, shifted into first gear, and rested her lean fingers on the black leather steering wheel; their pointed nails were professionally manicured and painted red. She took them smoothly out of the carpark under the block and along quayside walk into the Leeds traffic; thrown for a moment as they drove out of Leeds when Ayesha quietly suggested cruise control, rather than drive right up the arses of the cars in front, for the rest of the journey; she began to enjoy the sensation of the drive.

'I'm going to play four pieces; all of them my own.' Saskia announced unexpectedly.

'How Avant Garde of you. I'm impressed.'

'I'm petrified at the thought.'

'Imagine that you are playing just for me. I haven't heard you practising.'

Saskia shrugged. 'It'll be okay.'

'I am looking forward to it you know. You haven't played for me in weeks.'

'You never ask me to.'

'It doesn't mean that I haven't wanted you to.'

'We always seem to have other things to occupy us.'

'Is that all we are about: sex?'

'No, far from it! There are shoes. Bags. Jewellery.' They both began to laugh, quite merrily.

# Two

The drive and grounds of Claire's beautiful country home had been turned into an avenue of bright lights that led off into Claire's paddock, which had been designated a temporary carpark. Her dapple grey and its donkey companion had been stabled for the night. Saskia parked nose on with a vintage red Alfa Romeo convertible.

'I believe that belongs to Denise Cardray-Adams, she valued the contents of your houses for the firm,' Ayesha remarked.

They were met at the door by Claire, who looked incredibly sexy in a white wrap over dress that showed smooth tanned legs; it had a plunging neckline, which revealed the nude inner curves of her breasts; Saskia stared at her amazing legs. She had changed her hairstyle too since they had last seen her a couple of weeks before, and she was now sporting a blonde high-low bob. She smiled welcoming them into the spacious entrance hall of her eighteenth-century house. It was lit by lamps that created a warm ambience. The floor was flagged, and the ceiling heavily beamed; a broad staircase climbed to a gallery corridor. The furniture reflected Claire's period taste for Yew, maple, and walnut. A yew wood longcase clock by John Ellwood of Whitefriars was chiming seven as they came inside.

'You two look lovely,' she greeted, and kissed them both on their cheeks. 'About twenty guests are here. There will be about forty in all. I'll look after your Lute; I'll make sure it's safe. I'm really looking forward to you playing.' She took Saskia's cased Lute from her.

'Wow Claire, what about you?' Ayesha said, she leaned back to admire Claire's appearance.

'You're hot.' Saskia told her.

'Thank you, young ladies and so do you.' Claire smiled, grateful for their approval. 'Saskia you change every time I see you.'

'For the better I hope.'

'You're truly a beautiful young woman.'

Saskia's ears pinked, and her gaze fell away; compliments still took her by surprise. 'I've stopped hiding myself away. The rest is down to Ayesha.'

'Don't believe it. I only guide.'

'No, you inspire.'

Claire stared at Saskia's stunning antique necklace. 'Saskia your necklace, is it by Giuliano?'

'Yes. Ayesha bought it for my birthday. It was very naughty of her, but I adore it.'

'It suits you. It's beautiful. Everyone will admire it. Speaking of which, everyone is a friend here, magicians and some non-magicians, it's a safe place. Try to relax.'

'I will and thank you; you've been incredibly kind to me.'

Claire experienced an uncomfortable sense of guilt. She could almost feel herself squirming; she had arranged an attempt to have Saskia taken for her own protection by the Shee; it had failed and that comforted her, but the plan had originated with her, and that fact did not sit comfortably. She was grateful when Ayesha spoke.

'Come on little mantis, let's find the chardonnay.'

Saskia grinned and nodded; they passed on through the period entrance hall into the living room watched by Claire; she became aware of their interlocked fingers and smiled. She wondered how she had missed it for so long. They had visited her on several occasions over the weeks since Saskia had become Ayesha's charge, to practise entering her Place, but also because Claire enjoyed having them there. They had never given any sign that they were intimate, until only a couple of weeks ago, when Saskia had let it slip.

The living room continued the flagged and beamed theme of the house and was lit in the same ambient way, with a collection of figural lamps stationed on the polished period furniture. The fire was alight, logs sparking, it created a gleeful atmosphere, which appealed to Saskia. Across the fire breast, and about four feet in length, a fine Victorian reproduction of a medieval broadsword rested in iron hooks, which were sunk into the brickwork. It had belonged to Claire's father who had collected antique arms and armour. The rest of his collection was stored in the Place; the displayed broadsword was Claire's salute to her father. Saskia had intended to examine the sword during several of her visits but had never got around to it; she decided that tomorrow morning she would do so. Soft music was playing through speakers and about a dozen people were scattered about, holding relaxed conversations; a few interested looks were thrown in their direction, but they did not linger. Saskia could hear more conversation and some laughter coming from the large dining room next door.

'Don't stray, there are lots of awfully bad people here, who will try to steal you from me.' Ayesha deliberately raised her voice and tightened her hold playfully on Saskia's hand. 'Be particularly careful of this one. Hello Holly.'

A slight young woman immediately detached from a conversation with a couple of other guests, as she saw them enter through the opened doors; she approached them. She was pretty, with a straight brown symmetrical bob falling to her shoulders and laughing brown copper eyes. She had an elfin look. She was in a rust-coloured mini dress and red kitten heels; A cornelian choker glinted around her throat in the malevolent way cornelian can. She peered wide eyed at Saskia with open curiosity, even fascination. She brushed Ayesha's elbow in greeting and held out her hand to Saskia, who caught the slow flash of cornelian on her finger.

'Hello, Ayesha.'

'Holly Penn, meet Saskia Challoner.'

'You're famous Saskia,' Holly said grinning.

'Famous? Why am I famous?' Saskia's expression hardened.

'Ooh! Isn't she fierce? not that famous. Just among a few of us who care.' Holly seemed amused by Saskia's confrontational look. She held up an empty wine glass and released Saskia's hand.

'I need more alcohol. It's all very informal but there is an extremely cute young Cuban guy overseeing the bar, who I would probably take home with me tonight, if I wasn't staying over.' She led them to where the drinks were to be found, under a dramatic seascape of storm-tossed ships by Ivan Aivazovskiy. Ayesha cast no more than an indifferent glance at the bartender; Saskia because it was her way, appraised him more efficiently. Good looking, probably excellent in bed. Easily forgotten.

'Two glasses of Chardonnay,' she said. As they walked away with their drinks, Holly Penn resumed their conversation.

'You're famous because you are fettered, and you have a champion, the one next to you guzzling Chardonnay, who is apparently willing to defend you to the death against half an order, intent on seizing you for some mysterious purpose. Oh, and the small matter of a mortal covenant in your name, with the seals of three of the most powerful adepts in the UK attached. Four in fact, because you have a secret seal on your covenant and only a powerful adept can remain anonymous.'

'Shame that I can't.'

'No. Not now that you're the mysterious Saskia Challoner. I'm really looking forward to your Lute playing, by the way. Baroque or Renaissance?'

'Street,' replied Saskia coldly.

Holly grinned and giggled, unfazed. 'Even better.'

'Shall we get something to eat?' Ayesha asked. She was quietly enjoying Saskia's interaction with Holly Penn; it would do her good to mix with some different people, she thought. But they had only had the Pizza to eat since the previous evening and it was starting to tell.

'Yes, I'm starving,' Saskia said.

'The buffet is next door in the dining room, as you'd expect,' Holly supplied brightly. 'Do you mind if I tag along?'

'That would be nice,' Ayesha assured her, she glanced at Saskia; she smiled and pulled in her lower lip to trap between her teeth.

'I'll just rescue Diz from the secretions, she looks about ready to snap,' Holly said.

'I know the feeling. I want to throttle her,' Saskia said when Holly was out of hearing. Sullenly, she glanced at the unleashed amusement dancing in Ayesha's eyes.

'No, you don't. she's harmless.'

'She keeps giving me little silent giggles. She's like a little field mouse sitting on the end of a corn stalk, giggling.'

'There is not a bad bone in her body, I assure you. The wine's making her giggly. Make a friend of her, you won't regret it.'

'Why haven't you?'

'I don't make friends, to my shame.'

'Then why recommend me to?'

'Because I think that I might have been wrong. Until you came along, my only friend was Claire, and I believe even she thought that I was a lost cause. I weakened for a moment and took a chance on you, which surprised me. And look how that has turned out.'

'You were very doubtful. You almost sound regretful?'

'I was. And no, I'm not, it was the best decision I've ever made.'

'But you're not my friend you're much more.'

'Little mantis. You are my best friend, and you are my true love.'

She watched Saskia's expression melt. Saskia's head dropped forward and when she raised it again a few moments later she was smiling.

'Okay, I'll give her a chance. What does she do?'

'She's a professional artist and an incredibly good one.'

'Really? What size miniature or step ladder?'

'You can be a little cow sometimes. Her paintings sell for several thousands of pounds. She has her own gallery. And she shows in London and New York. She's a talented lady.'

'She hides it well.'

'Talk to her. Here she comes with Diz.'

'Ayesha, you already know.' Holly performed the introductions.

'Ayesha.'

'Hi Diz.'

'And this is Saskia Challoner.'

'Hello Diz.' Saskia was uncertain.

'Diz is fine, it's short for Denise. I'm frazzled. I've just been given the third degree by Amber and Pearl Shalako.'

'Who about?' Ayesha smiled. 'As if I didn't know.'

'You're not wrong; the two of you. More specifically, you.' Her blue eyes peered intensely at Saskia. Diz was slim, a cool good looking forty something, with a straight stance and a firm voice. She was in an off the shoulder knee length electric blue dress with a short v cut between her breasts; a diamond spider brooch glittered on her left. Her hair was straight and fair, brushed back and falling behind her shoulders revealing diamond drop earrings, matching her short azure diamond necklace. Her expression seemed mostly considered; her smile had remained a hint at the corners of her firm mouth. She was holding a glass of wine in either hand. She saw Saskia observe them.

'Exactly. After that I need alcohol. Avoid them if you can; they do hunt as a pair.'

'Saskia. Diz is Denise Cardray-Adams, the auctioneer who valued the contents of your properties.'

'Of course, I did! There were some fabulous things. Have you done anything with them?'

'Not yet. But I'm seriously thinking about spending a few days in Thirsk soon, so I can have a proper look.' This made Ayesha peer curiously at Saskia; it was the first she had heard about her intention, though it did make sense. Or maybe she was just making conversation. She could not decide if she felt slightly annoyed or slightly hurt that Saskia had not confided in her. She decided on both. Holly was speaking, asking her something. *What do I think? Of what?* she gave Holly her full attention. Well seventy percent of it anyway.

'If you need me, you know where to get in touch. No pressure.' Diz said.

'Absolutely. It would be good to be guided by a skilful hand.'

'You would have my undivided attention.'

'That's your vintage, Alfa Romeo convertible we parked next to in the paddock, isn't it?'

'Drop tops are called a Spyder.'

'A Spyder, why?' Saskia was genuinely interested. The name was evocative.

Diz smiled, but it was still restrained. Saskia could not decide if it was meant to be condescending.

'The bad boys in the Georgian aristocracy used to race each other in light carriages, they took extraordinary joy in terrorising the peasants. The carriages had large wheels with thin spokes that made them look like a spider; so, that is what they called them. The name stuck, so even now Later car manufacturers give it to sporty versions.'

'A history lesson too.'

'Just some of the crap hanging around in my head. When you come up, I'll take you out for a drive in it. We could have lunch.'

'Or dinner.'

Diz's eyebrows delved into an amused frown, her eyes searched Saskia's expression. She was a good auctioneer; she could interpret a poker face; this girl was hard to read.

'You're a bit different, aren't you?' she remarked dragging out her words.

'I suppose I am.'

'Come on you two time to eat,' Holly said breaking into their accord.

'I need more alcohol,' Diz announced, holding up her two empty glasses. 'I'm going for a top up. I'll follow you in.'

'Making friends?' Ayesha inquired falling into step beside Saskia as they made their way to the dining room. She tilted her body, and peered around, trying to see Saskia's expression.

'You said I should.'

'I did, didn't I?' Ayesha said with a wry smile.

It was filling up in both receptions, most of the guests had arrived and there was the buzz of laughter and conversation, permeated by the easy music. They went to the buffet which was starting to draw guests. Saskia stood next to Holly.

'There are drinks. Diz could have filled up here. Think she knew?'

'What do you think. She had other things on her mind though,' Holly grinned.

'Ayesha tells me you are quite an artist.'

'My daubs? I enjoy making them.' Holly's grin reduced to a wide smile.

'I would love to see some of your paintings.'

'I can usually tell when I'm being patronised.' Holly flashed her brows. The mask of laughter fell away for a moment and her expression became a little dark and a little sardonic, though the warmth in her eyes remained.

'Am I being patronising?' *Not to be underestimated then*, Saskia thought.

'I'll wait until you've played your Lute, then I can decide how I sound.'

'I don't care if I'm being patronised,' Saskia replied, her voice drawling into laughter.

'Then we understand one another, don't we?'

'I think we do.'

'Start afresh?'

'Why not?'

'Friends?'

'I'd like that.'

'Do you really want to see some of my paintings?'

'God yes. It might be a while though.'

'There are three of them in the house.'

'Here in Claire's house?'

'Have you been in her office?'

'No, I haven't.'

'I'll ask Claire if it's okay to take you in there.'

'Cool.'

Ayesha had stepped back from the buffet with a full plate. She relieved Saskia of hers. 'If you grab that chair, we can occupy the little couch and table next to the terrace doors. I think you'll like Holly's pictures. There's nothing pedestrian about them I promise you. Are you warming?'

'I'm getting there. She's okay.'

'You two sit, I'll get us fresh drinks.'

'I can see you're good for her,' Holly said when Ayesha left them. 'I like her, though I don't see that much of her, but she's never looked happier. I know that you'll hurt her but try not to hurt her too much will you?'

'She's good at hurting herself. I can't do anything about that.'

'You'll find a way. Has she hurt you?'

'I'm bullet proof.'

'Which means she has. She doesn't mean to.'

'That doesn't excuse it. But I swear it won't change how I feel about her. Are you an Archer of Lugh, Holly?'

'Where did that come from? Yes, I am.'

'What about Diz?'

'Diz is a lone player. Like most of the people at the party. Most magicians aren't members of orders or Associations.'

'And are there many Archers of Lugh here tonight, it just interests me?'

'There are a few. If you want me to count them, I will. There are some you should meet. Others maybe you should avoid.'

'Like the Shalako's. What did you call them? The secretions.'

'Amber and Pearl. Yes, they are Archers of Lugh.'

'You're not a fan?'

Holly gave a little shrug. 'Not many people are.'

'Then why are they here?'

'They are Claire's twin nieces. Her sister's daughters.'

'Is her sister here, I didn't know she had one?'

'Not unless she's in visitation.'

'Oh, how did she die?'

'She screwed one demon too many. I can't read that look!'

'It is inscrutable, isn't it?' Ayesha laughed as she returned with drinks on a small tray. 'I promise that she's not doubting you. I think she's processing whatever it is that you just told her. Which was?'

'Helen's death by demon.'

Ayesha began to chuckle. She sat down next to Saskia. She put down the drinks and cupped her fingers across her mouth and laughed into them. Saskia smiled, amused, liking the sight. Ayesha's laughter lasted for over a minute, while Saskia looked on indulgently, fingers interlocked in her lap.

'Fucked to death by a demon!' Ayesha gasped about half-way through her laughter. 'What a way to go.'

'Sorry Saskia,' she said at last. 'I don't know what came over me. Some of us take non-human lovers. Some of us do fuck with demons. Or in your case ghosts, Saskia.'

'I've been thinking that maybe I should revise my definition of them and refer to those ones as entities in the future,' Saskia remarked.

Holly's eyes widened and she gazed in curiosity from Ayesha to Saskia.

'Helen took demons as lovers,' Ayesha continued. 'Incubi and Succubae, Imps et al. Demons, and I am calling them that for convenience, enjoy intercourse with humans. They like sex as much as we do. Maybe more. But as time went on Helen's tastes became more exotic. In fact, abnormal. Never mention this to Claire. Or, that I laughed!'

They talked about ordinary things for a time, and then Ayesha and Holly began to point out Archers of Lugh, who were in the room or as they came to the buffet from the other reception room. Saskia watched them with interest, and the other guests, all who possessed magic, as they transited through; she realised how like ordinary everyday people they all appeared. Some were plain, others beautiful and stylish, old, and youthful, mean looking or happy, and all things in between. She considered the premise that if there were an equal number of people in the house without any magic, whether the two groups would be distinguishable from each other, and she decided that they would not be, there was nothing outwardly to tell them apart; not even a sense of difference; not to her, under ordinary circumstances anyway. She would ask Ayesha if she was aware of any sense of difference she decided. And the everyday worlds of magicians were no different to their counterparts; it was the individual who made the difference. And fucked Demons. She wondered if all the non-magicians were all aware that the rest were magicians, and which ones they were. Interesting; she would ask Ayesha, better still Claire.

Saskia realised that somehow it had got to eight-forty; she had become absorbed in conversation. A coolness transmitted from the glazed terrace doors. It touched her back with trailing fingers and she gave a little shiver. She turned peering at the heavy darkness beyond the illuminated terrace.

'I'm going to freshen up, and prepare I suppose.' She told Ayesha and Holly. 'I'm playing at nine, I don't know why I agreed to it.' She got up and headed to the downstairs bathroom; it was large with three toilets and had obviously been designed with party guests in mind. It had been declared the preserve of the female guests for the night. Saskia was familiar with it; she had been to Claire's house on several occasions by then and knew her way around most of it. She had her bag with her, containing anything that she might need; including a little toothbrush, she hated the idea of food in her teeth. She checked her white teeth in the mirror; they seemed okay, but she brushed them anyway. Then checked her lipstick. Had another look at herself. God, she looked quite hot! Ayesha had applied her makeup for her skilfully, and to be honest it made her feel quite good about herself. She knew that she was capable at least in part of low self-esteem; but tonight, that did not seem to be an issue; she felt relaxed and confident and even the thought of playing to an attentive audience, no longer seemed as intimidating.

She went to pee; while she was in the luxurious cubicle, she heard someone enter the bathroom. She emerged from the cubicle and found herself face to face with the secretions; Amber and Pearl Shalako.

They were identical twins, aged in their late twenties. They were very pretty and supple, and lightly freckled. One had her hair in a tangled pixie with a green rinse; she was wearing a short, green dress, off one shoulder, with a diagonal collar, and green stilettos; the other had her natural dirty blonde hair in an asymmetrical bob; she was dressed in a taut, black, faux leather, mini dress and black heels; they were short of Saskia's height by a couple of inches. Saskia found herself being appraised by two pairs of calculating grey-green eyes.

'Pearl,' said the twin with the green hair.

'Amber,' said the other. They introduced themselves in voices free of inflection. Neither friendly nor unfriendly.

'Saskia,' responded Saskia in the same impersonal tone.

'We were waiting to get you on your own,' Pearl said.

'I see. Do you mind if I take my jacket off before we start?'

'Start what?' inquired Amber, frowning.

'The fight. It's just that they always get so messy, and I don't want to tear my jacket.' Saskia slid the jacquard jacket from her shoulders, she held it up by the collar and went to hang it on the back of the door.

'Right. Ready, and no banging teeth into the edges of sinks; heads are fair game.'

'What are you on about? You don't sound common, so why do you think we've come for a fight.' Demanded Pearl.

'I just put the accent on, I'm common as muck really.'

'That is such bunny crap!' exclaimed Amber scornfully.

'You know that we haven't come for a fight.' Pearl folded her arms.

'Yeah, I know. I was taking my jacket off anyway. I'm playing in my shirt. What do you want to know? You've been talking to enough people about me; I don't know why you didn't come to me in the first instance.'

'There's absolutely no point starting at the end game. The journey is the fun part. Don't you want to know what other people are saying about you?' said Amber coyly.

'They can say what they like, it wouldn't be as dark as the truth.'

'You're fettered; it makes you interesting. And a couple of the dark orders were interested in you. What for?'

'Why should I tell you?'

'I heard that your mother fettered herself. And fettered you because she hated you.'

'Whoever told you that hit the nail on the head.'

'Is it true that you were a hooker?'

'Yeah, when Nathan Xavier found me, I was entertaining three Saudi businessmen at the same time. They pay well you know. And I almost didn't want to leave my old life behind. The sex was so good.'

'Nathan tells it differently. According to him, when he found you, you were turning tricks in an alley for a fiver. he says that you begged him to have sex with you and when he did, that you howled like a bitch in heat, and pleaded with him to comply you, so that he could humiliate you every day.'

'Did he tell you all of that, while you were in bed with him, sucking a ball each?'

'He is so not in our league. And yeah, I know, oh my god, what was auntie Claire thinking about? I mean the man will fuck just about anything on legs. You, Diz Adams, Holly Penn, Frances Kadman, your mother, our mother, Amelia... oh, yeah! Even miss bitch Ayesha Shah. And who hasn't fucked that? We only play together.'

'Why not?' Saskia shrugged, she pushed out her under lip and nodded. 'If I had a twin that looked as hot as me, why would I need anyone else?'

'We know that you're going down on Shah, everybody says so. Also, we're staying the night too. We know that you're sharing a bed. We are in the bedroom next to yours as a matter interest. If we get too noisy, don't bother banging on the walls, we'll not hear you.'

'Don't worry about it, we won't hear you over the noise that we'll be making.'

'Claire says that Shah was prepared to die for you. I get it. I'd die for Amber.' She looked directly at Amber, who stared straight back at her, deadpan.

'What? You know I would.' Amber insisted after a few seconds' unbroken silence.

Pearl redirected her attention to Saskia. 'I hope your playing is crap. And if you don't see us applauding it's not because we are doing it inside.'

Saskia grinned pleasantly.

'Much as I'd like to stay and chat on, I must go now. It's been an experience.'


'It's after nine I thought you'd bottled out,' Ayesha met Saskia in the hall, she looked anxious. 'I was coming to find you.'

'I got waylaid, by the Shalako's.'

'What did they say to you? Are you okay?'

'I think it was a draw. Here's Claire with my lute.'

'Hal and Amelia are here. Last to arrive of course.'

'I didn't know they were coming.'

'Why wouldn't they?'

'Are you ready sweetie,' Claire said as she came up to them. She handed Saskia her lute case. Saskia took it and passed her jacket to Ayesha.

'As I'll ever be. Where am I playing?'

'In the main reception. Alfredo the bartender has connected you a microphone and speakers, apparently, he's a DJ in another life.'

Saskia's breathing quickened and a little pleasureless orgasm of panic passed through her. She followed Claire into the main reception, Ayesha was right beside her, she felt her fingers flex between hers.

'We set you up a barstool, I looked for you to see if you needed anything.'

'I got delayed. I don't need the bar stool; I'll hitch one leg on the back of that armchair if that's okay.' Saskia felt her chest tighten, she could hear her own breathing, it was very loud, it sounded harsh and did not seem to be doing what it was designed to do.

She saw Hal, he was standing by the fire, his elbow rested on the sandstone mantlepiece which had been built into the brickwork below the broadsword; he was drinking a cocktail; a heavy-set man was talking at him. His strange eyes fell on Saskia, and he nodded a greeting, the corners of his mouth curved into a partial smile. He turned to the man and raised an index finger to his lips silencing him. Amelia was sitting with Holly Penn drinking a cocktail. Her platinum hair was shorter than when she had last seen her; her grey close-fitting dress more restrained and to the knee, and she was wearing kitten heels instead of stilettos. She smiled at Saskia and winked. Diz was standing and watching, head tilted to one side, her face expressionless: her eyes quite distant. She was aware of Claire removing the stool and moving the microphone closer to the back of the chair she had selected. She tried not to think about the forty sets of eyes on her as she walked into the space provided for her.

Her legs were trembling, and she really hoped all eyes were on her pale face and not her shaking knees. She hitched one side of her rear onto the back of the chair and braced with her other jerking leg. At some point she had taken her lute out of its case; she could not remember doing so. She looped its strap over her head. She straightened her upper body and raised her chin a little; she found herself looking directly into Ayesha's eyes; she saw an expression in them that she had never encountered there before; pride in her, and she knew that she felt incredibly good about it. She smiled briefly, almost shyly. Ayesha blew her a little kiss and released her; she moved her gaze and made a crooked reluctant half smile as she looked around all the watching eyes for the first time, each of them focused on her, centre stage. She had never experienced anything quite so horrific. A more detached part of herself noticed that Diz Cardray-Adams was no longer where she had seen her. In fact, no longer present. It noticed that the Shalako's had appeared; they were standing in the doorway, watching her, amused.

'Hi everyone,' she heard herself say, she felt and heard the nervous quaver in her voice. But it was a husky voice, deep, but not too deep, and it drawled just a little and it seemed to hide its nerves well. 'I'm Saskia Challoner, yes that one, the girl with the fetter. I've been asked to play the lute. I hope I don't disappoint. It's all my own music so there's only me to blame.' She released her breath in a little shudder that she kept away from the microphone. She was relieved; it was at perfect height. She felt the plectrum she had put in her trouser pocket, between her fingers, and she looked down at the strings of her lute and began to play the composition she had named several weeks ago, when she played it for Ayesha.

Hal was speaking to her. He studied her face with his heterochromic eyes; he smiled as she raised her eyes to his. 'Hi Hal,' she said, smiling back. She was aware of a ripple of fading applause, and guests transiting back into conversation. She had not been playing for at least a couple of minutes, and she knew that she had not acknowledged any of the applause.

'Hello Saskia. I'd ask for an encore, but you look as though you need a drink first.' Amelia appeared next to him, smiling also.

'I think you should get her one darling. I suggest a vodka martini.'

'That's an excellent choice,' Saskia agreed.

'And one for me, and I know that Ayesha's partial.'

'You can play that thing!' Amelia remarked, admiringly.

'She certainly can,' said Ayesha coming up beside her, she slipped an arm around Saskia's waist. 'I saw some condescension at first, you wiped that off their faces little Mantis!'

'There's an underlying trait throughout humanity,' Amelia remarked. 'So many of us enjoy seeing someone fail.'

A couple of minutes later Hal returned with four vodka martinis on a tray, he offered them around, retaining one.

'We're late to the party literally. Hal's fault. Though we were determined to be in time for your playing. I thought you might be good, but I was not expecting quite that level of skill.'

'We thought that we'd listen to you play and then eat,' said Hal. 'Will you join us?'

'I could manage a bit more. What about you Ayesha?' Saskia asked grinning as she squeezed Ayesha's waist.

'Just a morsel perhaps.' Ayesha allowed them to fall behind Amelia and Hal as they made for the dining room.

'This is kudos,' she said. 'Oh, and I saw you eyeing the hot taco fillings earlier. Nada, if we are having sex tonight.'

'Why?' Understanding dawned quickly. 'Oh, absolutely not.'

'I had an interesting conversation over the phone about you tonight, I asked an almighty favour of a man,' Hal said to Saskia when they were seated again and eating. 'It's why we were late.'

'About me?' Saskia gave Hal a worried stare, it gave her, Amelia noted, an almost sulky look. Saskia folded her arms and enclosed her elbows in her hands.

'What about me?' Saskia felt cold fingers creeping over her skin. There was still too much that she did not understand, and she knew that she was still far from secure, even with the mortal covenant in place.

'You're frightening her,' said Amelia.

'I don't mean to. We're proposing that we meet up in the morning. You, Ayesha, Claire and the two of us. There are some things that must be discussed. There is something that I don't have to keep until then. It has to do with your fetter.'

'In that case, I need to know if its good news or unwelcome news, before you go any further?'

Tears began to swim in Saskia's lambent eyes. She fought against them; Ayesha had put too much effort into her makeup to risk destroying it for the sake of a bit of emotion.

'It's positive news. The fetter can be undone. But the process is no quick fix. It's not straightforward. It is dangerous to you, there is a risk to your life. It is no walk in the park.'

'I never thought that it would be,' Saskia replied, she was aware of Ayesha squeezing into the chair with her, of her arms circled tightly around her upper arms and body, she felt her breath on the side of her face as she nuzzled. She could feel her trembling, even though she was trembling herself.

'Even the preparation is dangerous. The transaction is truly hazardous. And there will be pain, like none you have ever experienced. But before any of this can happen, there is something we must do and if we can't; we fall at the first hurdle.'

'What is that?' Saskia's lips had become numb, she was aware that she was excited and scared; but on a deeper psychological level Hal's announcement challenged her composure and her balance, and she had been unprepared for that. She found herself struggling desperately to stay calm.

'The Bran who originally constructed your fetter must be found to make any of this possible. But first you must decide if it is worth the risk, potentially to your life and if not your life, then perhaps to your mind. Take some time to think it through.'

Saskia responded at once, her expression dogged. 'To me it's worth the risk. I've had years to think it through, whatever the risks, whatever the consequences, I'm prepared for them, I hope.'

'And that's your decision?

'That is my decision.'

'So be it Saskia. But we need to find the Bran. I promise you that you will not be alone in all of this.'

'You know where I'll be little Mantis,' said Ayesha with quiet determination. 'Every step of the way.'

'You can count on me too,' Amelia promised. 'Maybe you should have left this until tomorrow, Hal. She's shaken.'

'She can take it. Can you Saskia?'

'Yes, I can take it. I'll take anything that's thrown at me. But I think that I need another drink.'

By midnight, the party buzz had ceased. Claire had called time at eleven, and all but a couple of the guests who were not invited to stay over had driven away. Holly came to find Saskia and led her away from Hal, Amelia, and Ayesha where they had settled by the fire. Saskia's thoughts had gone into overdrive after Hal's revelation about her fetter, she had them under control now, but she felt stressed and stifled; she realised she wanted space; she was grateful when Holly came for her. They ascended the staircase in the hall to the second floor and made for Claire's office at the end of the main corridor where Claire had hung Holly Penn's paintings. Saskia was familiar with Claire's house by then, but there remained rooms she had never seen.

Holly opened the door and felt for the switch, flooding the room with stark light. Claire's home office was a very personal workspace. It held nothing that was related to business. A Georgian knee-hole desk in the warm Yew wood that she favoured, stood in the centre of the room; the sash window to its right looked out over her paddock. It was carpeted and an older style radiator was located under the window. A bookcase occupied an entire wall, crammed with books and boxes. Five bronze Chinese Koros occupied the top between the shelf and the ceiling; they were Qing dynasty though Holly and Saskia were unaware of that. There were lamps on small tables, and a desk lamp next to Claire's computer. The wall facing the desk was occupied by a trio of oil paintings in identical plain gilded frames.

Saskia gasped. Her eyes widened in amused surprise and appreciation as they flickered over the pictures.

'Oh wow!' she said. 'They are wonderful. Were they naked when they sat for you?'

'Yes of course they were. I insist on it.'

'Are they true to life? Is Claire really that beautiful, and Hal that muscley and well... well-hung!'

'Yes, they are accurately portrayed.'

'And the other; is that Claire's sister? There are similarities.' She was referring to a beautiful woman with short dark-blonde hair, who crawled catlike along a bed towards an unseen occupant. Slender curved white horns appeared from her head above her ears. Her face was turned towards the viewer, and she was smiling in anticipation.

'Yes, it is. Beautiful, isn't she? She was lovely; I miss her.'

'And did they choose their personas or was that your choice?'

'No. Claire chose to be Medusa. Hal chose to be a Faun. And the thought of being a succubus appealed to Helen.'

'I'm so impressed. You're an amazing artist.'

'Well, your musical skill impressed me Saskia, I don't think anyone expected that apart from Ayesha. I couldn't take my eyes off you when you played. You were so intense, the way you looked into Ayesha's eyes.'

'I can't remember. But I often lose myself in them.'

'I want to paint you Saskia?'

'Naked and in persona?'

'It is my speciality. But it must be with that look in your eyes and while you play the Lute. Seen enough?'

'I could look at them all night.'

'Well, you'll have to come back later then because I need a cup of tea.'

'I need to clear my head to be honest. I'm going outside in the air, just for ten minutes. I have some heavy stuff to think about.'

The lights dimmed to less than half radiance as they left the office and shadows were thrown up along the corridor.

'The power supply,' commented Holly. 'It happens regularly at my house. Plays hell with the tv.'

Halfway along the corridor Saskia narrowed her eyes and peered intently at the head of the staircase where the upper spindles passed behind and seemed to merge with the spindles of the gallery.

'Has Claire acquired another cat bigger than Robespierre?' She said curiously. Robespierre and Talleyrand were Claire's Savanna cats.

'It would be some going for it to be bigger than Robespierre, why?'

'I thought that I saw something on all fours at the top of the stairs just briefly. I assumed it was one of the cats.'

'I didn't see anything, sorry,' said Holly. 'It was probably the shadows.' She was not trying to be dismissive, but she could normally sense presence. She opened the centre at her brow, reached out, but felt nothing.

Saskia did not press the point. She had seen something; she knew that it was not a trick of shadows. She decided that it had been Robespierre on his way downstairs, but she failed to convince herself. She had not seen any ghosts during her visits to Claire's house over recent weeks, and had they been in residence she would have noticed them, and Claire had never mentioned anything in the house. She did not believe that Claire kept a guardian like Ayesha kept Snuggles, she was certain that she would have seen it, and none had ever been mentioned. Claire's father's old guardian, Soth, was in residence in the Place, he never left it, he was dormant and just hung around in a dark corner, cocooned entirely in leathery wings. Saskia had surprised Claire when she told her that she could see him, on the first occasion she had gone down into Archie Bosola's Place, with its arched ceilings and medieval look. Curious.

Saskia knew that everyone who was invited to stay over had gathered in the living room, apart from the Secretions who she had not seen for some time; they had presumably gone to bed. She was disappointed not to have spoken more with Diz, she liked her and wanted to get to know her. She had wanted to ask her about her auction room, and about maybe spending some time together when she went up to Thirsk.

'I'm going for that fresh air,' she said to Holly; she touched the crook of Holly's arm and trailed her fingers away as she made for the dining room. 'Anyone asks, I'll only be a few minutes; I'm going to circuit the house.' She made for the terrace, through the glazed doors that exited the dining room.

It was cool out in the night air; she could feel it entering the fabric of her shirt. She excluded it, like she did when she walked home in one of her skimpy dresses, from her drop off on Culverin Road. The house was surrounded on one side by the paddock with a path between them, and on three sides by garden, with woodland beyond that, at the back and down the remaining side where the garden was quite narrow. The whole of the outside was floodlit and in places draped with lights hung through shrubbery and on ornamental trees. The power supply was still at a reduced level and the lighting had assumed a moody effect, the shadows becoming deeper and more prevalent. Saskia walked along the back of the house, skirting Claire's orangery which was accessed from inside the house from the library; or from the outside via a door set next to the wall. She continued past the kitchen where the lights had been left on. Mrs Rowe had gone home; she was returning in the morning with help, to restore order. Saskia continued taking the path between the side of the house and the paddock. She heard restless hooves being stamped in the little stable block. Neither horse nor donkey were used to being locked away. To her surprise a car engine started, a late leaving guest obviously; she saw the flash of headlights as it started across the grass; then exited the paddock gate in front of her. It was a red Alfa Romeo Spyder, with Diz in the driving seat. She could make out a figure in the passenger seat, it was the Cuban bartender, Alfredo. Lucky Alfredo Saskia thought. Maybe lucky Diz too. She had been caught in the headlight stream as it had searched over the paddock and the house, and she saw Diz's eyes fall on her; she raised her hand expecting Diz to acknowledge her in reply, but she did not, and her face remained expressionless as their gazes met momentarily. Saskia watched the car's taillights disappear along the drive towards the lane. She shrugged, maybe Diz was embarrassed by being caught in the act. She would not hold it against her, she decided. The engine noise receded but there was never silence; she listened to her breathing, though it was not so cold that her breaths plumed; she listened to the pea gravel scrunching under her feet enjoying the noise as she strode out across the front of the house. Small creatures rustled among the dead leaves around the roots of the trees at the side of the house. There was something up in the trees to her left among the naked branches, close to the middle of a low extended sycamore limb, which had served Claire, so she claimed, as a tree swing when she was a child, and later Hal.

'Hello mister owl,' said Saskia as she glimpsed the feathered face peering at her through the lattice of slender nude boughs. She had forgotten about the gate, a painted wooden vertical bar gate on a spring that accessed the enclosure, where Claire kept her Orpingtons' and Silkies; there was no direct route into the back garden this way, she had to pass through the enclosure; it was grassed but there was a paved path set in the ground. She lifted the latch and pushed the gate inwards entering the enclosure. Saskia paused and huffed to herself through her nostrils; she considered backtracking, but decided to press on, albeit a bit cautiously. The enclosure was lit; it always was in case of foxes, Claire had told her, but there were shadows and obstacles and hen shit. She made for the two large gable shaped hen houses which stood sideways-on, next to the wire mesh fence; the exit she recalled was an identical gate to the one she had entered by; it was to be found just the other side of the hen houses. She could make out the grey expanses of roofing felt on their steep pitched sides.

She heard a high-pitched night creature sort of call off to her left and movement in the branches of the trees. She glanced towards it, looking for the owl; it might be keeping pace with her she supposed, in the event she disturbed something edible. Were they that clever? there were gaps in her education she decided. But she was certain that Roger had told her that they avoided humans. She located the owl, not far off, its face was visible above a thick tree limb in the act of gazing down on her; she gave it a little wave. She peered up at it, she had a soft spot for owls; it peered straight back; there was something quite remorseless about its gaze and it made her frown. It began to move closer; a pale spindly arm followed its progress, and after that a pale spindly body.

'What the fuck are you?' Saskia breathed.

With mad urgency she hopped from one foot to the other as she wrenched off her kitten heels and hurled them away; then she fled. The creature's harsh call clawed at her ears; she heard the crash of its body through breaking branches as it plunged through them to reach her.

Saskia concentrated on flight. She knew that she had plenty of power in her legs, but alcohol reduced efficiency and co-ordination, and there was plenty of it in her system.

On the other side of the hen houses was a wire mesh fence almost hidden on both sides by dense swathes of ivy and honeysuckle, roughly five feet in height; not as high as the apex of the hen houses; beyond that the garden; rose beds, lethal Mahonia, a killer sundial on a stone column. She sprinted fifteen meters across grass and a patch of slippery disturbed ground. Buff Orpingtons' and Silkies might be pure breeds, but it was still chicken shit that she was running in she thought, grimacing. The soles of her feet connected with a rough felt surface on a steep slant; to her intense pleasure she ran the slope easily, three strides and she launched herself from the apex. She glimpsed a partial moon above the wrythen chimney pots as she gained height and lost sight of it again, as she descended; she scanned what lay below and in front of her, desperately. Claire's Lilley Pond thank God, its population of Koi carp ravaged for three years in succession, by a grey Heron apparently. If there was nothing unexpected under the water to impede or injure her, she could probably land on her feet; she knew that the pond weed would impede her, and she apologised to Claire in absentia, for any damage she would do to her Lilly plants. As the surface of the water hurtled up to meet her, she glimpsed movement in Claire's

Garden swing which was situated for getting the best of any sunshine and for koi viewing. She could not make out what it contained, but it was mound like, and it undulated. Her heart leapt into her throat at the thought that it might be another creature; she could even hear little moans issuing from the mound before the water erupted around her and the splash of her impact drowned everything out. The pond was far deeper at the other end she recalled thankfully.

'What the fuck is happening?' shouted Amber Shalako rearing up from between her twin sister's thighs; she threw off the blanket they had used to cover themselves and exposed their nude bodies.

'You're sitting on my fucking face!' exclaimed the muffled voice of her twin.

'You don't usually complain!'

'You don't usually try to suffocate me! Get off; what's the matter with you?'

'It's fetter bitch. What were you doing in Claire's Chicken preserve and why were you jumping off the roof into the fucking pond? Whatever you're on I want some.'

They wriggled apart and swung their legs off the seat to sit up, managing to appear quite demure despite being flushed and naked. A half-consumed bottle of vodka stood on the newly mowed lawn under the swing.

'Fuck me so it is. More to the point what the fuck is that?' Pearl pointed towards the roof of the chicken house.

'Not a clue!' gasped Saskia who had a fairly good idea what Pearl was pointing towards; she climbed on her knees from the pond and dragged herself to her feet and moved, dripping water and oxygenating plant, away from the pond; she was suddenly hit by the effects of the cold water and her fright, her body started to shudder. 'It reminds me of something by Hieronymus Bosch.' She hugged her body and turned to gaze in the direction of the hen house, inexplicably she wondered if it held the Silkies or the Orpington's. The creature had paused and squatted on the roof; it peered down at them. The owl head tilted to one side, listening to something it had heard inside the hen house as it had sprung up the side, though the chickens were mostly preserving a studied silence. The thing was naked, it had a sinewy body, with arms and legs that appeared to be all tendon and taut sinew; each one ended in three horrific talons, which had ripped through the felt of the roof. It was braced on three of its limbs, the other an arm, bent at a skinny elbow, the forearm rested across its long thigh. A thin, long, red fleshed penis dangled between its thighs. The creatures owl-like head observed them with large remorseless eyes, and a thin black tongue flicked in and out of a mouth resembling a vicious beak. Saskia backed towards Amber and Pearl. The Shalako's had risen to their feet apparently unconcerned about their nakedness, or unphased by the presence of a creature that had not been spawned on their world.

'She's not wrong Amber,' Pearl observed. 'I'd say second circle. Pandemonium.'

'Come on fuck face!' Amber taunted. 'We'll send you back to hell in a fucking sack.'

The owl head shrilled at them. '*Caahtu!*'

'It speaks!' Pearl laughed.

'I wonder what it's saying?' Amber said, tilting her head to one side. 'I wonder which tongue it's speaking in.'

'Take your pick. I don't know any of them.'

'I think it's saying Fuck you!' Saskia said and began to back off towards the house.

'What's the matter fetter bitch, can't you hack it?' Amber jeered.

'I'm going to the house for help!'

'Why don't you think that we're capable of handling the skinny shit?' Pearl inquired scathingly.

'To be honest I think that you are more than capable of handling the ugly bastard. But I'm not sure you can handle them!' She pointed down the garden and started to run towards the house.

Amber bit her lower lip and unleashed vis ultima on the thing on the hen house with a vindictive back hand slap. It shrieked in pain; its limbs flailed as it was catapulted twenty feet through the air back into the chicken enclosure. Only then did Amber follow her sister's wide-eyed stare in the direction that Saskia had indicated.

'Fuck me!' she exclaimed.

Past the big vinery greenhouse on the left, almost as far as the orchard, in front of which Claire had planted a miniature maze, the upper part of an enormous bald head three meters or so in height and of equivalent width, had appeared out of nowhere, it might have risen up out of the ground if there had been no disturbance to the lawned ground around it, or signs of ruin or debris from the maze tumbling from it; it had made no sound as it appeared. It seemed to be submerged to just below its under lip; this was covered by a glistening purple tongue that was several feet in width and protruded a good couple of meters onto Claire's lawn. Huge, round, opaque eyes bulged from its head above mound like cheeks; it appeared to be constructed with bricks of flesh which shifted and undulated with the movements of the face. It gave voice to a low hooning moan, which sent shivers through Saskia. Its mouth gaped like a cavern, revealing gums lacking any teeth; its interior walls glistened dark red; its cavity was filled with shadowy movement. Outlandish figures were appearing from it; they spilled from its tongue, out across the lawn.

'No pressure fetter bitch!' Amber called after Saskia. 'But tell Hal he'd better kick his arse into gear!'


'Bastard!' Saskia swore, as she fought with the stiff handle of the terrace doors. The mechanism gave at last, and she staggered into the room, looking like a drowned ghost girl, drenched and with bits of pond plant adhering to her clothing. She felt the warm air welcome and penetrate her, but she had no time to appreciate it. Hal was already half risen out of his chair; Claire, Amelia, and Holly shot her almost startled looks. They had turned in their chairs at the fire, in reaction to her dramatic entrance. Only Ayesha was missing from the group.

'Who's energising intent!' Hal snapped, he moved towards her, eyes flickering over her, taking in her drenched appearance, the scared look in her eyes.

'Amber and Pearl in the garden! It's filling with creatures and they're coming out of a giant head! I saw dwarves with enormous feet, and they were dressed in armour, and they had tails!' Saskia jabbered at him.

'Have you had something psychedelic Saskia?' Claire asked somewhere between worried and hopeful.

'I've never had anything psychedelic that caused me to see things like that!' Saskia responded, surprised that she could manage indignation. 'Amber says they are from the second circle of hell, Pandemonium she said, and that you had better kick your arse into gear Hal!'

Hal went past her like a dagger in flight. 'They were by the pond!' She shouted helpfully as he disappeared through the doors. Amelia followed him kicking away her kitten heels to run in bare feet, she was like an amazon, Saskia decided, quite magnificent. Amelia paused as she passed her; she trailed long beautiful fingers down her wet arm and acquired her gaze with reassuring silver-grey eyes. 'Stay well back. Let us handle this.'

'This is on me, isn't it?' Saskia looked and sounded fragile.

'Nothings on you.'

'Please stay safe,' Saskia whispered to her.

'Our purpose is your safety. Stay here.' Then she was gone after Hal; Claire followed her, an incongruously dangerous look on her face.

'Go to the Place with Holly. And stay there,' she said.

Saskia turned to Holly, the only other person still in the room. Holly appeared stressed; she was smoothing her short dress against her thighs with both hands. She kept eye contact with Saskia; she was breathing rapidly; Saskia could see that she was torn.

'I'm not going to the Place.'

'But Claire said...'

'I don't care what Claire said!'

'Alright don't bite my head off!'

'I'm sorry! I'm stressed. Where is Ayesha?' Saskia demanded.

'She went looking for you! just a couple of minutes ago. She was fretting about you. When I told her what you were doing, she decided to go and look for you at the front. She'll be fine, I promise.'

'You want to go into the garden, don't you?'

'I'm not going to leave you don't worry.'

'I'm not worried. But you should go. You might want to paint it later or something. Go on Holly. I'll be fine.'

Holly ceased to smooth the front of her dress. She stood more erect. Her mouth set into a determined line.

'Are you sure?'

'Yes, go on.'

Holly nodded. 'You are going to find Ayesha, aren't you?'

'Yes of course I bloody am! Wouldn't you if you were me?'

'Yes of course I bloody would.'

Saskia watched as Holly strode from the room. She could hear shouting, and bizarre squeals and brays echoing in from the garden. This was insane, she thought; utterly, totally, insane. Her ears tightened and tightened again as energised intent was released. She strode purposefully to the fireplace and lifted the broadsword from its brackets; It was heavy; much heavier than she had expected. She was about to leave when Claire's two Savana cats Robespierre and Talleyrand loped into the room; they had kept themselves to themselves during the party, until now staying upstairs; their long bodies were taut and stressed; all their fur was standing on end and every sense that they had was telling them that something was wrong. They cried plaintively in their strange voices to Saskia, whom they recognised. Robespierre made to go outside but changed his mind and looped back to Saskia.

'Come on boys,' she said. She led them back out of the room, and they went with her because they trusted her. They were tall and they flowed against her legs; she felt as if she was being flanked by a pair of Cheetahs. She did the only thing she could think of, she led them under the staircase.

'*It is not down on any map; true places never are.*' She could dispense with the words, but she was not yet ready to do so. Shaking, she thought her way in and led the two cats into the Place with her; guiltily, she left them at the top of the stone stair that led down into the chamber that had been Claire's fathers, and where Claire so rarely went. 'I'll come back for you,' she promised them, bending down to pet their heads. What else could she do? She was sure that she felt a cold draught sweep up from the chamber stirring her hair, but she knew that it was her imagination.

A dozen bizarre figures had appeared from the interior of the giant head. The strange company appeared to be led by a beautiful Lilû, with an air of authority. She was slender and she had raven black hair and large gleaming jet eyes. Her fingers and toes possessed slim claws. She wore stockings from her ankles to her upper thighs constructed of fine silver chain mail and sleeves the length of her arms made of the same fine mesh, supported by straps, as were her stockings; on her head she wore a flare brimmed, fifteenth century style, Burgundian, wrythen kettle helmet, also forged from silver; otherwise, she was naked. She was carrying a long whip in one hand and a slender javelin constructed of bone in her other hand. Two midget-like creatures clunked in bronze armour as they advanced in front of her, one had the face of a grinning child behind the bars of its visor, the other a face resembling a Mr punch, from a punch and Judy show; both had tapering tales and large feet, in sturdy studded boots. The punch head carried a large, spiked club, the child a hefty bronze hammer. Behind them came an assortment of the weird and the horrific; There were two owl heads and a squat naked red imp its body apelike; it carried a spear and its enormous penis trailed on the ground; a spider-scorpion walked beside the Lilû like a dog, its skin was formed into thick armour overlapped across its legs and its body, it was as big as a giant tortoise and had the white heart shaped face of a pretty woman with eight black dispassionate eyes; above its pincers there grew a pair of slender human female arms. A contingent had faces like goats, their white, rangy, almost human bodies were protected in part by leather armour, some were male, others female. The males carried spears the female's short bows. Others looked human, thin gaunt humans, with mottled skin like a frog.

When Hal and the others appeared from the house the Lilû spoke; calling out to them in English as she advanced, her voice had a cold edge, it was matter of fact.

'In your tongue I am Satran Saradina!' She spoke in an accent that might have been taken for eastern European. 'My chief is Bereth lord of covenants. And I am commissioned to end a covenant of mortal need. Resistance is pointless. Surrender yourselves; the end will be quick.'

'This sphere is forbidden to Pandemonium unless you're invited,' Claire yelled. She almost added: *Get out of my fucking garden!* but refrained.

'Oh, I've been invited!' Satran Saradina laughed. 'Heaven forbids, that I came without an invitation.' She wielded her whip and it unrolled with a brutal crack; in response a coruscant sphere of sulphur yellow brightness appeared from the mouth of the giant head. It climbed into the air above the house and began to expand across the sky. It grew at an astonishing rate and curved back to the ground. It shut off the woodland and the night sky and the lane beyond the house. As it completed its hemisphere, the already dimmed lighting outside and inside the house cut out altogether, and everything was permeated by its alien yellow radiance.

'There we are sequestered. Now I feel like I'm at home!' the Lilû cried.

'Hal, it's the bowling alley from hell,' Amber exclaimed. 'I keep knocking the fuckers over, they keep getting up. You should know: the fetter bitch... I mean Saskia was being hunted down by an owl head; one that arrived before this lot. Before the head came. I've hit him twice already he's rooting somewhere around the enclosure. My point is there will probably be others. This might be the main attack, but it could be a diversion too.' She and Pearl had retreated almost as far as the terrace. They were standing next to a massive granite column, on top of which was fixed a striking armillary sundial, in engineered steel.

'We decided to lob this onto them,' said Pearl.

'Good idea,' Amelia agreed as she arrived; surprised that she had the opportunity to say that to either of the Shalako girls.

'Together then!'

The three of them screamed like banshees desiring their power under the stone; the ground groaned and lurched under their feet as the column broke free from where it had stood for fifty years; when six strong men and a tractor had laboured nearly a full day to position it under Claire's mother's supervision. It appeared almost stately as it rotated, ponderously skimming above the lawn. They hurled it in the direction of Satran Saradina, and she was almost too late seeing it as it passed directly between her midgets. She reacted with snake like speed and struck it with her whip; she was quick to realize that discard was not an option, she was powerful, but she knew her limitations. Desperately she deflected trying to send it into the ground but only succeeded in deflecting into her own company. She heard the impact and the squeals of agony behind her; but by then Hal's vis ultima had struck her and hurled her fifty feet backwards into the nineteen-fifties iron framed vinery greenhouse, demolishing more than two thirds of its entire twenty-foot structure.

The spider scorpion screamed with a woman's voice and hurtled across the lawn towards Hal. It shouted as it scurried towards him in an alien language, words that appeared to be made entirely of harsh unfamiliar syllables. It performed gestures with the two long female arms above its snapping pincers. Hal saw distortion in the air between the creature's fingers; it was years since he had faced elemental magic. He struck with intent, but the air was already full of rust-red tentacles swarming towards him. Half of them broke against his intent, turning to filaments of smoke which returned to the spider-scorpion; the rest greedily acquired him, and he felt an instant sensation of heat where they touched him. He quickly realised that they were not the source of the heat, it was coming from within himself; his own energy centres were being leeched. He reacted at once, recognising that it was too late to employ Aspis; he struck at the Spider-Scorpion before it could start further magic, sending it tumbling back towards the giant head; meanwhile raising a thoughtform in his solar plexus to counter the tentacles and hopefully any added elemental attacks. Ribbons of light flowed across his field of vision, he was aware of their cool texture, more of them touching where the tentacles had bunched transforming them to twists of smoke. Hal realised at once that he was receiving help from another source. He grinned malevolently as Holly Pen appeared on his right; she formed the elemental ribbons of shimmering light between her hands and sent them streaming towards him, until the last of the tentacles had dissipated. Saskia knew her own mind, he decided; She had either gone to the Place alone or understandably, she had gone after Ayesha. He took in the rest of the events which had begun to play out in the garden and gave no further thoughts for the present, to either of them.

The sun dial had crushed two creatures, a frog skin, and a goat face female, both were horribly injured and writhed beneath the mass of the column which had crushed them. Claire was duelling one of the armoured midgets with intent, Amelia the other, as they advanced across the lawn. The Shalako's had moved to the right side of the garden, positioning themselves near Claire's beautiful Acer, attempting to deny the rest of the company from Pandemonium access to the house. Most of the creatures lacked intent but they were hard to stop or kill. They had advanced to the rose garden. A goat face directed an arrow at Pearl; it plucked at her hair close to her ear; she felt frantically for blood scared of the poison in the metal of Pandemonium. Amber shrieked in rage and savagely drove the goat face back and down with vis ultima; her intent hurled it into the rose garden causing a huge furrow through the middle of it and uprooting a dozen rose bushes in the process. It was clear to Hal that the Shalako's would be eventually overrun by the creatures moving towards them; the thought form in his solar plexus remained without definitive form; he gave it legs and jaws, its form that of a massive grey hound, its body like surging smoke, with a head the size of a bulls. It issued from his solar plexus and loped on great long legs into the body of the creatures from Pandemonium and began to create havoc among them.

'Yay! Uncle Hal!' Yowled Pearl.

At the same instant, the Lilû, Satran Saradina, stalked in a fury from the ruins of the greenhouse. She had lost her helmet; yellow blood trickled from several wounds to her head and sides, caused by brutal connection with the iron framework; her silver mail had protected her limbs. Iron excelled against many of the otherworld lifeforms, where modern weaponry had little or no effect, and the Lilû's wounds were edged in creeping black where the poison from contact with the old, feared metal had penetrated her flesh. Her shoulders were hunched like a cobra; her face had twisted, mixing incandescent rage with pure malice. Her appearance caught Holly Penn's imagination as she appeared from the wreckage, Holly visualized her painted as a twenties flapper, enraged that her cocktail had been so badly mixed.

The Spider-Scorpion cast a mass of swirling threads of elemental intent at Holly Penn and scuttled to the Lilû, it dribbled a milky ooze into its hands from a beautiful female mouth and anointed Satran Saradina's poisoned wounds with the fluid; as she worked the Lilû defended; her whip lashed out to deflect Hal's fresh strike of intent and she deployed her own at once. The Spider-Scorpion returned to the fight and immediately engaged Holly Penn who was finishing off the last of the threads with elemental intent. Amelia and Claire were locked in a relentless battle of attrition with the two midgets. Their discards and deflections were destroying Claire's Garden, piece by piece. Claire broke the deadlock by declining time, a skill she was always reluctant to employ because it invariably caused her a migraine. She felt the physical universe stretch, pause. She could decline time for a more extended moment than most. She used it with clinical efficiency. She was aware of Amelia about to release vis ultima at the punch headed midget, Amelia surprisingly was unable to decline; Claire's own opponent, the child headed midget was staring directly at her and she saw comprehension in its wide, slightly deranged eyes. She struck her own opponent and Amelia's with vis ultima twice each, then desired at the eyes of the child-head, using grim intent in the form of an imagined misericord thrust into each eye. The great deceiver reclaimed event, disallowing her the opportunity to desire into the eyes of Amelia's opponent. But mayhem was already guaranteed.

The house was plunged into darkness as the power failed at last. Saskia froze half-way across the hall. A thin, sinister yellow light spilled through the windows and filled the space with restless shadows. She thought she heard a noise upstairs, a creak indicating something moving about. Not Ayesha, why would she go upstairs? Something scuttled along the landing into the corridor; another creature, it had to be. She heard rustling, then more scuttling and a squeal. She wondered how they were gaining entry. Her thoughts went to the monstrous head in the garden; but she suspected some other means employed by her owl-head and whatever was moving about upstairs. Saskia continued hurriedly to the door, she peered cautiously through the side window, before partially opening the door and slipping outside. She peered curiously at the yellow sky and the alien yellow light that permeated everywhere. The grounds at the front of the house were still and silent; Saskia shivered in her wet clothing, she felt annoyed with Ayesha for not staying with the others. She wondered what had motivated her; she had told Holly that she would be only minutes. Perhaps Ayesha had felt it was time to go to bed; to find her and lead her away from the living room and further conversation; time for Saskia to remove her clothing and draw off her stockings in the manner she enjoyed. Saskia smiled fondly. She heard a loud impact on the other side of the house; it sounded like a head on car crash some way off. It motivated her to action.

'Ayesha!' She moved to the centre of the hemisphere of gravel in front of the house, cautious in her bare feet. She saw no purpose in hissing Ayesha's name or speaking softly; so, she said her lover's name loudly and clearly, highlighting the smoky timbre of her voice in the stillness of the air. She could hear distant voices; it sounded almost like an outdoor party in full sway, without music.

'You look ready for war?' It was a sibilant, purred, accented voice that flattened its words. It came not from directly behind, but from behind and off to her left.

Saskia had rested the blade of the broadsword on her right shoulder, she kept it there. She took a deep breath and turned about; she was careful not to appear disturbed at what might confront her. She knew that she was breathing through her mouth, with her white teeth separated. She lowered her head slightly so that her irises slipped partly under her upper eyelids; she knew that it made her expression appear dark and uncompromising. It could be adopted either for sex, or intimidation.

He had appeared from shrubbery, composed of Rhododendron and Euonymus. Saskia supposed that he was more Ermine than man, about four feet tall, whiskered, and furry. He was dressed in black quilting that looked like velvet, covered in silver studs. Very renaissance, genuinely like a creature in a Bosch painting portrayed in the act of murdering a man up against an overturned table. What was it called? Oh yes, *the garden of earthly delights*. This creature wore an Ermine poncho with two flat tapering tails and a hood; it was thrown over his right shoulder to make his swept hilt silver sword accessible. He regarded her with eyes that were likely to be as black as his soul. They were utterly pitiless.

'I will die trying to kill you,' Saskia told it, realising that it sounded dramatic, though she did mean it.

'I'm not here to kill you. I'm here to take you. You are valuable alive.'

'I won't go easily. I will fight. I will scream!'

'Scream if you want to. You will go with me though, if I must beat you unconscious and drag you by the hair; what there is of it.'

He would too, she could read it in his mean, black eyes, so filled with mockery; he would knock her out and drag her away bleeding.

'Where do you intend to take me?' She needed time; time to think.

'To my world for a short while.'

'Just where is your world.

'In the second circle of imagination; deep in the boundless edge. It is a bitter-sweet place called Pandemonium. My name is Alarin Laz, and I know that you are Saskia.' He pronounced it Sasskyaa.

'Well, Al whatever your name is, I don't want to go there.'

'You may like it, there's something about you that says you might. But it will only be for a while anyway, until they send for you.'

'Until who, sends for me?'

'My paymaster.'

'I won't go.'

'You have no choice. And that is an extremely sweet pleasure.'

'I prefer a choice. A free will.'

'You no longer have one.'

'How much are you being paid for this? Who are you working for? Who is this paymaster? Whatever you're being paid...!'

'Questions! Questions! I'm not being paid in gelt.' He raised an Ermine gloved hand to silence her; his finger in front of a mouth lined with pointed teeth.

'My friends will come for me. They'll find me and make you pay!' She threatened.

He shrugged. 'Ah, that is another matter, and not my task or that of my crew. Your friends are not to be afforded the luxury of living. They will not find you; they will not come for you. Everything ends tonight. Lay down your sword now, come with me.' He gestured with his fingers, bending them towards the palm quickly, twice.

'Fuck you!' Saskia snarled. She brought the sword down from her shoulder and swung it in an expansive arc. She heard it hum in the air. The Ermine hopped back, peering at the point of the sword with respect as it passed a few inches in front of his pointed face. He huffed and drew his own sword.

He began to circle her, becoming predatory. Saskia thought that he must have sensed something, his black eyes flashed, and he showed his sharp teeth in a snarl as he whirled about with speed that astonished her. He stopped, frozen in motion halfway in his turn, too late. This close to declining, Saskia's thoughts turned to an elasticated moment without cogency, and her vision to a couple of blurred stills. As the deceiver resumed, Saskia breathed, and the world piled in.

The ermine, Alarin Laz had sprawled to the ground, his body driving into the pea gravel. He began to contort. His sword was still in flight, and it plunged into the gravel several meters away. Ayesha was standing over the Ermine a look of pure malevolence on her face.

'What did you do to him?'

'I put vis ultima into his evil little body three times. I was stalking him, then you came outside. It won't kill him, but that might. It's iron.' She nodded towards the broadsword still gripped in Saskia's fists. As she spoke, Saskia saw, with interest, the tiny muscles around her eyes flexing, as she delivered vis ultima into the Ermine's body for a fourth time.

'What's happening at the back? I thought I heard a car crash, but there's only a little track beyond Claire's wood. Go on whack him in the head with your sword, quickly,' Ayesha encouraged, seeing Saskia's hesitant expression. 'This little bastard is from pandemonium. I probably don't have the power to kill him, and we don't have the luxury of keeping him subdued Sask…'

She did not finish her sentence; she was too distracted by the impact of the broadsword as Saskia swung its tapering end into the side of the Ermine's head. Alarin Laz twisted away sending gravel in every direction; he gave a high-pitched shriek and fell still. An instant later, unexpectedly he jerked and threw himself up onto one knee with alarming speed, making them both jump. He hissed at them. Yellow liquid was streaming from a large delve in the side of his head, it had very quickly begun to turn black around its edges. He swayed and shook his head; his black eyes fixed on them with pure loathing. Ayesha was about to react with force but then his outline flickered and blurred, and he disappeared from their sight.

'Did I kill him?' Saskia asked.

'I doubt it. I think he's returned to Pandemonium. Iron poisons them supposedly, like their metal poisons us; did you see the blackness eating into his head where you hit him.' Ayesha felt herself begin to shake; she decided not to waste energy fighting it.

'Something chased me a few minutes ago. Its head looked like an owl,' Saskia told her. She took a very deep breath and watched Ayesha's face closely. 'Also, there's a giant bald head squatting in the garden where Claire's maze used to be; all sorts of creatures marched out of its mouth. Everybody has gone to fight them. That's what all the noise is around the back!'

'Fuck me Saskia! This is getting out of hand!'

'What are we going to do?'

For the briefest instant Ayesha's gaze flickered towards her BMW parked in Claire's paddock. Her hands tightened into fists at her sides; she rolled, then flashed her eyes and set her mouth into a determined little line. She stared emotionally at Saskia.

'No!' the word came from Saskia's throat and mouth, softened, almost pathetic.

'Saskia, if you run you stand a chance,' Ayesha pleaded.

'I will not leave you and you can't make me.'

Ayesha saw the resolve in Saskia's eyes, it was unequivocal. She nodded. Her voice fell to an emotional whisper.

'Just stay close to me little Mantis.' She set off towards the house with a resolute if somewhat jerky stride.

Saskia followed; she cradled the broadsword's heavy blade in the crook of one arm; throwing cautious glances over her shoulder as she scanned the bushes for glimpses of anything resembling an owl.

'Fuck! Shit! What the fuck is that!?' Ayesha exclaimed in alarm; she froze as she entered the house, pitching her gaze at something suspended below the upstairs gallery, directly in front of them. She halted so abruptly that Saskia almost collided with her; she followed Ayesha's stare, prepared for the worst, and lowered her sword from her arm in anticipation of needing to use it. She saw Ayesha tense as she prepared to unleash intent and laid her free hand on her shoulder to prevent her.

'Don't,' she said softly. 'It's Soth in form. Claire's dad's guardian, he's just doing his job. I think I let him out when I put Claire's cats in the Place.

Ayesha relaxed against her, releasing a relieved breath. Saskia found the experience pleasant and quite comforting. She heeled the door shut behind them feeling safer that way.

'He's grown big,' she had seen him on a couple of occasions in form, but never like this.

'Do they all change size?'

'They can, but not all. Some don't need to. I'll tell you later.'

'I sort of expected the rest of him to look like a bat too.'

'Me too.'

'Lots of tentacles,' Saskia remarked. 'He concealed those well under his wings. Have you read any H P Lovecraft?'

'Yes; I get your point.'

'I think Claire's dad probably did.'

'Probably.' They made for the main lounge; they had to pass within a few feet of Soth, watched indifferently by his large yellow eyes.

Soth was holding something in his long, dark blue tentacles, almost embracing it in fact; something that strove to break his grip, wriggling ineffectively. Saskia glimpsed a single visible, round red eye which was rotating in desperation, and a partial view of spike like vomerine teeth. The creature had long limbs and a rangy body, though little of it was visible; Saskia could however just make out that it was covered in dark hairs. As they passed Soth, a long spidery appendage extended from between his tentacles stretching out for them. It had a sucker and two hook like talons at its tip. As it reached out, some of Soth's tentacles extended and coiled about it and drew it back inside the mass; they flexed as one, tightening inexorably on his victim, and Saskia and Ayesha heard cracking and a hiss.

'Can't it just go back to Pandemonium?'

'Nope. Soth's hold is elemental too, he obviously needs energising otherwise he'd have gobbled that thing up by now. Come on, let's join the others.' Ayesha grabbed her hand, she squeezed it with an attempt at reassurance, and pulled her along.

'Ready for this little Mantis?'

'Well, it is my war, I suppose.' She gave a humourless chuckle. 'Saskia's war.'

In a shrill piping voice, the punch head midget screamed as it was struck by Amelia's vis ultima and by Claire's double strike. It was hurled off its large, armoured feet and pitched across Claire's mangled lawn; its body tried to contort inside its armour; it sprawled into the Lilly Pond, displacing a surge of water; the water engulfed it and only the churning surface indicated its whereabouts. Claire's intent flung her own opponent almost in front of Satran Saradina; its screech rang across the garden as it sprawled away, its bronze hammer had been torn from its grasp and it clawed at its visor trying to reach the *desired* misericord that had plunged into either eye. The red imp with the huge penis charged ape like across the garden. It veered as the bronze hammer spun towards it; it came to an abrupt halt and struck its fists together angrily, as it hurled intent at Claire.

Claire shielded. She felt bereft. Her beautiful garden was wreckage. It resembled a World War One battle scene. It was an opportunity she supposed to re-landscape; it was a good thing that Graham was no longer living there, because he would have been a real pain. She drew a long breath surprised at the tingle of excitement it drew up through her. It had been twenty years since she had been in battle, with a cold thrill she realised that she might not live. She would mourn the garden later. Time to do what she excelled at. She saw more figures appearing from the mouth of the giant head; time also for Hal to do what he excelled at. She felt a hand on her arm. She glanced to her right and saw that it was Ayesha. She thought of the young woman like a daughter; perhaps it was time that she told her. He eyelids flexed in her stony face as she discarded the red Imp's intent and lobbed it back on it with the addition of her own.

'Where's Saskia?'

'The terrace. Others came from Pandemonium Claire.'

Claire became concerned; she looked glumly towards the house.

'We dealt with it, with some input from your dad's old Guardian,' Ayesha told her. 'One of the guests must have enabled this incursion.'

'I think so too. If this isn't a sound rationale for keeping guardians, I don't know what is.' She had, illogically, always resisted the idea, even keeping Soth mostly in hibernation. 'Look we are getting seriously outnumbered. Can you deal with our friend with the enormous thingy, while I motivate Hal?'

'Done, fresh to the fray and all that.' Ayesha gave Claire a perplexed look, wondering what further motivation Hal required, and to do what exactly.

Without turning her attention away from the conflict; Claire stepped elegantly back. She had already discarded her stilettos to avoid sinking into the lawn. She saw Hal stride past her on her right, shoulders stiff, determined. His eyes were fixed on Satran Saradina, the captain from Pandemonium, and her fresh cohorts.

'Hal!'

'Yes!' He paused mid stride and looked over his shoulder at her. He eyed her impatiently. Perhaps resentfully.

'I don't mind re-landscaping my garden, but I don't want my house in ruins before you decide to end this!'

He gave her a wolfish look.

'Act now little brother,' she said uncompromisingly.

Hal nodded grimly; he turned about and went to stand a few paces behind Claire. He began to remove his clothes.

'About time Hal!' Amelia called out to him, as she engaged with Satran Saradina.

Saskia watched proceedings from the foot of the steps. Ayesha had left her on the terrace, but she had gradually gravitated down the steps to the lawn, whilst keeping Ayesha in sight.

Saskia jammed the blade of her broadsword about a foot into the ground, so that it stood on its own; it was getting a little heavy to lug about, but she was reluctant to give it up for the present.

'Wow fetter bitch! That's a big one!'

She had watched the Shalako's as they had gradually given ground, they had been the hardest pressed; they retreated across the lawn diagonally. They must be cold, she thought. Pearl whistled, deafeningly, fingers in her mouth, at Holly Penn, who glanced over her shoulder; she nodded and began to fall back towards them. Hal's thought form was still active but had begun to lose integrity of form.

Saskia surprised Amber by grabbing her arms and forcing her to take a step to one side. A hurled spear passed them by inches quivering and humming in the air next to them; they heard it rattle into the steps of the terrace, a few yards behind them. Saskia received only a slight widening of Amber Shalako's eyes, in response to her action.

'Keep behind us!' she told Saskia. 'Watch for stuff. Are you prepared to use that sword?'

'I already have.'

'Good enough! This is hairy. But I think we may only have to hang on a couple more minutes. Hal's up to something.'

Saskia had begun to think that she might have to re-evaluate the Shalako's. She wondered what Hal was about to do.

The Punch midget re-emerged from Claire's Pond; water streamed from its armour. It began to clunk across the expanse of the ruined lawn back towards them. The child head had begun to walk round in circles clutching its helmet with its gauntlet encased hands. Claire decided it was badly hurt and no longer posed a threat. However, three more midgets had appeared from the giant head; each one was accompanied by a grey spider the size of an Irish wolfhound; they possessed blood red eyes and spiky vomerine mouths. Saskia saw a slender girl with a catlike face; she had fine white fur with feathering on her legs and arms and back and head, and lower abdomen; she was dressed in a closely fitting tabard of fine silver mesh; she carried a slender silver dagger and a finely spun net also of finely meshed silver in her clawed hands. She had a rather sad expression on her strange pretty face, or perhaps it was an expression of sullenness, Saskia thought. Her stride was purposeful however and she made straight for Saskia.

'She's hot,' commented Pearl, following Saskia's stare.

Hal by then had stripped naked; he stood very straight; he pressed his palms to his forehead and began to chant; like a head monk at Vespers, Saskia decided.

*'The crawler on the paths knows me, the pursuer in the stars knows me, Chaos walks at my side and the king in the cold emptiness fears me. I am the dweller in the deep; the Wurm whose eyes are lightning and falling skies. Hear me in the limitless dark. I call you.'*

Hal lowered his hands to his sides. His heterochromatic eyes appeared luminous. Hundreds of tiny points of light appeared from every part of his body. Points of incandescent light. Perhaps a thousand, thought Saskia. Most were pure white, though some were pink like sapphires, and others glowed with an uncanny black light. They formed a rotating helix about him and as they grew brighter Hal's appearance became less solid; he became his own spectre. The helix of light ascended, it stretched to a height of twenty metres or so and extended over the garden and began to coil in on itself; it became a hundred metres long, more. It left the ghost memory of Hal standing alone.

Saskia began to step towards him, but Amber caught her by the hand. She turned and peered at her.

'Best not,' Amber said.

Saskia withdrew her hand as Amber relaxed her grip. Ayesha appeared at her other side; her stare was still fixed on the red imp; her face grimly determined as she continued to deliver intent.

Saskia saw the others drawing together forming a hub of power, in the form of an extended arc. They were keeping up relentless energised intent, but they were by now well outnumbered.

'Shit!' Amber snarled.

The Cat girl had begun to run towards them, she flowed on long supple legs. She glanced up at the snake of light in the yellow sky above them and yowled fiendishly; she extended her dagger in front of her and deployed the net like a paso-doble cape, it undulated sinuously in the air behind her. She appeared, Saskia decided, to be coming directly for her. She pulled the broadsword out of the ground, and hefted it, she obtained moderate comfort from the feel of its weight in her hands.

Amber threw vis ultima; the cat girl brushed it away with impunity and came on hard. She threw again with the same result. She glanced towards her twin, but Pearl was beset. Unable to help.

Ayesha reached out one handed to her, across Saskia, and clutched at her hand. Surprised, she allowed; she felt Ayesha decline time, their joined hands allowing them to occupy the same declined moment. Game on! Amber thought. She struck at the cat girl with vis ultima three times in succession. Ayesha spared one strike for the cat girl; kept two for her imp.

For the second time in the space of a half an hour Saskia felt elastication and saw event in the blurring of a few separated images. She had been in the act of levelling the broadsword; it was extended above Ayesha's and Amber's linked hands. She felt vertigo as the weight of the sword pulled at her as event returned. She swayed and caught herself before she pitched forward.

The cat girl spun like a dancer, an elegant capering puppet dancer. Like an extended cat leaping for moths in the moonlight. The succession of vis ultima lifted her off the ground; they struck her with dreadful, penetrating impacts; they contorted her, and her dagger was flung from her grip, but not her net. They devoured every mote of strength that she owned. Willpower alone kept her upright, as she landed crouched and catlike on her feet; it alone propelled her forwards. She stumbled onto Saskia's extended blade; its point penetrated her side below her ribs where, her tabard of silver mesh had flowed aside and did not protect her.

She screamed in agony, shocking Saskia who pulled the tip of her sword free, spilling dark blood through the cat girl's fur. Saskia tried to see if the wound had poisoned but the fur was too darkly bloodied to see; she thought that it probably was. Yellow eyes flashed at her malevolently and she was aware of small exposed pointed teeth. The cat girl had fallen to her knees, she was beyond spent. Yet somehow, she cast her net at Saskia as she pitched forward onto her hands, but if fell ineffectually on the ground at Saskia's feet where it shimmered and writhed, apparently animated with a vitality of its own.

'Careful,' Amber advised. 'I think that she came for you. That thing will probably take you straight to pandemonium.'

She closed her hands around Saskia's grip on the sword hilt and levelled the blade at the cat girl's upturned face.

'Together, yes?'

'No!' Saskia diverted the blade down into the net, driving it into the ground. The cat girl threw her a surprised look.

'What the ...!' Amber began. She shrugged and released her hold on Saskia's hands.

'She is cute I suppose. But think about this; if she was taking you for herself instead of someone else, she'd keep you for sex and beat you mercilessly. She's from Pandemonium, after all.'

'Get lost!' Saskia snapped coldly to the cat girl, who hissed defiantly at her, her yellow eyes were still puzzled; she began to push herself backwards across the lawn, clutching her side in pain. She glanced back once at Saskia, curiously; then she stared into the air directly above her, a searching stare, and as her returning strength allowed, she turned over and began to scramble away.

Hostilities seemed suddenly to have been suspended. Everyone, every-thing it appeared had paused to gaze upwards. There the helical serpent coiled, now hundreds of metres long, its body coruscant white, flecked with pink amethyst and black light. Like an enormous, glowing Cumberland sausage, Saskia thought. A loud bellow got Saskia's attention, it issued from the gaping mouth of the giant head and was followed at once by another and then another; they continued; there was an urgency about them. Satran Saradina stalked over to the head. She was joined by the Spider Scorpion; it scuttled forward to aid the cat girl to her feet and dribbled its milky fluid to bathe her poisoned wound; then supported her slumping figure to the head. Two of the armoured midgets returned to the head with their spider hounds. The rest of the creatures from Pandemonium looked about in confusion. Satran Saradina directed a final cold look straight at Saskia, then turned about and led her small cohort into the gaping mouth.

Saskia felt Ayesha's hand in hers. She looked at her in surprise. She realised that everyone else had disappeared, except Hal's spectral figure.

'Quickly!' Claire called out. 'All of you, get inside.' She was urgent. Ayesha dragged at her hand, and they began to run.

The bellowing ended as the rain began. Saskia turned in the doorway. She saw the giant head close its mouth and collapse in on itself like the folds of a fan until nothing of it was left in her world. Burning slugs of raw white fire pelted down from the Wurm, a brutal hail that hummed and sizzled through the air. They crackled angrily where they hit the earth; where they struck creatures of Pandemonium, they burned them through, turning them to columns of seared flesh. Even the armour of the midgets succumbed, splitting, and melting. The shrieks of the creatures filled the air, but within a few seconds they fell still. Saskia could not feel sorry for them; though for some reason it pleased her that the cat girl had got away. She relaxed her grip on Ayesha's hand; she looked down as her nails relented in Ayesha's flesh.

'I've hurt you.'

Ayesha shrugged. 'So?'

'Hal!'

'Hal's okay, I think. There may be a revelation or two tonight though.'

Ayesha stepped back outside into a hushed night. Saskia followed her. The burning rain had ceased. The glowing helical coils had disappeared, as had the yellow sky of Pandemonium.

Nothing remained. A bat piped suddenly overhead, in pursuit of insects in the moonlight.

Hal was solid again no longer a spectre; he had fallen to his knees on the ground where he had stood. He was vomiting and Amelia and Claire went to help him.

'God! I feel like I've been on a seventy-two-hour bender!'

'Hal, you wouldn't know what one looked like!' Amelia pointed out.

Hal was dressed again, though he had not bothered with his shoes. He felt cold and he was sitting in an armchair by the fire with a glass of whisky in his hand. His face was drawn and his complexion almost grey; every movement appeared to give him discomfort.

'You know until tonight I thought Cockatrice was mythical,' Holly Penn said.

'I've heard of it. But I've never given it much thought,' said Ayesha. 'It was impressive Hal.'

'It was dangerous,' he replied coldly. 'If it had gone wrong, we could have all been lost.'

'It was necessary,' Claire said. She was standing behind Hal's chair, and she laid a reassuring hand on his shoulder. 'We could not have gone toe to toe with them for much longer.'

'Isn't a Cockatrice some sort of dragon?' Saskia remarked.

'I thought so,' Amber agreed.

'Wasn't that what we saw?' Pearl reasoned. 'Some sort of dragon.'

The Shalako's had fetched clothes from the bedroom, jumpers, and jeans; they had occupied the settee with Ayesha and Saskia. Claire looked at the four of them sympathetically. They looked done in, all of them together, drinking tea; even Saskia with no magic had played her part tonight, and she was grateful to her for getting Robespierre and Talleyrand into the Place.

'How long have you had that up your sleeve uncle Hal?'

'Long enough. I never deliberately kept it secret.'

'It's rare,' Holly Penn remarked.

'Really rare. Ancient magic: I suppose in a sense its primordial too. It chimes with whatever underpins the magic in your Wild Saskia.'

'I don't know what you mean?' Saskia was surprised that Holly had any knowledge of the Wild; or that the Shalako's expressed no curiosity as it was mentioned.

'You're too tired to think about it fetter, so don't go there,' Amber said to her, she was surprisingly amiable. Saskia wondered if she could get to like her.

'Amber's right!' Claire announced. 'We're all tired. We all need sleep. I'm going to bed, and I advise everyone to do the same.' She frowned and massaged her brow; she could feel a headache coming on. She was mildly pensive.

'Watch out for Soth and his victim as you go into the entrance hall: I'll sort them tomorrow. Goodnight.'


Saskia was tired but did not allow herself to fall asleep. She waited until she heard Ayesha's steady breathing and got up. She slipped on a jumper and trainers and went down into the darkened house. She turned on the light in the entrance hall and slipped by Soth, who was still enjoying his leggy prize. She smiled at the glowing fire in the living room, behind its guard and went out through the terrace doors and into the ruined garden.

She did not expect to find what she was looking for. She suspected that it had been destroyed by the burning rain; like everything else from Pandemonium. Nothing else seemed harmed by it; though Claire was adamant that it was dangerous to anyone.

She knew the area to look in, she had seen it fall, leaping and tumbling like a living creature. After five minutes she thought it was lost. Then she saw it, it gleamed beneath an overturned urn that stuck out of the ripped turf and where she had seen it come to rest. Only the handle was visible, looked at from the side, all the blade was buried in the ground at an angle. Saskia reached under the urn and pulled out the silver dagger dislodged from the grasp of the cat girl. It was slender and beautiful, and there were black symbols that resembled runes etched into both sides of the tapering blade. It felt cold in her hands. Satisfied she returned to the house, passing the broadsword, which was still upright in the lawn, where it had impaled the cat girl's net. Of the net there was no sign, it had burned with the rest of Pandemonium.

Saskia returned to their bedroom; her stealthy movements as quiet as she could make them. She quietly hid the dagger among her things. She slid into bed next to Ayesha, sliding an arm around her.

Ayesha stirred, semi-awake. 'Oh, you're cold. Cuddle up.'

Saskia smiled, cuddled, and fell sleep.

# Three

'God, I need bacon and eggs Mrs Rowe,' Saskia slid onto the pew bench between the wall and the antique kitchen table, its surface was patinated a dark honey tone, and here and there it was just slightly uneven.

'I thought you might love.'

Ayesha slipped in next to her; she grinned nuzzling Saskia's shoulder. They were both in jeans and fitted jumpers.

'Bacon sandwiches for me Grace,' she said.

'One or two?'

'Two please.'

'Do you want beans Saskia?'

'Love some beans.'

'What's been happening? I came back this morning, the greenhouse is wrecked, in fact most of it is demolished. The sundial is buried upside down. The garden doesn't exist anymore.'

'Things got out of hand Mrs Rowe. People indulged in unseemly behaviour. The Shalako's were involved,' Saskia said.

'That adds up.'

'Have you been into the hall yet?'

'No.' Mrs Rowe frowned.

Saskia exchanged an amused smile with Ayesha.

'We kept well out of it didn't we Ayesha. Is Claire up yet?'

'Not yet. She has a migraine apparently and might not get up at all. It was Holly Penn told me; she's around somewhere. Hal and Amelia have gone for a walk; they looked absolute wrecks when they came down. I haven't seen Amber and Pearl.'

'No great loss there then,' Ayesha remarked.

Mrs Rowe smiled indulgently. She set Saskia's and Ayesha's breakfasts down in front of them.

'I'm so pleased that I left at ten-thirty.'

'It was a wise move Mrs Rowe.' Saskia destroyed the yolk of one of her fried eggs with a piece of bacon on the end of her fork and pushed it into her mouth. She watched Ayesha sink her teeth into one of her bacon sandwiches; Ayesha chewed, mouth full and closed; she locked eyes with her lover. Saskia's tongue appeared from her mouth and suggestively licked a dribble of egg yolk from her underlip.

'You might have been dragged in.'

'You never know. Anyway, we've had our laugh. Things got hairy here last night, didn't they? No point denying it the place reeks of dire and elemental intent at present. I'm sure you two were in the middle of it as well. And I don't want to know what happened; Claire will tell me if she wants me to know. Tea?'

'God yeah!'

'I'll have a cup of that Grace if there's one going spare,' said Holly Penn. She came into the kitchen removing her coat and an open fleece shirt, she hung them up on the wall rack by the door. She was in boots, needle-cords, and a strappy white vest top; Saskia realised how tiny she was, four-foot ten of supple delight.

She reached into her coat pocket before coming to the table, extracting items; she brought them with her and after first laying out a napkin on the patinated timber, she set them down upon it one after another.

'I found these: one inside the house and two at the front, and one in the rear garden; they were well hidden.' she told them.

'What have you got there?' asked Hal. He entered the kitchen from the interior passage; Amelia was directly behind him; they both looked sharper than when they had left for their walk thought Grace Rowe, but the strain was still visible on both their faces, more so on Hal's. They had come in at the front door. Hal was not one who adhered to the old superstition that you should always return by way of the door by which you left. His question stilled Saskia's own intended: *'What are they?'*

'Invitations,' Holly replied.

She had distributed four circular tablets, roughly the size of a coaster, over the paper napkin; three were made of black clay, one of yellow, hardened in a kiln. They were decorated in curious symbols and a strange slanting script.

Hal occupied an Elm wheelback carver at the end of the table having taken up Grace Rowe's offer of bacon and eggs; Amelia sat down opposite Ayesha, with a bowl of muesli.

Scenting a faint odour Saskia leaned forward and sniffed at one of the discs.

'What is that smell?'

'It's like potassium nitrate, add essence of dank tomb and there you have it.' Amelia was makeup free and exceptionally beautiful and perhaps a little wan; she watched Saskia's expression, her pliant mouth curving indulgently.

'The smell of Pandemonium.' Ayesha added. Amelia continued to smile at Saskia, her gaze not shifting towards Ayesha.

'This is how they found their destination, and opened portals,' Hal said. 'Beacons. Someone must have placed them. Someone at the party last night. Where precisely did you find them Holly?'

'The yellow one, concealed in the miniature dry stone wall near what's left of the Maze. One in the shrubbery at the front, another at the side. One on the gallery between the aspidistra and the Savonarola; you saw something starting to form on our way back from Claire's office, Saskia. Soth put paid to it. They were not particularly well concealed; I don't believe that was the intention.'

'Who would...?' Saskia began. 'No, strike that. We might never find out. Why though? everyone at the party knew Claire and all of you. Many of them are Claire's friends, and your friends too.'

'The usual suspects. Gain, loyalty, or love,' said Holly, compressing her lips. 'I think I'll have a bacon sandwich.'

'Whoever initiated last night's forays took a very grave risk,' Hal said. 'They must be greedy for power. I suppose they could be desperate. They are prepared for dire consequences. They must want what you have very badly.'

'I'm endangering everyone now.'

'You are endangering no one little mantis.'

'Someone new has dealt themselves into the game. Someone powerful enough and hungry enough, to allow it to drive them to this type of extreme.'

'What makes you think that, Hal?' Amelia inquired, she frowned, an expression of doubt, she was more inclined to lay the blame at the door of one of the dark orders.

'Isn't it obvious?'

'Their actions are in the present,' Saskia said, she glanced at Hal, he shrugged.

'Go on Saskia,' said Ayesha.

Saskia continued. 'Had they known about the Wild before, I don't believe that Trevor Challoner would have been safe. I don't believe anyone would have been safe. They are immensely determined whoever they are, and they don't give a damn about a mortal covenant. I'm sorry.'

'I think you're wrong; they will be afraid of the consequences,' Ayesha asserted.

'How do you make that out?' Saskia asked; she frowned, a little put out by Ayesha's challenge.

'Last night was a big throw of the dice. To involve entities from Pandemonium, demons from the abyss in Christian etymology. Lesser agencies though they were. That is heavy stuff. But whoever their paymaster is, whether they represent their own interests or those of another, their options are limited; they believed it was the only choice available to them. To come for you personally on their and our physical plane, he or she sees as too much of a risk or they would have done just that, despite the covenant.'

'You are saying that I'm safe?'

'For the present.'

'Why? I really want to believe you.'

'Because little mantis, when they came for you, they came for us all. The ermine creature you whacked on the head confirmed it.

I find that flattering. They needed us gone. The covenant scares them. We were victorious so it continues to serve its purpose; indeed, by virtue of our success against their agents, we can only be enhanced in their eyes.'

'What if he or she sends more agents for us?'

'You can't just dial pandemonium and ask for more hit men. What happened last night took planning. Resource, contracts that used to be signed in blood. Serious commitments will have been made, he... they, whatever, took an enormous risk and have nothing to show for it.'

'Surely that will make them more desperate.'

'If I were them, and I don't give a damn who they are, I would be avoiding contact with pandemonium for a long time.'

'I agree,' Amelia announced softly. 'The mortgage will be enormous. It will not be something they can pay off with the sacrifice of a couple of virgins, or babies.'

Saskia wondered if she was being serious, but she appeared sincere. Amelia must have realized that Saskia's attention was focused on her, because she stared directly into her eyes when she continued to speak.

'Or sex and pain for that matter,' she continued; Saskia sensed a hidden barb. 'Ayesha is wily, even cunning; I recommend that you listen to her. There are some matters where you wouldn't rely on her counsel but in this, she's quite impeccable.'

Resentment entered Ayesha's expression, it quickly changed to hostility. She exchanged a look with Amelia that held daggers. Saskia watched curiously as Amelia locked gazes with her and within a few moments had stared her down. Ayesha's gaze fell away; any colour that she owned drained from her face. Saskia wondered what was going on there; she had not noticed any vibe between Ayesha and Amelia until then, though they had not spent that much time in Amelia's company. Interesting.

'What do you know about my Place Hal?' Saskia asked. She had not meant to be so direct, but she wanted to diffuse the tension between Ayesha and Amelia. Ayesha flashed her a grateful look, Amelia shot her a surprised one. She sensed a current of tension pass around the table.

'Shall I leave?' Holly asked guardedly.

'Why?' Saskia asked, 'I suspect you're in the know.'

Grace Rowe glanced at Saskia and then at Hal. 'I don't want to know. I'm going to see how Claire is. I'll take her some tea.'

When she had gone Hal replied to Saskia's question. 'Enough to enter into mortal covenant to keep it out of the wrong hands.'

'It's alright I did know it wasn't to keep me safe.'

'It does that too,' Hal gave a one shoulder shrug.

'I'll take what's on offer. I'm envious of all of you; you know that don't you? I covet what you have. And I have what you want to protect. Are you sure that I'm a fit person to be entrusted with it?'

'We can't do anything about that. The Wild will only answer to you; not to any of us.'

'It wouldn't allow Claire and me in,' Ayesha remarked, 'it wanted its mistress, no one else. I entered the mortal covenant to protect you, by the way.'

'I didn't suspect otherwise.'

'Thankyou darling.' Saskia was aware that Amelia's eyes transited from her to Ayesha and back again, and they were filled with curiosity.

'All my own. What will I do with it?' Saskia stretched her arms above her head showing her litheness and the firmness of her breasts under her close fitted wine-red jumper; her smile conveyed a sense of wry contentment; she lowered her arms and rested her hands back in her lap. 'You know at first, I didn't care. I just wanted my fetter gone and to regain my intent. But now I've grown possessive. In my head, I know the Place inside out on a basic map, as good as. But I don't know it at all really.'

'Do you know what it looks like Hal?'

'I've never seen it.'

'I have briefly. Could you go there? Would you know the way?'

'I do know the way, but I've never been there. Trevor Challoner offered to take me over twenty years ago. I knew him, though not particularly well. He was a close friend of my fathers. It's why Claire's firm, our father's old firm, is entrusted with his affairs. I can only tell you that he was afraid of the Place; he said to me that there was something incredibly old there, that in the wrong hands could do great harm in the mortal world; something that is presently asleep, and I believed him. He insisted that he didn't want to be the one to re-awaken it. Do you?'

'I'm thinking no further than getting rid of my fetter. When that's done, if it can be done, and when I feel ready, I intend to travel to the Wild; but I have no intention of waking anything up. Just out of interest, to who else might Trevor Challoner have talked? What other connections had he?'

Hal frowned and shook his head. 'He kept himself to himself. He made few connections. My father was his only friend.'

At midday when Saskia and Ayesha were on the point of leaving, Hal approached them on his own; he wore a serious expression. They had loaded their overnight case and Saskia's Lute in Ayesha's BMW; he stood with them on the gravel, almost on the exact spot where Saskia had struck the ermine with the broadsword.

'I've spoken on the phone, with the adept who agreed to attempt the removal of your Fetter.' He told Saskia. 'I informed him of your decision to go ahead. The nature of the thing absorbs him, and he intends to begin at once. His name is Theodor Bacchus. He's expecting a call from you this evening between six and seven. Here's his number.'

Hal passed Saskia one of his personal cards with a London number written in biro on the back. He fixed Saskia with his strange gaze.

'Saskia when this begins don't let your life come to a halt. Continue being you; conduct your plans; live life; because ultimately if it fails, that is all you have.'

'For me, that's not an easy thing to do,' she replied.

'I know that it isn't. As we say: Be prepared for failure but anticipate success.'

'There's nothing wrong with deviance. There's a lot of it about.' Saskia made the statement as they came to the outskirts of Leeds.

'Are you suddenly an expert on the matter?' Ayesha was curious, wondering where this was heading.

'Last night was the only proper party I've ever been to.'

'Really? What other types of parties have you been to?' Ayesha had not been to that many proper parties herself and usually at Claire's. Most of the other parties she had attended were her uncles, and she was not particularly sure how one classified those; she had been honest with Saskia about her past, including her uncle's gatherings, where until her late teens she had allowed herself to be used for sex.

'The previous were three were BDSM, when I was eighteen; though last night sort of puts anything into fresh perspective,' Saskia continued. 'I had sex for a few weeks with a forty-five-year-old woman at the time, who was into it. I quite enjoyed some of it, though I mostly took a back seat. There's a lot of it about, take it from me.'

Ayesha drove on in silence while she digested Saskia's latest revelation. She was driving them home; Saskia had remained mostly silent, deep in her own thoughts. Ayesha wondered where she was taking this.

'Now I'm in love. With my beautiful Ayesha, who enjoys intense pain, driven by desiring into silver thorns which are buried under her skin. If that's not deviance I don't know what is. And you know that I find it quite sensual, I genuinely do; even though the desiring is driven by her other lover.'

'I see. For a start Khalid is not my other lover. I make love with you, nearly every night and most mornings. You are my lover.'

'Alright so Khalid is your Sado-masochistic sex partner, with whom you occasionally have straight sex.'

'I see him twice a month now. Three at most. What is your point? Or are you simply trying to make me rise to the bait?'

'If you think that I'm trying to antagonise you, I'm not.'

'You could have fooled me.'

'I love you. I don't want to make you angry.'

'What are you getting at then?' said Ayesha suspiciously.

'Okay; serious question. Are you emotionally invested in your relationship with Khalid?'

'No, I am not emotionally invested in my relationship with Khalid. But I am emotionally invested in my relationship with pain. It's a significant difference. But more to the point I am totally emotionally invested in my relationship with you.'

Saskia was not sure that Ayesha was being totally honest; she knew from experience that the easiest person to lie to was oneself. She wondered if Khalid meant more to her than she was willing to admit.

'There, does that satisfy you? If it doesn't, I don't know if there's anything else that I can say.'

'There isn't and I believe you.'

'That's big of you,' Ayesha could not help allowing a faint note of sarcasm to creep into her voice. 'Can we move on?'

'I'm not done. Do you remember I told you that I had finished being cruel to you? That I wasn't going to detail my sexual exploits anymore.'

If Ayesha had not been driving, she would have crossed her arms defensively; as it was, she threw Saskia a dark little sideways look.

'Yes.' Her voice came out in a little growl.

'I've decided not to seek out sex with strangers anymore either. Not on the nights you go to Khalid or any other night.'

'Oh!' Ayesha was genuinely surprised.

'But I do intend to have a regular sexual accomplice.'

'A regular sexual what!?'

'Accomplice. Not on the night's that you go to Khalid. I realise that is a pointless exercise because you are consumed by your deviant need. I will still be jealous when you go to Khalid, and I can't guarantee that I'll not wait up for you.'

'You originally said there was no quid pro quo, well it really has felt like one.' Ayesha was mildly rebuking.

'I think I was lying to myself. But I've realised I was burying myself in sex and the point was getting lost.'

'And the point being?'

'To make you jealous of course!'

'I wasn't jealous on the nights I was with Khalid.'

'But you were when you came back, and you were miserable when I told you what I'd been doing; the nights I went out when you weren't with Khalid sent you up the wall. It's why you reduced the number of times you saw Khalid, so I wouldn't go out and leave you in alone, think about it.'

'That was cunning of you. What are you proposing now?'

'I have found someone, who I think might suit my taste. But I'm not sure yet. You'll be the first to know I promise if I go through with it. This is simply advisory.'

'Okaay. Let's hear it.'

'If I decided to make them my regular go to, it wouldn't be often. It wouldn't be at night either. I mean the evening's wasted on something like that really, isn't it? When you could be all tangled with someone who matters, or watching the tv, or playing chess, or just squeezing a foot.'

'I see. If you did this then, would you be doing this to punish me?'

Saskia frowned and pursed her lips.

'I suppose that I would be,' She admitted.

\*

When Saskia rang the number Hal had given her that morning, just after seven in the evening, a young woman's voice answered the phone; it was a quiet voice and sounded somewhat aloof.

'Bacchus residence.'

'Hi. It's Saskia Challoner. Theodor Bacchus is expecting my call.'

'Dad's busy; he's occupied with something for you at present. He asked me if I would take your call. I'm Selene.'

'Hello Selene. Can you tell me what I need to do?'

'You must come to London; Dad needs to see you. Can you be at Bacchus house tomorrow night?'

'I think so, I will have a companion with me, I'll check with her.'

'Mister Bosola said that you probably would be accompanied.'

Saskia's voice fell away. 'Are you speaking to me yet?' The words were just audible. Selene Bacchus allowed herself a little smile.

'Yes. What time do you want us there?' Saskia's voice was louder again.

'Be here for six. The address is Bacchus House, 1 Black Lion Square, Mortalwell. Will you wear a loose-fitting top or a camisole top please; the camisole might be preferable; You need to undergo a small procedure.'

\*

The black cab dropped them outside Bacchus House, it was a huge corner residence built of black brick, its frontage elegantly remodelled by Sir John Soanes. It was the largest of the mansions on the square by a long way. Eight broad granite steps climbed to its shiny black front door. They stood inside the tall archway and listened to the sound of the doorbell shrilling within. A minute later it opened. Selene Bacchus was seventeen. With long straight, ice blonde hair and fine ice blonde eyebrows above large icy blue eyes, which did not easily give back friendliness. Her nose and cheeks had freckling in a fine gold dust; she was cool and composed and exceptionally pretty, with potential to beauty. She was in tight jeans and brown leather lace up shoes, she wore a cream shirt outside her jeans, its sleeves rolled almost to her elbows, it's top four buttons remained unfastened.

'Come in.' She opened the door fully and stood to one side as they entered.

'Dad shouldn't be long. I've made tea in anticipation of you being on time, is that okay?'

She took them into a warmly lit study, and they sat in club chairs covered in dark red leather and drank tea.

'I understand that you're fettered against your will, which must be awful for you. Does it affect you in any way? I presume there are issues.' Selene spoke to Saskia; her words expressed sympathy but there was a cool dispassion in her stare. 'I don't mean to pry, but all of the different aspects of magic interest me.'

'It's alright, I don't mind. My head gets a hot pressure inside that can build until its unbearable. Ayesha draws that away now for me. Until recent weeks it was not as bad, it worked its way out in other ways. My mother had herself fettered; it killed her when she was only forty.'

'My mother died before her time too.'

'I never forgave mine for fettering me.'

'Do you miss her?'

'No.'

'I miss mine.'

'I'm sorry.'

'It's okay. It's my loss. I understand you. Why has the pain in your head worsened?'

'I came into connection with something that I believe had some sort of effect on it.'

'Something?'

Something that I'm not at liberty to discuss.'

'I see. Okay. Anything else?'

'It's the continuous aching frustration that gets to me.'

Selene watched her expression closely with a detached appraisal. Saskia had a sense that she was waiting for more; she felt like a laboratory experiment in its last stages; the rat being scrutinized as it stood on its hind legs before pegging out under the weight of implanted electrodes.

'Dad will remove it if it's possible. He's capable of most things.'

'I see ghosts too.' Saskia announced. She had not intended to tell her, but she decided that she would after all. 'Often. Other things too. I believe that's down to my fetter; mostly. I saw a blonde-haired woman on the stairs as we came inside.'

Selene appeared interested; her face tensed.

'A blonde woman you say, could you see her clearly?'

'Yes, she was small and pretty with straight platinum hair.'

'Oh,' Selene seemed disappointed. 'Please tell me if you see any others.'

'I will. I promise.'

'Here's Dad.'

Theodor Bacchus entered the study. He was powerfully built; over six feet in height. His straight white hair was shoulder length and he looked to be in his late thirties. He was good looking in a cold way and his eyes were the colour of glacial melt water. He was wearing a white silk shirt and grey trousers and black leather, handmade shoes. A gold ring set with a massive table cut ruby flashed on his hand.

'I see that Selene has made you welcome,' he said in a voice of pleasing depth, which was very slightly accented. Hal had told them that Bacchus's mother was Danish. He had been born in England and educated in both countries. Hal considered him to be the most powerful magician in the UK and possibly Europe, and a great master of 'real' alchemy, whatever that meant.

'I was longer than I anticipated.'

'It's okay, we enjoyed our tea and chat with Selene,' said Ayesha.

'It was not an apology.'

Saskia and Ayesha exchanged looks; Selene closed an amused smile. Bacchus sat in the large comfortable club settee; he leaned forward over the coffee table and placed a wooden box with a hinged lid down in front of him and settled into an elbow on knees position.

'Selene, will you get me a southern comfort please.'

'Yes dad.' Selene responded, unhurriedly she got up from her chair. She poured her father the requested liquor into a chunky glass at the oak drinks' sideboard; she half-filled it and set it down in front and to the left of him, before she resumed her chair.

'I am told that you are without reservation.' he spoke directly to Saskia, fixing her with his intense stare. He had already decided that she was beautiful, remarkably so. The other one was also beautiful. He could not sense any evil in them, but there was an element of darkness in both their natures; it added to their beauty. A dark thread that wound in and out of them, intertwined; it hinted at being unbreakable. The smaller one had entered some form of alchemical bonding at some point, he could feel its reach, it felt cruel, and elegant even, but not malefic; unlike Saskia's fetter; which was something else altogether. That felt freakish, anomalous, queer; it felt alive. He found himself looking forward to becoming better acquainted with it.

'I told Hal I can take anything that's thrown at me. I meant it.'

'I can see that you do. We begin the process tonight. The action, the alchemy, will come later, dependent on other things being successful.'

'I know that we need to find the Bran. I can't help you; I never knew his name. I only knew that he claimed to be Irish, though he spoke with an English accent.'

'He's not in Wilmslow anymore where he fettered you,' Selene informed her. 'His name is Tadgh Byrne he is regarded quite highly among his fellow sons of Bran. He is an Alchemical magician, more to the point, a skin magician, a Pellisomancer. He is one of only a couple of people in the UK who can perform the alchemical fetter. The other one is a woman.'

'Oh, my God. How did you find that out?'

'I have my ways,' Selene replied. 'Tadhg Byrne lives under the radar. But I think that I can find him.'

'Thankyou. Selene, thank you!'

Selene shrugged. 'It's okay.'

Saskia looked from daughter to father. She felt tears brimming.

'Why are you doing this for me? I am north of the Lhoegyr you are south.'

'I make no such distinction,' Bacchus replied. 'I find the old division to be stupid. I am a cartomancer by choice and when I set out my cards on this action it was clear to me that I should help you. Why I should do this, was in shadow. I am not a natural philanthropist. But I'm sure that in the future, that shadow will be dispelled. This is a challenge to me. But bear in mind the outcome is not guaranteed, even with me performing the transaction.'

'I'm helping because I want to,' said Selene. 'That was a terrible thing to do to you.' Despite her sincerity, she was still showing no emotion.

'What do I need to do?' Saskia asked taking a deep breath, she felt suddenly purposeful.

'When Selene finds the Bran, you must confront him. You must obtain from him an amount of the original distillations and ink made for the purpose of fettering you, that must be done in less than ten days from now, or we lose our window of opportunity for a couple of months. All of it will still be in his possession; if he denies that, it will be a lie. We need details of the making, the hours, and the astrological houses during which his alchemy was constructed. They will be written down in a Log. It must be given into your hands, at least the page about your fettering or a copy. But he will have used a symbol as a seal for the imagining that goes into the alchemy. That will be in his head. And if he is not co-operative; that is why you will have Amelia with you, or so I am told.'

'I don't need your menstrual blood, I thought at first that I might.'

'I only menstruate three or four times a year. My most recent one was last month.'

Ayesha levelled a curious look at Saskia; a little bit here, a little bit there, she thought.

'But I do need some blood from you.' Bacchus opened the wooden box in front of him, laying the lid back on its hinges. It held a couple of small silver topped jars and a choice of silver instruments. He selected one and held it up for her to see; it was an odd little instrument like a single bladed razor, but less than an inch in width.

'This is for the removal of skin. It's called a Flay,' he told Saskia. 'I need to remove some from your tattoo. It will not be a comfortable experience for you. There can be no anaesthetic. Now, when I come to removing the tattoo and introducing the alchemy into the fetter, no drugs, including painkillers or alcohol can pass your lips, until the fetter is destroyed. Be prepared for pain, like no other.' Saskia heard Ayesha issue a little ooph! under her breath.

'Ayesha, you must bring her in a car when we perform the transaction. You will not be able to take her home on a train.'

'But we'll discuss that and other things closer to the time when it is relevant. Now we concentrate on the moment. I see that you are wearing a camisole top as suggested. Remove your jacket.' Unhesitant, Saskia slipped out of her black, quilted jacket. She turned in her chair so that her fetter was visible to everyone.

'He's used elemental making to bind,' commented Selene. 'Part of his own essence is in that red weave. They'll need to get something else off the Bran.'

'That's his own undoing. His own fault. In a sense it works for us. He would never expect to be involved in his creation's removal. Are you still alright finding him?'

'He made his bed,' said Selene. 'Fuck him.'

'Don't swear.'

'Sorry dad.'

'Ready Saskia? you may want to grip the arm of the chair. You are going to feel a smarting pain. Be reassured my instruments are sanitized. More so than in any place of surgery.'

'Ooh!' Saskia winced at the application of the razor edge. 'That wasn't so bad,' she grimaced. 'It stings a bit.' She had heard it slice her skin away.

Bacchus had removed an inch long section of bloodied skin from the blade with a pair of tweezers he had got from the box. Saskia watched as he dropped the skin into one of the jars, which Selene was extending towards him; she replaced the silver lid and put the jar back in the box. She then extracted the other jar from the box, together with a silver scalpel, which she handed to her father in exchange for the Flay.

'I must cut you I'm afraid. I do require the jar to be at least a quarter full.'

'Where do you suggest?' Saskia said in a grim little voice.

'Your back, close to the fetter.'

'Okay. Whenever you are ready.'

'Selene have you a dressing for the two wounds?'

'Yes.'

'Something to stop the blood running down and getting on her clothes too.'

Selene nodded and produced a clean white towel and pressed it to Saskia's back above the edge of her camisole. Ayesha followed the entire procedure with eyes that were dark with intense fascination; just as she had watched what she could of her own procedure, the insertion of the silver thorns several years previously. The Bacchus's were being considerate she thought, appreciatively.

Saskia gave a tiny flinch as Bacchus cut her pale skin but made no sound. The blood flowed and he caught it, pressing the rim of the jar into her back beneath the wound so that it ran into it. He let it run until the flow slowed down and the jar was about a third full. Then he took it away and replaced the cap.

'Done,' he announced.

Selene caught the remaining trickle of blood with the towel.

'Will you hold this?' she asked Ayesha. 'While I put a dressing on.'

Ayesha nodded and sat down on the arm of the chair; she pressed her own hand against the towel. Selene fetched an expensive looking first aid box from the top of the desk.

'Are you okay?' Ayesha asked Saskia in a soft voice.

'I'm fine. This is nothing compared to what is to come. I know that.'

Selene had already prepared a couple of dressings, but with the wounds being so close together she only had to use one of them. She did apply antiseptic, which stung a little, before she covered the wounds. Ayesha slid down to be level with Saskia and Selene. Three pairs of large, beautiful eyes exchanged looks.

'We can't use anything when dad undertakes the transaction,' Selene said. 'The slightest thing could interfere with the action. You understand, don't you? I'm not usually involved in dad's alchemy. But I will be on this occasion. I'll do all I can; it will not be much. And I'll find the Bran for you, I promise.'

'I'm so grateful to you,' Saskia told her.

'It's okay.'

'Saskia you'll need this.' Bacchus extended a tiny bottle towards her. Saskia accepted it and examined it between her fingers. It was cylindrical and it was made of green glass, of antique manufacture, with a glass stopper that had a square handle.

'Every morning, beginning tomorrow, take no more than two drops in filtered water before you breakfast. It will probably make you vomit, though that should settle after a few days. It may interfere with your sleep and there may be other side effects. But you need to take it every day until the day of the transaction. Yes?'

'Yes. I understand.'

'I am going to reiterate and impress on you that you must consume no alcohol or use any drugs; any type of pain killer from now, until the Transaction is entirely over; is that clear?'

'Yes, clear.'

'Good. Now the Bran. He has bound your fetter with himself. This helps us. But we need more from him now. About a hundred mil of his blood.'

'Frankly, I would bleed him dry!' said Saskia malevolently.

'He signed himself in your fetter. Into you. I'm sorry. It's part of the alchemy. And you need to understand what is going to happen to you.'

'I'm listening.'

'This is no walk in the park, Saskia. What I intend is a kill to cure solution; unless something goes dramatically wrong, you are unlikely to die though.'

'That's comforting,' Ayesha commented glumly.

'It may break her, and her purpose will fail if it does. Your role is vital. Sakia is inviting in a fiend, though I believe you know that don't you Saskia?'

'I think that I do.'

'The alchemy will permeate your body, it will enact physical torture on it, and on your mind. Your mind will flee to escape the pain, which is a given; it will meet altered consciousness. Perhaps nightmare: it will trip and badly. This will go on, back and forth. I can offer you only meagre solace, in the form of a sleeping draught; it will give you oblivion for a couple of hours, but that's all. You are permitted no pain killers, no opioids, no muscle relaxants. No intersession from a magician; do you understand that? I must impress that on you Ayesha because every instinct you have will drive you to intervene, and you must resist them, understood? This will be torture for you too. There are three more applications of the venom and the veil, Saskia; each twelve hours apart; as one relents you will have the unfortunate knowledge that you are about to plunge yourself deliberately, back into nightmare. Some say that the best revenge is to live well. I say that there is a place for revenge in most hearts. Take your revenge Saskia, because this will harm the Bran; he had no consideration for you when he took this on. Keep that thought; use it. The spirit of the Bran is bound to the earth; as a kind they are beloved of the Fae, as you've discovered. He has bound you, through your fetter and through himself. There is in you some part of him; blood, being and will, and that is what I meant by kill to cure; the venom and the veil will kill the part of you that is the Bran. What your mother and Tadgh Byrne did to you is obscene; part of this man lives in you, and I intend to kill that part. It may, probably will, change you; how or to what degree, I don't know. It may give, it may take away. I can't guarantee that you will regain your ability, but it I believe it is likely that you will. So, are you resolved, Saskia Challoner?

*

'Are you okay?'

'Tired. My back's a bit sore.' They had just exited the lift on the penthouse floor at home.

These were the first words they had exchanged since leaving the Bacchus residence. Saskia had become brooding on the return journey. Ayesha had thought that she was being moody, but now and again she heard her sniff and saw her blink at tears.

'I thought you still weren't talking to me. I was a bit of a bitch I know.'

'I know. I've just been giving you space.'

'I'm feeling sorry for myself.'

'I know you are.' Ayesha aided Saskia off with her jacket. 'Are you hungry?'

'I'm starving.'

'Pizza then?'

'I might have broken if it hadn't been for you. I still might.' Saskia looked forlorn.

'I know you better than that,' Ayesha said gently.

'Are you okay?' Ayesha dropped to her knees next to Saskia who was face down in the toilet. The waves of nausea had struck

Saskia twenty minutes after she had taken the first draught of potion that Theodor Bacchus had given her.

'Noh! I'm throwing up.'

'Bacchus said that you probably would. Anything else?'

'I feel cold and shaky, and my eyes are all blurry; they were like that before I threw up.'

'Poor little thing!'

'Don't make fun of me.'

'I'm not, I'm mummying you. Is that it, do you think?'

'I don't think there's anything left in there. I'll clean the loo.'

'No, you'll wash your face, rinse your mouth, and brush your teeth, and I'll find you a comfortable T-shirt. I'll clean the loo. Do you want to go back to bed? Or have a duvet on the couch?'

'Duvet on the couch.'

Saskia woke with a start and gasped. She woke from a dream in which she was sitting in Claire's Garden next to the Lilley Pond; Selene Bacchus was carefully peeling away the skin from her face with the flay, her expression one of extreme concentration; she had just begun to slice and roll up her eyebrows when Saskia jerked awake. She was drenched in sweat; she unwrapped the blanket from around her body. The baggy T-shirt Ayesha had found her clung to her like a second skin. Ayesha came from the kitchen when she heard her wake up.

'Feeling better?' she smiled as she ran cool smooth fingers over Saskia's damp brow.

'Yes, how did you know?'

'The distillation Bacchus gave you is not unique. I had the same before my thorns were driven.'

'And you were on your own. I'm pathetic.'

'You aren't. Go and have a shower. Face the jet and be careful of your back, on second thoughts I'll come with you.'

Saskia had no appetite during the morning and day, and Ayesha nibbled. Saskia paced and could not settle into anything. They went out for a long walk in the afternoon and when they returned Saskia still could not settle; she told Ayesha that she felt almost fraught. Ayesha reassured her that she had experienced similar effects. In the early evening Saskia regained her appetite and they finished a lasagne from the fridge, and a salad, which she devoured with genuine hunger. She was even hungrier in bed, and Ayesha was not inclined to deny her own sexual appetite; it was after midnight before they stopped sex, and they lay on the bed sweating and exhausted. Saskia leaned over Ayesha, her small perfectly formed breasts pressed against her, rising, and falling rapidly; she kissed her mouth, and caressed her face and hair, her eyes were still flooded with the aftermath of pleasure; Ayesha panted as she stared into them, enjoying the sight of it in them.

'I adore you,' Ayesha whispered to her.

'Does it bother you what I need to do?'

'What are you talking about?'

'The Bran. This. The fetter.'

'It seems a strange time to ask me that, but my darling little mantis, you are strange. To answer your question: it doesn't. We do what we must. We are different the likes of you and I, we live in a different world to most other people, the ordinaries. Your fetter has chained you to a world that isn't your own. You didn't bat an eyelid when I killed that man, Rod.'

'He got what he deserved.'

'And you didn't hesitate to bash the pandemonium things head in with a sword. It was a living sentient being too, despite its press.'

'I don't think I killed it.'

'You'll get it next time.' They laughed.

In the morning, after she took her potion, Saskia was sick again. She was prepared on this occasion, kneeling at the toilet in anticipation of the nausea to come. It did not disappoint. Ayesha soothed again and cleaned up. When Saskia emerged from her shower she was shaking and felt utterly dreadful; Ayesha wrapped her in a robe and held her in her arms on the bed until the shaking subsided. That day she felt low, depressed, and tears flowed intermittently. She had no appetite and managed only some toast, which Ayesha insisted was spread with honey. Her mood lifted in the evening, but she was still quiet and introspective. They played chess, and then went to bed early and Ayesha cradled Saskia until she fell asleep.

# Four

The frost gleamed white and hard on the grass on either side, in her headlights. The rutted track was not user friendly to a Ferrari, and Rachel Zimpara observed unfamiliar caution as she drove along it. Beyond her stream of light, the blackness hid the uncompromising expanse of the north Yorkshire moors; by daylight they would be bleak, at this time of year, and she would have appreciated their barren beauty, as she had in past visits, though she had never been to this particular corner of them before. Her keen, sly eyes, glimpsed her turn off immediately, as it appeared on the right, and she halted the car as she nudged off the track opposite a heavy five bar tube steel gate, set in a dry-stone wall. She climbed out, leaving her door opened wide, and twenty-four hours from Tulsa spilling into the frozen still of the night. The ground was hard under her three-inch heels, a mixture of short grass, grit, and dirt. She ignored the icy bite of the air; her short Ferrari red skirt and white cotton camisole top were the barest of barriers. She released the frosted mechanism and pushed the gate, making it swing away into the darkness. She climbed back into her car, drove it through the gateway and along a straight upward sloping track. About a hundred metres away she made out the shape of a building, and the shimmer of outside lights.

She drove the Ferrari onto a wide expanse of chipped granite, she heard it crunch under her wheels, as she stopped the engine. She saw a man emerge from the side of the house and stand in the spotlight; she presumed she had passed by a sensor at the gate. She climbed out of the cock pit and drew on a short jacket, matching her skirt, then reached back inside to retrieve a slim leather document case from the passenger seat.

'Around the side,' the man called out. 'I'm in the kitchen.' He owned a deep bass voice, with a dark rough quality. He turned and disappeared again behind the house, not bothering to wait for her. She shrugged philosophically, her wide mouth forming a sardonic smile. She stepped carefully off the gravel, her heels burrowing into it, onto a path of old sandstone slabs, with expanding patches of ice across their surfaces. She followed the man, towards the light of an open doorway, set in the dressed stone wall on her left. Zimpara slid into the kitchen, like a little mouse looking wickedly coy; her slim shoulders were slightly raised, her wide mouth hinted at roguishness; she carried her document case in two hands, behind her back.

'Hello Max,' she said, pitching her voice low. 'We meet at last. Ooh! It's nice and warm in here.' Something was bubbling on an aga in a blue le Creuset casserole dish, the lid set to one side, the smell was not unpleasant: quite appetising in fact. She caught the scent of something else too that appealed to her; Max smelled of Bvlgari, but it was not that.

'You usually make do with an email or a phone call,' he growled. 'To what do I owe the...honour, of a visit.' Max added a couple of twists of black pepper to his recipe and mixed in the remaining wine from a bottle of red, before replacing the lid on the casserole. He moved to the island in the centre, still not looking directly at her, his gaze down, concentrating on what he was doing. Zimpara's eyes took in a mixing bowl, and ingredients in containers or dishes, also a stoneware cream jug. A radio was playing, turned almost imperceptibly low, tuned into a music station.

'Curiosity.' She answered. 'Put a face to the mysterious voice? After three years.'

'Bollocks!'

'It's true! Why bollocks?'

'Because I know you well enough by now, to know you do nothing without purpose.' Now he looked up; he had dark eyes, slightly moody, and they checked her out. She enjoyed what she saw in them; curiosity first followed by appreciation. She had already classified him as her type. Big, well-muscled, used to weights, big hands, the backs covered in black hair, jaw black stubbled, dark hair, shaved short.

'You know me that well after a few phone calls!' she replied dryly.

'Close the door, you're letting cold air in.'

'It couldn't get much colder in here,' she replied. Obligingly she pushed the door to and leant against it until the mechanism engaged.

'You just said it was warm! what do you mean its... I see, now you can't blame me for being suspicious. Why are you here Rachel?'

She ignored the question. 'Do you always cook from scratch? that chili con carne smells not half bad.'

'You assumed I'd be a ready meals man because I live alone.'

She gazed about the room; her eyes contained an element of mischief. 'Was this kitchen here when you moved in?' she asked feigning interest.

'I didn't have it fitted. I wouldn't have chosen it.'

'Grey Shaker, just doesn't seem you, somehow?'

'I don't mind it. What colour's yours.'

'Mine?'

'Kitchen.'

'Red.' She moved closer to him and laid her document case on the granite work surface. She peered at his food preparations; her nostrils flared delicately as she located what she had been scenting. She tapped the cream jug with an elegant nail, painted Ferrari red to match her suit. 'But not as dark as what's in this. More of a chili red. Pig's blood?'

'I'm making black pudding, to have with my breakfast.'

Zimpara's lips curved whimsically. 'Before you start kneading that concoction then, and add the pigs blood, have a look at the dossier I brought with me. It was essential that I came in person, Max; it was to impress on you the urgency involved. Also, there is someone, in entity form, in regular visitation at my house and I did not want them to overhear any phone conversations or witness any interaction between you and me, about this matter. It has skin in the game, so to speak. I don't trust it, but I am keeping it around for the moment.'

'Is it likely to have come with you.' He frowned, revealing just a tad of uneasiness. He decided not to ask why she wanted it around.

'Are you worried?' Zimpara was amused, her eyes widened and glinted mockingly; she removed her jacket and draped it over the back of a white leather barstool, standing on a chrome column and base. Her delicate camisole top revealed the petiteness of her figure. She kicked off her three-inch heels and propelled herself with the balls of her feet from the slate tiled floor, with limber ease, and sat on the edge of the work surface. She continued. 'No, I didn't want it following you either, in the circumstances. I set a ward on my car.' Max had no magic, she knew that, but he understood it and often moved in its sphere. He could find things, he could find people, he had a nose for it, like no other.

Max nodded, satisfied. He picked up the dossier case and extracted a file, replacing the case on the work surface. He opened the slim red file and peered at the contents. He frowned, puzzled.

'All it says here is: He's in your fiefdom.'

'He is. The rest of the information is in my head, for the same reason I'm here in person.' She picked up the white jug of pigs blood by means of a couple of fingers through the handle. She raised it to her nose and sniffed delicately; unhesitant, she immersed her forefinger into the contents and withdrew it, bloody to the knuckle; she parted her wide pliant lips and inserted the finger between them into, her mouth; she proceeded to suck it dry. 'I'd have preferred it warm,' she remarked.

He cast the file onto the work surface, dismissively, and moved to stand in front of her. He removed the jug from her grasp; she eyed his powerful fingers thoughtfully; she allowed.

'We don't want drips, do we? On that nice white top,' he said, setting the jug aside.

'I could always take it off, though a girl could die of thirst around here,' she complained, letting her lower lip jut, ever so slightly.

'I'll take the hint; would you like a drink?'

'What have you got?'

'Diet Pepsi?'

'The hard stuff! I'd like a whisky.'

He nodded and turned away, going to the cupboard where he kept some bottles of alcohol.

'His name is Tadgh Byrne,' Zimpara said. 'He's known as the Bran; he's an alchemical tattooist, one of the very best. I'll tell you everything I know over a bowl of chili.' She watched his broad back as he went to fetch her drink, he was wearing jeans and a black denim shirt, it hugged his powerful torso, revealing the bulge of muscles. She heard the chink of glass and he returned with a half bottle of whisky and a square chunky glass.

'You want me to feed you as well?' He said gruffly, he shrugged. 'I can't say I've heard the name, Tadgh Byrne. Single malt. Do you want ice? Soda?'

'I'll take it neat.' He placed the glass down next to her and unscrewed the top from the bottle of Glenmorangie; he poured her a generous measure. 'This is important Max, it's urgent. That's why I can pay double the usual fee.' She raised the glass of Glenmorangie between her fingers; her eyes roamed from its pleasing colour to the look of fresh interest as it took residence in his eyes, at her reference to a double fee. She set the glass to her lips and drank the contents in three successive mouthfuls, pausing appreciatively between each. She presented him with the empty glass. 'Pour me another.'

'Aren't you driving?' he cautioned.

She laughed, a soft chortle, the tone pleasing. She bent a bare leg at the knee, her short skirt riding up her smooth thigh. She pressed the ball of her small, beautifully maintained foot against his chest; she spread her toes; their nails were painted in the same Ferrari red as her fingers. She ran them into the thick dark hairs, visible at the upper part of his chest where the top three buttons of his shirt were unfastened. She savoured the sensation of the hairs between her toes, and the heat of his skin, for a few moments, before moving them up, over the dark stubble of his chin and jaw. She let them rest, curled, the tips barely touching his lower lip. She was aware of his gaze assessing her, of new considerations stirring in it.

'Who said I was driving?' she replied. 'I'm looking forward to my black pudding in the morning.'

*

Saskia woke to the sound of the phone; her eyes fell on Ayesha who was curled on the couch; she had been watching her while she slept. She saw Ayesha's mouth tighten glumly as she got up to answer the phone. She knew that it was Khalid before a word was spoken. She listened to what was said, it was not a lengthy conversation.

'Yes...alright...tonight...I need to talk to you anyway...No, I'll choose what I want to wear. I'll see you then.'

The previous day Saskia had been unwell and nauseous, throwing up randomly throughout the day as the effects of Theo Bacchus's alchemy appeared to worsen. She had felt dispirited and full of self-doubt. She experienced the familiar burning inside her head and Ayesha had drawn her energy to counter it. Sleep had eluded her in the night, and Ayesha lay awake with her for as long as she could, conversing and making gentle love, until sleep overcame her, and Saskia lay waiting for morning. When it came, she had felt a change, as if something heavy had been lifted from her, and everything seemed sharper, less shadow edged, as they had been. After the alchemy she threw up only once, and she regained her appetite. She studied the Wild in the afternoon with Ayesha, and in the evening, she played her lute for her. When they went to bed Ayesha had fallen asleep in her arms, but sleep had still eluded Saskia, and she watched Ayesha shift and murmur in slumber all night in soft dim light. That morning after her alchemy she had not thrown up at all. She felt only mild nausea, and ill temper from lack of sleep. At last, she had fallen asleep in a chair, her face in the crook of her elbow, rested on the chair arm. When Khalid's call woke her, she listened to the phone conversation feeling hungry and sulky.

'You'll be alright Saskia,' Ayesha said as she replaced the phone on the hub. 'Tonight, I'll be back before midnight, I promise.'

'Do what you want,' Saskia shrugged. 'You usually do.' Though she regretted her words the instant they had left her lips and she had seen the expression on Ayesha's face.

The driver held open the door of the Bentley. Ayesha climbed into the back, disposing herself elegantly onto the seat. Her clothing and makeup were restrained for a liaison with Khalid. She was in a simple, pale, iridescent, lamé dress, strapless and to her mid-thigh. She had naked sandals on her feet, with stiletto heels. She had a one carat diamond stud set in platinum in each ear lobe. Her eyes were dark and her lips red. She had highlighted her two tiny, beautiful moles in black. Saskia ignored her when she had paused in the doorway to announce that she would see her in a few hours. Her face had been buried, determinedly in a book. Her profile had been beautiful, resolute, sulky. Ayesha was delivered to Khalid's exclusive hotel restaurant. Khalid kept a luxury apartment there on the top floor where he entertained mistresses, and occasionally some of his dubious friends. It overlooked the glazed rooftop restaurant that attracted the best clientele that Leeds and its environs could offer. Ayesha entered by a private door at the rear of the hotel and took a cosy, private lift to Khalid's suite. When she entered, Khalid was standing in the window of his chic apartment, looking down over the park; he sipped his customary Laphroaig whisky. He was dressed in a black silk shirt and linen trousers; he had bare feet. Music was just audible and a girl with a pleasing voice was singing contemporary songs in Arabic.

'Osha,' It was the pet name they used for her, back in the days when she was sexually exploited, at her uncle's gatherings. He usually employed it when she had earned his displeasure.

'Hello Khalid,' she said a little breathlessly, she had never ceased to feel excited when she entered this place. She had learned how to find genuine pleasure in the sex act here. How to pleasure a man for hours, and in turn be pleasured for hours. Here, she had let her deviant self, first appear; Khalid had recognised it quickly and educated its evolution with relish. Meanwhile he had appreciated another evolution; that of Ayesha Shah herself as she developed into a sophisticated and beautiful young woman. This over time had changed his own perceptions and certain of his preferences, which included her bed as his playground of choice. That was now out of the question, and he was still smarting inwardly; he was not accustomed to her denying him.

Ayesha smiled and went to him. He looked down at her from his towering, height and showed strong white teeth, prominent behind his broad, dry lips. He bent to receive her kiss on his mouth and laid a long hand over her shoulder, a gold ring gleamed on his middle finger, set with polished black onyx, the intaglio seal of a spider cut into its surface, his seal. She felt nervous too, this was not a routine liaison. and she felt that he would not welcome what she had to say. They did not usually eat when they were together, and they drank economically. Their connection was driven by a powerful sexual impulse, which had existed for ten of Ayesha's twenty-four years. It was the one link that had survived from Ayesha's exploitation at her uncle's hands. One she had actively sought out, after Hal had intervened. She had never dreamed that she would question its durability, it had always seemed so much a part of her life, but she realised that she was beginning to do exactly that. She poured herself a glass of chilled wine from the bottle in the cooler and lowered herself into the luxurious hide couch. Khalid sat down close to her, studying her. Ayesha drew up her legs folding them on the cushion, her knees towards Khalid, her short dress riding up to reveal most of her smooth thighs. Khalid poured Laphroaig into his mouth, a long swallow, then placed the almost empty glass on the low table in front of them.

'Six days,' Ayesha chided cautiously. 'We agreed ten.'

'I recall that you agreed ten, not I.'

'It was bad of you.'

'Yet you came.'

'Yes, I came. Because we have things to discuss, you and I.'

'Because you wanted to.' He reached for her glass and removed it from her hand, placing it on the table next to his own. He drew her to him and kissed her and she melded to him, returning his kiss, she accepted his tongue. Her body became pliant; responsive and submissive. The fingers of his right hand loosened the strapping of her stilettos, and she shrugged them from her feet; the long fingertips stroked her left foot, he curled them under her toes separating them.

Khalid was a Nubian. His oiled skin intensely black, smooth, and taut over a rangy muscular frame. He claimed descent from the Kushite Pharoah Taharqa, and who was to dispute his claim, Ayesha thought. In her world many strange things had more than a grain of truth in them. The male line in his family were adepts, and who was to know what lay buried in his family history. He was powerful. Not as powerful as Hal or Theodor Bacchus, but powerful enough; more powerful than her, and truthfully that had always been something of a turn on for her. He was arrogant and dominant and capable of cruelty; these were the things that attracted her to his personality.

She felt arousal kick in, a strong sexual need. When they were naked it would increase intensely. The oil on his skin acted to increase desire and intensify pleasure. The intoxicating smell of his alchemical lure was already accessing that part of her brain that induced desire and willingness. The oil had already absorbed into

Khalid's skin, stimulating him; it would absorb into hers the more they touched. The oil and the lure were expensive agents; created by an artisan; a woman, Khalid had told her; she made a mental note to discover her name and her location; she was certain that Saskia would not shy away from a little experimentation. There she was thinking of sex with Saskia even while she engaged in carnal pursuits with Khalid. She smiled and shook her head slightly in mild disbelief. Khalid caught the gesture and searched her expression; his eyes questioned.

'You're amused?'

'I'm aroused.' Her smile continued. He watched her lower eyelids flex, lifting and drawing out; it was a peculiarly Asian gesture and Khalid always wondered how she had acquired it. Saskia considered it to be quite delightful and wondered if she was even aware of it.

'As are you.'

She stroked the elongated shape of his erect penis, visible below the waistband of his linen trousers.

'Just take me to bed Khalid, we don't need to fight.'

'You're unusually impatient.'

'I'm only staying until midnight. We have limited time.'

'That's ridiculous. Why?'

'You contrived this liaison. And I came, didn't I? So, I should set the parameters. I could simply have told you to phone me on another day.'

'Then why didn't you?' He was surly.

'Because there are matters that you and I need to discuss. I thought that they could be postponed, but now I realise that they need addressing, ASAP. Sex first, then words.'

He was tempted to cross swords with her, he was not accustomed to her being this assertive and it had begun to occur more often; he was also curious to hear what she had to say to him; he found it enticing. Perhaps she needed a more serious commitment, he had long suspected it; he also had his own revelation to make tonight.

He invited her to precede him, spreading his hand, a faint smile on his handsome, elongated face. Ayesha inclined her head gracefully; she got the lacquered box that held her goad, from her bag. She led the way to where they usually pleasured. The silence of it filled her as she entered the Place. It was pyramidal in shape, internally, the walls paper white, the light stark by contrast to the subdued lighting in the apartment. Khalid preferred his sexual activities well illuminated. The floor was black, it had the appearance of onyx. It was cool under her bare feet. A low, large, red leather bed occupied the Place, it was structured in places, to augment and enable sexual position.

She placed the lacquered box by the bed, on an elegant bronze torchiere stand, in the form of the Egyptian god Anubis; then turned to Khalid; she unfastened her dress and let it fall, revealing her impeccable nudity. She reached to him, opening his shirt with slim fingers, and pushed it back from his shoulders; then glided her red nails down over the Black skin of his smooth chest and impressively defined abdominal muscles. She drew his belt and ran it through her hand smiling, she recalled he had used it on her occasionally, when she wanted it.

She knelt and removed the trousers from around his naked feet, pulling them from each in turn. She straightened her upper body, rising off her heels. She grasped his large erect penis and aligned it with her mouth. She extended her tongue running the tip of it over the glans with little darting movements, then licking from the base of the underside of the head, she inserted the tip of her tongue into the aperture and moved it delicately within for several minutes. She withdrew her tongue and ran her cheek against his penis, nuzzling against the sac.

'You shouldn't be jealous.' She almost said to him: you have no right to be jealous.

'Do I need to be jealous?'

She gained her feet suddenly, nimbly and taking him by the penis led him to the bed. She lay down on it and drew him down on top of her. They began to lock into shapes and shift into movement. Ayesha arched her frame and began to encourage him with softly phrased obscenities.

Ayesha arched back against Khalid's upright thighs, as orgasm contracted her around his rhythmed hardness; it flooded her lower body, and tentacles of pleasure reached into her anus and through her back, and others into her breasts. She reached to him pressing her palms against his chest, as pleasure subsided. She laughed, panting, her heart thudding. He returned her laughter, peering into her eyes, searching for remnants of bliss. They had fucked for well over an hour in this manner; both had climaxed, Ayesha more than once. He placed two fingertips on her underlip at her opened mouth, she extended, and he probed inside with them, her tongue licked at them. His gaze questioned, she grinned in response, her eyes conveying an eagerness, a glee. Khalid drew his fingers from her mouth; he reached for the lacquered box and extracted the silver goad, he could feel the charge inside it; Ayesha watched his actions; her pelvis rising and falling still in arousal, small movements pushing against the hardness still inside her. Khalid smiled, a little cruelly, studying her eyes as he pressed it to her skin, where a silver compliance thorn lay buried inside her. Ayesha's eyes widened becoming dark avenues of pain; she contorted, and she moaned as the familiar agony pressed into her shoulders. Khalid persisted for several minutes before withdrawing intent; as it did so, Ayesha relaxed again, she searched him with her dark, fierce eyes, waiting expectantly. Again, he dispatched intent into the goad, and the agony of the barbs around her lower spine rocked her backwards; then she jerked forward, arching, as he pressed the goad to various parts of her, and harder, daggers of pain pushed unforgivingly into her shoulder and breast.

Khalid felt near to orgasm. He had applied Ayesha's goad for thirty minutes, inducing her pain, alternating its location along the path of her compliance. She was sheened in sweat and her body shuddered; the breath hissed between her sobs of pain. Khalid regarded the red limning that had risen along that part of her tattoo that was visible to him. He knew that it would extend over the whole of it. He did not understand her need for torture, but he did find it enjoyable. He paused her pain, sensing the approach of her own orgasm; he pulled her close to him pushing his size deeper into her. She climaxed, clawing at his back, voicing little cries of pleasure in her throat. He hissed, intense pleasure taking him also, and he ejaculated into her.

Ayesha rode out the sensations of pleasure allowing them to subside; ordinarily she would exhaust herself before calling a halt, but she subdued the instinct that urged her to continue with the pain and the sex. She plucked the goad from Khalid's fingers and twisted her body to lever herself up by bracing her arm on his knees; she drew herself from his hardness and crawled on all fours across the bed, away from him. She lay on her front leaning on her arms, cobra-like; she was breathing hard, and half laughing, half disappointed to end her diversion into pain. He made to reach across the bed for her.

'Enough. That's enough.'

'You meant it!' He sank back onto his elbow, frowning at her disbelievingly.

'Of course, I meant it.'

'You, have changed.' He huffed, annoyed.

'I probably have.'

'Is it because your life is suddenly more complicated?'

'Careful, remember that its mine to complicate.'

'I believe that It's down to this girl Saskia. She occupies too much of your time. Isn't it time she moved on?'

'Your animosity is showing.'

'I am going to divorce my wife.' He announced suddenly. He peered at her in expectation. Ayesha was unsure how to respond. She wondered what response he expected or hoped for.

'Why? She behaves. She tolerates your adulteries.'

'Is that how you see them?' he frowned, and his voice darkened.

She smiled and shook her head, becoming a little cautious.

'That is how she sees them. Whereas I am in a way polyamorous by nature.'

'We have grown apart, she and I.'

'You mean that you've grown tired of her.'

'She is no longer beautiful. I intend to divorce her. I want something exquisite to show off and to occupy my bed. I am considering marrying you. In fact, I intend to marry you.'

She laughed, surprised. He cast her a jackal's look.

'What's funny?'

'You're serious, aren't you!'

'Yes, why wouldn't I be?'

'You expected me to be overjoyed, didn't you?'

She was studying his expression; she knew that he took himself seriously, but he had just excelled himself in her eyes. She became suddenly sober as realisation sank in. She took a deep breath. Ayesha did not let people down gently. She believed in individuals living with the consequences of their own actions and their own assumptions. She had often enjoyed, sensual, even obscene hours with this man, she had performed any act that he wanted of her. Then she had gone home to get on with her life, and that was what she intended to continue to do.

'Not happening!'

He looked nonplussed. Khalid was a man used to getting his own way. When he made assumptions, they were usually complied with. He stared at Ayesha's expression, and he was surprised to see an element of anger where he had expected to see pleasure, if not pleasure then satisfaction.

Ayesha realized that it was time she took this particular bull by the horns. Better to level. If the bunny dies, best to tell the child, was her philosophy.

'You may as well know that I am in a relationship with this Saskia, who you are so dismissive of! We've been sharing a bed for the last few weeks!'

He stared at her in silence as she made her announcement. His expression gave her nothing to work on. She could see his thoughts processing behind his piercing eyes. They moved quickly over her face and body, from point to point as if he was joining up lines. She realised that she had shocked him to silence. She edged closer, peering into his face for some sign.

'I'm sorry Khalid, but this is how it is! You cannot go on feeling so entitled, that you think that you can demand my company whenever you want. Saskia has been understanding and I know that it's caused her emotional pain, my insisting that I go on seeing you. And I will go on seeing you. But I realise now that it must be on my terms.'

'You'd choose a slip of a girl over me?'

Ayesha felt surprised. He was sulking she realised.

'You don't know her! Don't you dare make assumptions. She is charismatic, intelligent, beautiful!'

'Listen to yourself. You are infatuated. Is the attraction that she is fettered. A tragic little waif!' His face became animated, releasing his thoughts.

'Khalid listen to yourself. You don't know her, so you can't judge. What do you think I am! I'm not flattered by some simpering little girl; even Hal and Amelia are smitten by her. Call your car for me. On second thoughts I'll get a taxi.'

He appeared concerned, nonplussed at her reactions. He shook his head, experiencing unfamiliar bewilderment. He was as angry as he had ever been, and resentful. But he was also a man who valued things, and Ayesha represented a high value to him; he was not prepared to lose her. Not for misplaced pride. She was a prize, a trophy, he had always thought that. Khalid had the patience of a spider; he was prepared to bide his time. He released a long, thoughtful breath as he subdued his anger.

'I'll summon the car. I suggest we dampen this down, before we go too far along a path, I assume neither of us want to take.'

'I think we agree there.'

'I want to continue to see you. I had no idea that I had a rival; it's been a shock.'

'Yes, I do want to continue to see you, and Saskia understands that. Sort of. But you must understand that you can't dictate to me. You can't muscle in when you choose. It was at my discretion anyway Khalid; it's just that now I'm prepared to exercise it. Yes. You're part of my life. I feel affection for you. But I don't love you Khalid, I believe you assumed that you were my obsession. Sex and pain are my obsession, and Saskia.'

'Then I want to meet her. I want to meet Saskia,' he announced, unexpectedly.

*

Eleven p.m. was the earliest that Ayesha had ever returned from a liaison with Khalid. If Saskia was surprised, she did not show it. When she heard Ayesha come in, she was still occupying the couch as she watched snuggles roam about near the ceiling; she reached for her book which she had finished almost an hour before and re-opened it a few pages from the end. She had snacked during the evening, but the only sign was an inch or two of sparkling water in a glass and an empty wispa wrapper. Ayesha perched on the edge of the couch at Saskia's bare feet and studied her. Saskia would never know what it had taken for her to stand up to Khalid. She was aware that her body was soiled, this was not unusual, but on this occasion that awareness was somehow heightened, and uncomfortably intense. She invariably showered immediately she returned to her apartment. Occasionally requiring a cool drink; not tonight. She had slipped back into her dress and collected her sandals on her way out of Khalid's; she had carried them, making the return journey barefoot. Her revelation had laid her bare to Khalid and in a sense herself, she felt denuded; even unmasked. She felt the urge to lay herself bare to Saskia, but at present she might only receive barbs in exchange.

'Don't you want to pass comment?'
'About the fact that you stink.'
'Fuck you Saskia!' She bridled.
'And fuck you, Ayesha!'
'I'm going for a shower.'
'Good, you need it.'

Ayesha sighed, decided to indulge. 'That I'm back so early.'

Saskia shrugged, she had no intention of offering solace; even though she was both surprised and reassured.

'I want to finish my book.'

'Okay! we'll talk in a few minutes.'

'I've made some tea.' Saskia announced. She was feeling contrite and even sympathetic. She had not discussed Khalid much with Ayesha, but she had the impression that he was a dominant personality, who was accustomed to getting his own way, and that he was used to Ayesha playing a submissive role. This was the guy she had chosen to torture her, with her compliance of thorns for god's sake! They went back a long way, this was an awkward and inconvenient situation for Ayesha; Saskia knew that it must be putting a strain on her; how it affected Khalid, Saskia could not give a monkey's shit.

Ayesha had emerged from her shower feeling cleansed but anxious. She had thought of going to bed but rejected the idea; she realised that she wanted this time with Saskia; it felt somehow risky, a walk in the wild wood; cool and different. She wondered if Saskia felt even remotely the same. Ayesha was in a silk dressing gown, white on this occasion, and white backless slippers. She had not dried her hair. Saskia decided that she looked a little bit lost.

'Would you like something to eat? I could do you some toast.'

'Is there any chocolate cake left?'

Saskia smiled. She would have laid money on that reply. She wondered which of the two experiences, the compliance of thorns or Khalid, invariably made Ayesha need chocolate when she returned home.

'I'll fetch you some.'

'Did you enjoy the book? What was it?' Ayesha had seen the title, but requesting it was not the true reason for her question, she was sounding Saskia out. It was looking more promising.

'Eyes of the overworld. I enjoyed it.'

'I like Jack Vance. Try Dragon masters next, it should be on the shelves.'

'I will.'

Saskia returned with a tray a few minutes later; tea and their remaining two slices of triple layered chocolate cake on a plate; also, a cake fork.

'Oh, yes!' exclaimed Ayesha; she clutched the plate from the tray as Saskia was in the act of lowering it to the coffee table; she placed it on her knee and began to devour slivers of cake.

'One of these isn't yours, is it?' she asked.

'No, both are for you,' Saskia replied, amused; she had moved into position next to Ayesha, ensuring that they had contact, because she found it comforting. She was surprised when Ayesha rested the side of her head against her shoulder. She was aware of her damp hair through her T-shirt, the showered warmth of her penetrating to her skin. Her scent.

'I told Khalid about us,' Ayesha announced.

A dozen responses jumped up and down inside Saskia's head. Malevolent gratification stole into her lambent eyes, and she kept them averted; she allowed no satisfaction to creep over her expression in case Ayesha glanced around at her. She selected the responses that would cause the least and the worst disharmony.

*I hope it really fucked him off! It was time he knew.* She chose neither.

'Are you okay?' she said softly; she slipped her arm around Ayesha's waist.

'I'm fine little mantis. It was time he knew anyway. Now he won't assume he can just call me whenever he wants and expect me to go running to him. He was angry, though he hid it well. Shocked too. I still intend to see him, you know that.'

'I know. I'm part realist. How often?'

'I don't know. When I need to, I suppose. You see with Khalid it's not a matter of need. It's a matter of want. He's greedy. Entitled. He informed me that he's divorcing his wife.' She laughed through her words. 'Then he told me that he wants to marry me.

Oh, look at your face.' Ayesha smiled tenderly. 'He doesn't love me. He told me that; he wants a trophy to show off, and to keep his bed hot. Fuck that!'

A sensation like creeping ice had spread through Saskia. Ayesha appeared to be treating it as a joke though, which was reassuring.

'You know he assumed I would. I'm sure that he had the idea that I would jump up and down in celebratory glee. You should have seen his face when I told him it simply was not going to happen.' Ayesha finished her chocolate cake and returned the plate to the tray, she intended to pick up a napkin for her mouth, but Saskia's next words prevented her.

'Are you sure?'

'Saskia!' Ayesha turned to her and grabbed for her hands. She searched her eyes; was there a shade of green for worried. 'I'm certain.'

'You, say that now. The best way I can phrase it is like this. What if he had wanted you to marry him and I had not been in your life?'

'Same reply. Not a moment's hesitation. I swear it!'

'Okay. Anything else I should know?'

'He slagged you off, he was scathing but not too overt.' Ayesha watched Saskia's expression closely, she felt relief when Saskia grinned.

'Of course. He probably thinks you've fallen for a silly little girl. That is really insulting to you.'

'I put him right, on a few things. Then he said that he wanted to meet you.' She had been building herself up to this. She did not want to overplay it. Softly, softly, catchee monkey.

'Not happening! Nada!' The expected response.

'Think about it. I wouldn't keep you on a leash. You could show your pointy little horns. Your decision.' She stroked Saskia's dark brows with the back of her fingers, then dabbed her, unexpectedly, on the tip of her nose with her index finger, causing Saskia to smile.

Saskia leaned towards her and kissed her on the side of her mouth, then licked something from the middle of her upper lip.

'Chocolate cake,' she breathed.

'That, was mine.' Ayesha was smilingly artful.

At that point, the phone rang, and they exchanged mutual frowns. Ayesha went to answer it. She felt her heart quicken when she saw the number on the screen. She lifted the phone from the hub.

'Ayesha.'

'Hello Ayesha, I'm sorry to ring this late. But I thought that you'd want to know straight away, so I chanced it.'

'It's fine, hang on while I put you on speaker.... It's Selene Bacchus.'

Saskia almost leapt from the couch to join Ayesha. She gripped Ayesha's hand so fiercely that it hurt, but Ayesha did not care.

'I'm listening. Hi Selene.'

'Saskia, I've found the Bran!'

# Five

The pub was old and atmospheric. It was popular for that reason. People travelled from town, several miles away, to enjoy its low, age darkened beams and spacious flagged floor and leaping fire. It had a tradition of witchcraft, things discovered in the chimneys and under floorboards, when work was undertaken, and a reputation for ghosts. Saskia could see several, mingling with the clientele; some long present, others not so long; but all held there by familiarity and pleasure. They did not know each other and did not associate; ghosts rarely did, in Saskia's experience. She avoided them, and avoided looking at them, she did not want to attract any of them.

Saskia had become familiar with pubs and bars over recent weeks, for the reason she used to habitually avoid them in the past, the presence of predatory males. There were several unaccompanied males in the Horseshoe, occasionally watching her with hunger. Her companion was the deterrent. He was intimidating, with close cut black hair and heavy stubble, and dark, hard eyes. He was dressed in a denim shirt and jeans, the fabrics stressed by muscle; his sleeves were rolled to reveal hair and tanned skin; a genuine gold Rolex on his thick left wrist. He was drinking halves of Guinness; Saskia was drinking diet Pepsi. His name was Max Angus, and he had found the Bran.

'He shouldn't be long,' he said; he kept his voice subdued, it had a deep pitch, pleasingly dark. His eyes flickered over her; Saskia had sensed his attraction when he introduced himself, but also an element of caution.

'You should get his attention. He prefers younger women.'

'Are you sure he'll come?'

'Every Monday, Thursday, and Saturday. Eight o'clock, give or take a few minutes.'

'What if he has someone with him?'

'He won't. He always arrives alone. He leaves around ten, usually accompanied. Never the same one; it's a popular place.'

'You seem to know quite a bit about him.'

'It's my business to find people, for other people and find out about them.'

'Is that all you do?'

'No. I do other things. I don't draw the line at much.'

She did not imagine that he did.

'I can see that you keep very fit. What do you do for pleasure?'

He shrugged. His pupils were circles of black onyx fixed on her eyes. He liked her green eyes. They smouldered and they lacked innocence.

'I like my toys.'

'What sort of toys?'

'Women mostly.'

Saskia's mouth shaped into a little twist of sardonic humour. She felt intimidated which she liked; turned on.

'And when not 'mostly' what then?'

'Cars. I hunt with a crossbow.'

Saskia nodded politely, metal and spanners; she yawned inwardly; the crossbow tweaked her interest though. She reached for her glass, she sipped her drink and decided to bring the conversation back to the business in hand.

'Do you know this man; Conel?'

'Not personally. I know him by sight.'

'Has he lived around here long?'

'Just a few years. He lives in the forest past the Roman camp. I hunt there occasionally. You need to avoid the Rangers. But that's easy enough.'

She was about to respond; her eyebrows furrowed with interest, but the pub door opened behind her, it was an inner door and opened to the side, directly behind their table. He had arranged for her to meet him there early to ensure they got that very table. Max's face showed sudden irritation, his eyes threw hostility at her.

'It's just how the fuck it is!' he snapped, telling her that the Bran had arrived.

'Fuck you! One call and you ditch me for that bitch! What's the matter with me?' Saskia was angry, bitter, her voice rising.

Max shrugged. He got up to leave; he yanked his car keys from the front pocket of his jeans. He widened his eyes, to indicate to her that the Bran had walked past them. She glanced to the side, locating the back of the man walking between the pubgoers towards the bar, by then out of ear shot; but he was not alone, he had a companion, dressed in long black garb, who walked beside him and stayed with him until he had almost reached the bar; where they separated and the companion moved away and went to stand by the hearth, to gaze into the fire. So, the Bran did not come alone after all. Saskia frowned, puzzled; a little thrown; but pulled herself together, then returned her gaze to Max and smiled, her mouth forming a thin curved line, her expression filled with contempt. She didn't mention the companion, he probably could not see it.

'Just fuck off,' she told him.

'You know where I am,' he muttered.

She watched his brawny shoulders out of the door; she waited, making tears, then got to her feet and took her empty glass with her to the bar.

She was wearing fitted black jeans, black suede ankle boots with a kitten heel, and a burgundy mohair jumper, snugly moulded to her breasts and hugging her slender waistline. She had accessorized with a cherry amber bracelet and earrings courtesy of Ayesha and had kept her makeup demure. She said excuse me to a bearded man discussing Top Gear with his friend and squeezed in next to the Bran, she jarred his arm where it rested on the bar just enough to gain his attention.

'Sorry!'

'No problem.' He was holding a twenty-pound note between his fingers, waiting to pay for his drink. Saskia got out her own money and leaned her elbows on the bar. A tall well-built girl with straight mousey hair and a chunky body, dressed in tight designer jeans and top, came with the Bran's drink, a pint of John Smith's; a girl who had found her niche in life thought Saskia cattily.

'Thankyou Laura,' said the Bran, 'and whatever this young woman's having.'

'No that's okay, really.'

'What are you having?' Laura inquired, big eyed, big faced, stressed. 'I've got other customers.' The Bran had not released his money to her.

'Diet Pepsi, ice and lemon,' Saskia smiled.

'Same glass?'

'No, a fresh glass.'

'Right!' Laura plucked the twenty-pound note from the Bran's fingers and went away to get change, and Saskia's drink.

'She'd have made you wait ten minutes otherwise. She has a bit of a complex. And she is struggling with a biggish arse.'

Saskia vented a brief callous laugh. She put her money away.

'And there's nothing at all wrong with you by the way.'

'What do you mean?' Saskia showed a still despondent face.

'It's what you asked that twat you were with. I couldn't help hearing what was said when I came through the door. You're better than him. He's not in your league.'

'I wouldn't know. He made me feel sort of this big.' She showed with her index finger hovering an inch over the bar. She allowed her voice to strangle just enough.

'What's your name?'

'Stevie. Yours?' She turned to him smiling, brave.

'Conel. Pleased to meet you, Stevie.' Laura returned with the Bran's change and Saskia's diet Pepsi.

'Thanks for the drink.'

Saskia made to move off, she paused as though reviewing a sudden thought.

'Join me.' She offered.

'I thought you weren't going to ask,' he replied affably.

They sat down together at Saskia's table. The Bran nodded towards her coat and bag hung on the back of her chair.

'That was trusting.'

'It should be safe here surely.'

'Should it? Were you going to eat?'

'We were, but I've lost my appetite. I think I'd just like to talk.'

'It suits me. You do know that you are incredibly beautiful, don't you? And that fool was a man with no ability to appreciate it.'

The Bran had piercing blue eyes that looked right into her. His hair was black and choppy with long sideburns, a hint at late regency. Shots of grey threaded it. He had pale skin, a wide face and small nose. He was clean shaven, a tiny fresh wet razor cut blobbed under his chin. He appeared fifteen years younger than his probable, fifty plus years. His face looked just how Saskia remembered it. She felt relieved, because she had carried a doubt that this man, called Conel, might not have turned out to be the Bran Tadhg Byrne, the man who had fettered her. But here he was, sitting across from her, as large as life, unaware of who she was and totally absorbed with getting her into his bed. He was wearing a blue almost black jacket and collarless white shirt, dark blue fitted jeans, and pointed black leather shoes. A leather belt was drawn to its final notch through a silver buckle; she recalled that he had been much fitter and leaner the last occasion that she had seen him. But he had charisma, and he was erudite and charming, which had understandably been lost on her at twelve; she felt her body relax and her mind sharpen.

'You're not from round here!'

'That sounded more of a statement than a question.'

'I suppose it was. It's just an impression. I've a sixth sense, it's the Irishness coming out in me.'

'You don't sound Irish.'

'I've family there. My roots are there. I rarely visit though. But you haven't answered my statement. Am I right?'

'You're right, spookily, I'm visiting my sister in Whitby for a few days, we were out together last night; that's when Max picked me up. I live in Leeds.'

'What do you do? College? Work?'

'I'm doing a business management degree at the city of Leeds university.'

'Clever girl? How old are you?'

'Twenty.' *Patronising bastard.*

'You come across as more sophisticated than your average twenty-year-old student.'

'Are you familiar with many twenty-year-old students then?'

'It was a compliment.'

'Okay. I'll accept it. No, I am different. I don't swim with the other fish.'

'Are you ambitious?'

'Yes of course I'm ambitious.'

'Do you want to get married? Have kids?'

'No and no. I told you I'm ambitious. I don't want to tie myself down.'

'Do you have a boyfriend back in Leeds?'

'No. I have occasional men friends. What about you? Have you got a girlfriend, or a wife at home?'

'Neither. I prefer not to tie myself down either. And I'm not even ambitious. Are you ready for another drink?' He had finished his John Smith's and her glass had been empty for a couple of minutes.

'Yes, I am. Same again. Let me get them.'

'No, it's okay. Are you sure you just want diet Pepsi?'

'I'm certain. I don't drink alcohol.'

'That's a lie,' he grinned.

'Yes, it is a lie. I don't drink alcohol presently.'

'I see. Can I persuade you to make an exception tonight?'

'Afraid not. And don't bring me back anything with alcohol in it, in case I'll think what the hell! I won't, but I will walk straight out of the door. I don't need alcohol to lower my inhibitions. I don't have any.'

He shrugged. 'Fair enough.'

The companion had stood by the fire until then, gazing down into its depth, as though lost inside its burning heart. Unseen by those close to it and others who had walked against it or inadvertently touched it, yet not been aware that they had. It left the fire, as Conel went to the bar, and approached Saskia. The dark habit that covered it, and hooded it, flowed away, flowing around its back as slender arms and hands appeared. It was a woman, lithe and small, more petite even than Holly Penn. Her walk was graceful, almost not a walk, a progression.

The sound of the pub stilled, and silence fell as the companion declined time. A familiar sensation of being stretched on the inside passed through Saskia, but stronger than she had previously known it; like the string on her lute being overstressed. She gasped as she understood that the declined moment had extended its reach to her and had already endured for longer than the earlier occasions when she had experienced it. She was participant, not observer.

The companion seated herself at the opposite side of the table. She was nude, Saskia saw, and she considered her to be beautiful, though many would think she was a monster. Her face was narrow, its skin was covered with fine feathering or soft scales like on a butterfly's wing, in shades of blue and occasional green, iridescence. Her unblinking eyes were dark red, like the amber of Saskia's earrings. Her small mouth opened in a cold, cruel little smile, to reveal tiny, pointed teeth. Her hair was pine needles, the length of porcupine quills. The membrane over her body looked like fluttering iridescent feathers, but like the skin of her face, it was not feathers. The sensual shadow, which had covered her body as she entered the pub, trailed from her slim shoulders like a cape, Saskia could see now that its gossamer darkness was part of her too, though a deeper blue than her body; it shifted and moved with the same subtle undulations.

'I Felt your eyes touch me when I came in with my man,' she said. Her soft tones lilted and lisped pleasingly. 'Now, few see me, even among those with the sight. So how is it you can see me, I ask?'

'I see ghosts, other things too.'

'Do you see ghosts now?'

'No. They all left when you came into the pub.'

'They usually do.' She leaned across the table resting on slender elbows, her eyes burning into Saskia's. 'You could have any man you wanted. If you simply needed to be mauled and thrown about and fucked senseless, you should have stayed with the caveman you were with. Why then do you want to fuck Tadgh because he will disappoint?'

'Why? are you jealous?'

'Why should I be jealous of a fuck? He's fucked hundreds.'

'Are you some sort of family spirit?'

'That, I am not.'

'What are you then, Shee? *Sidfhir?*'

'Ooh, I thought you'd say *Sidhe*, *Sidfhir* will do well enough.' she said her tone faintly mocking.

'Not Irish though?'

'I don't come from that place. But neither does he.' Her brows delved suddenly in concentration. 'Are you going with him when he leaves?'

'I must.'

'Must? The great liar reimposes the lie, can you feel it?'

'I wish that I could.' Saskia had the sense of travelling backwards, she felt almost disorientated. The *Sidfhir* appeared to move with incredible speed, rising and passing through the busy room as it stirred back into life; Saskia realised that she was experiencing the effect of withdrawing from the source of declining. The *Sidfhir* was gazing into the fire again, her dark habit drawn about her, by the time the first voices rose in conversation. The Bran, Tadgh Byrne, who called himself Conel, came back with their drinks a few minutes later.

'What do you do Conel?' Saskia inquired as he resumed his seat.

'Me? I'm a tattooist. But not in the ordinary sense,' he replied, casually.

'A tattooist? How do you mean, not in the ordinary sense?' Saskia appeared fascinated, her eyes had widened, becoming large, and she leant across the table, much as the *Sidfhir* had done with her. She rested her chin on her interlocked fingers and waited expectantly for his response.

'I work in Japanese Tebori. Berber, Innuit, I scarify too. I use traditional tools and methods, and my skills are second to none if I say so myself.'

'Is that legal though? You can't do that sort of work in an ordinary tattooist parlour surely?'

'It's very specialised. I work on commissions only; Sometimes I travel to where my services are needed; mostly they come to me. My work is highly sort after.' She could see him preening, he could not help but bask, as she devoured. He did have an easy charm though; he was enigmatic, and his blue eyes had the ability to acquire. She had felt the tug of him inside her; she understood why he was successful with the opposite sex. If they had met by chance, without her knowing who he was, she might have shared his bed.

'Wow! That's amazing. What type of person wants work like that performed on them.?'

'You'd be surprised. But mostly those with a very particular reason requiring it. I can advise the kind of tattoo they need, to symbolize a very particular requirement. It doesn't come cheap.'

She had no intention of pushing him too hard on that score, in the event he became suspicious, so she directed his attention to thoughts of her body.

'It sounds fascinating, really.' She said, looking enthralled. 'I have a small tattoo on my back, but I'd love more. I'd really love some scarification, all those little beads of skin.'

'Where would you have them?' He smiled, an element of licentiousness seeping into his eyes.

'All across my stomach and breasts, the thought is really quite sexy.' She grinned and bit on her under lip, feigning playfulness.

'It's often about attraction and about sex too; arousal; you know a penis can be modified by scarifying, to increase sexual stimulation.'

'My god! You're loving this! Conel, have you done anything like that?'

'No, I haven't. I'd have to draw the line there I think, handling some blokes cock!'

'I do see your point,' she grinned. 'Are you here until late. Lock in maybe?'

'Not my scene. You think these are my kind of people?'

'Not really.' Saskia went all in, following instinct, and discarded caution. 'Would you rather take me to bed?'

'I think that you know the answer to that.' His blue eyes revealed his pleasure.

'Do you live close?'

'I'm a little bit remote. Does that deter you?'

'I'm in my own vehicle. I'll follow you home then.'

*

'There are two faces to the forest,' said Saskia's strange little passenger. 'One old, one new. Yet the new is still the same ground it always was. It's the trees that are newcomers. The old life beat of the forest survives. You only need to listen. It's why we came to live here; when things in the world became difficult for Tadgh.' She was curled in the passenger seat of Saskia's jeep, her legs drawn up under her, her body side on; she peered at Saskia. She had not bothered with the seat belt; Saskia had not pressured her about wearing it. They had left a grass centred little lane and joined a narrow-rutted track flanked by old woods, frost forming as the temperature outside the car fell. The milometer had counted six miles. There was no habitation only trees made stark in her headlights, and total blackness behind them, and the taillights of the Bran's land rover, fifty metres ahead.

'Difficult? How?'

'He lacks friendships, but not antagonists. At least he has me.'

'How do you know him, Ta...Conel?'

'He was promised to me before his grandfather was born. He has an ancient lineage, though you wouldn't think it. You came seeking Tadgh, not Conel. Don't bother to hide it!'

Saskia compressed her mouth and tensed her hands round the steering wheel, angry with herself.

'It was not your slip. It's not a fuck you want tonight, it's another errand entirely that brought you here. Have a care with your reply. I am not a fool. You gave yourself away when you called me by O'Reilly's name for us, *Sidfhir.* Immortal men.'

'You knew that I could see you. There was no point hiding it. Why didn't you tell him?'

'Oh, it's hard to think like you! Don't you know that? To converse like this.'

'He can't see you, can he?'

'He knows that I am there. I hide myself out of design; I am seen when I want to be seen. Or in lover's bliss. For I come to him in the night when there is no other in his bed. He knows I'm there. He loves me. He knows that I will protect him. I am his legacy. He is a Bran. He worships old gods...though they do little for him. What did he do to you?'

'He fettered me.'

The companion tensed; her slim hand closed around the edge of her seat back. Her strange eyes searched Saskia's face, seeking a purpose.

'He's fettered six in his time. Four chose to be fettered. One was fettered for slavery. The sixth was fettered at her mother's request. The mother was one who had made the personal choice to be fettered.'

She extended a slender hand. Saskia allowed her touch. She felt the pressure of cool velvet fingers against her cheek.

'I recall you. You were too young to be fettered. But your mother was persistent and willing, and exceptionally beautiful.'

'And that's why he did it? Performed this horrible alchemy on me? On a child. In exchange for sex!'

'Don't judge him harshly. He's silly, just that. His cock rules him. He touches the old deeper than most, but it doesn't make him less of an idiot. It's the whimsy of his kind in him. He doesn't see the ill it does.'

'It killed my mother within a few years. It might have killed me eventually!'

'Have you come for revenge?'

'I feel vengeful. But not on her behalf, I don't know which of them I despise most.'

'I'll not let you harm him.'

'I'm not here to harm him; I'm willing to forgo revenge. I want the alchemy, the making. So that it can be reversed.'

'It can't be undone.'

'Yes, it can. He took away what was mine. Part of me and I want it back!'

'I am sympathetic. But alchemy such as that is part of him. If it is undone it will harm him, eventually. Something from the dark will be let in. It will reach for him and diminish him. He'll wither before his time.'

'I don't care.'

'You are beautiful, and I am sure persuasive. But he won't give you what you want.'

'Then I'll take it,' Saskia replied grimly.

'And I will not let you. Do you know what I am?'

'You're Shee, I think we established that.'

'I am *Leanhaun Shee,* as the old language of Tadgh's people call my kind. A *Sidfhir* who takes a human lover. It's not as simple as the old stories though. Tadgh was promised to me before his five times grandfather was born. He is mine, so that I can have knowing of the physical realm, in ways that you would not understand. In your parlance: I've a lot invested.'

Saskia smiled thinly. 'I'm sorry, I can't help that.'

'How old do you think he is?'

'He looks forty. But I believe he's mid-fifties.'

'He is seventy.'

'No way!'

'I sustain him. The more he sees me, the less I can do that, and the bond that tethers us has gradually lessened. Something like this might break it. Then he will go from me and come again and forget me. It is the way the great liar makes slaves of you, forgetfulness. I'll deny that for as long as I can, and by any means.'

'Are you going to kill me?' Saskia felt a surge of cold fear gather around the area of her fetter.

'I wouldn't choose to kill. I have killed, but never one who could look into my eyes whilst I did it.'

'What are you going to do? Run me off the road? Strangle me? You'd regret it!'

'Why so? Ah! Let me.' She reached out again to touch Saskia. On this occasion her fingers became hot, and Saskia thought that they might burn her if they continued their contact with her, though she did not draw away from it.

'I see,' said the *Leanhaun Shee* at last. Her voice sounded suddenly like the stirring of fallen leaves. She looked down at her hands, now clasped on her knees.

'Once my people and yours had affinity and loved too, you know. Long ago, in a time unremembered by your histories. Before the great liar crawled through the darkness and spoke about his jealousy and caused the blindness. Made men want. Like the bartender in the pub. Oh how she wants. There were magicians then, as there still are magicians. And I know Tadgh performs services for them. And he envies them you know and resents them, because he has no Desiring, and maybe in part it was a cruelness in him that made him chain six of you. And I know that he's done other things, though not so wicked.'

'You agree that it's a wicked act.'

'I never said otherwise. My beloved's life was charmed from the start. I made it so. But now his past seeks him out and I can't protect him. You have powerful friends.' She paused and peered at Saskia intently, before continuing.

'You're no innocent though, are you? So, go carefully, because yours could be a dark little soul if you allowed it. Take it from me.'

'Don't worry about me, I'll look a...' She ceased speaking when she glanced to the side and realised that she was alone in the jeep. The terrain had grown steep, and the track clung to an escarpment; it moved diagonally across its tree clad slope. After a few minutes, almost at the top, another narrow track almost hidden by the trees struck to the left. The Bran threw his land rover onto this, and Saskia followed. A hundred metres further on and the Bran pulled over and climbed out of his vehicle to swing open a timber barred gate. He waved her through into a broad clearing, before following her in his vehicle. She could see the lights from a dwelling a few yards away. She had reached the home of the Bran.

Saskia climbed out of the jeep. She looked up at the cloudless night sky, blue black velvet displaying the milky way as she had rarely seen it. In this remote woodland and at this level, light pollution was at a minimum and the stars rewarded. A soft breeze soughed in the upper branches of the trees, stirring them.

The Bran closed the gate behind them and walked towards her smiling, He left on his vehicle headlights, and the beams bathed them in light. A few feet separated them when the smile left his face, and his eyes became daggers.

'You are a fucking, deceitful bitch!' He snarled.

'Are you angry because I lied to you? or because you know that you aren't going to get to have sex with me? I do come highly recommended; you're really going to miss out.'

'Fuck you! Fucking little cow!'

'What's the matter, you got to see your *Leanhaun Shee* didn't you. That doesn't happen every day; she told me so.' Saskia was crowing; elated.

'How the fuck can you see her when she's hidden? you miserable, gobby little piece of duplicitous shite!'

'I think that's your fault, I reckon that it's a by-product of you fettering me, you fuck faced bastard. I see the dead because of you. All the fucking time! And worse!'

Tadgh Byrne laughed, it emerged as a short, savage, humourless bark; he turned his head to the side gazing down at the low grazed grass around them. Saskia wondered if he kept a couple of sheep or goats, or if there were just lots of bunnies about. She realised that he probably was not looking at anything; his face was frozen in a mask of genuine distorted anger; he appeared to be having an inner struggle with himself because his mouth had started to work, compressing and uncompressing.

When he looked at her again, he was calmer, and his rage had descended to a cold anger.

'How did you find me?'

'Think I'd tell you?' Saskia stretched the surrounds of her eyes making them appear bigger and grinned maliciously. She almost crossed them at him but decided against it. She had decided that she was not in any real danger. She supposed the Bran might try to beat her up, but the *Leanhaun Shee* was unlikely to move against her; she was too aware that hell would follow in that event. Saskia was feeling excitement, and she was having trouble keeping it contained. She had dreamed about this moment, but always with a sense of dire consequence and the implication of menace. She stepped away turning towards the Bran's home, her eyes scanning for the *Leanhaun Shee*. She forced down her elation and felt it at once replaced by a bitter little sense of anger.

'A cave house; It looks really cool.' She studied the lengthy frontage. There were several windows. A couple of doors. It had a contemporary look. Two metal chimneys emerged from the rock.

'What do you want from me?'

'You thought you were under the radar, afraid not. You couldn't hide from us. Is it rented?'

'It belonged to my mother. It's mine now. Though you wouldn't recognise the name on the deed.'

'Why under the radar though? Is someone else after you? Have you been a very naughty boy? I'm told that you haven't worked for nearly three years, and I don't believe that's because your services aren't required. Your sort of skill is much in demand.'

'What have you come for? What do you want?'

'My mother died just over two years ago.'

'A shame, I'm sure, and I'm sorry. But what has that got to do with me?'

'Her fetter contributed to her death, in the sense that it caused it. She suffered pain and depression. I suffer pain, though I'm not depressed, you couldn't exactly call me normal.'

'That's a certainty. So, you blame me for your mother?'

'I couldn't give a toss about her. I hope her soul is in a cold dark place.'

'You're quite a piece of work, aren't you?'

'As one to another, yes, I am. I was twelve when you fettered me for her. Didn't you feel a bit of shame?'

'No. I didn't then, and I don't feel any now.'

'I think that you are a bastard!'

'Your mother was beautiful. Mad as a fucking march hare. But beautiful. Almost as beautiful as you are. And if you are half as good in bed as she was, then I really have missed out. I thought I recognised something about you, but only something. There have been so many women through my life, I didn't think too much about it.' His voice had taken on a jeering note.

'How long did you know her?'

'From when she was in the Belit order; I did workings for them. Later I fettered her when she asked me to. Then years later she appeared again, begging me to fetter you. I think she visited me over three months, while she persuaded me.'

'So, you had reservations.'

'I did for the first couple of weeks. In the end they counted for extraordinarily little. Now what are you here for? before you fuck off.'

'The Alchemy of my fetter. I want it. Including your elemental seal. And about fifty mil of your blood.'

The *Leanhaun Shee* appeared beside the Bran. Suddenly there. She glowered at Saskia from beneath her cowl of skin. A small, brooding figure.

'You can whistle for that. Huh! So, someone thinks they can undo my fetter, do they? Good luck with that!'

'You owe it to me,' Saskia said reasonably.

'I owe you nothing.'

'Make him see reason.' She looked directly at the *Leanhaun Shee*, her expression one of calm expectancy.

'You think that you know me?' responded the Leanhaun Shee.

'Broacha, you're there?' Tadgh searched the space around him for a glimpse of her, genuine longing in his eyes. Saskia almost felt sympathy for him, but the feeling lacked endurance.

'I don't have to know you. Resent me all you like. Persuade him please, Broacha...is that your name? We haven't long you know!'

The *Leanhaun Shee* looked at her resentfully. Saskia shrugged her shoulders. 'What would you have done?' she asked.

Tadgh came about then; his face was drawn, and his eyes were hot with excitement. He gazed down at his *Leanhaun Shee*, and he was not a tall man. This was the second occasion he had seen her within the same hour. He sensed her presence often, glimpsed her, spectre like, occasionally. Saw her in her skin as he put it, rarely. He wanted to crush her to him, take her to his bed, burn the sight and touch of her into himself again, because he knew that she would not linger in his sight and for his touch.

'Come with me Tadgh Byrne you silly son of Bran, we must talk,' she said to him; she took him by the hand and led him towards the cave house.

Saskia watched them disappear inside; then thoughtfully sauntered over to his land rover to switch off its headlights. Ten minutes later another set of headlights lit the little cropped-grass compound from beyond the gate, as Amelia manoeuvred her black Mercedes cautiously along the narrow track. It came to a halt; waited. Saskia passed through the gate and went up to the driver's side door. The window lowered.

'Has he seen reason?' Amelia inquired.

'I think we'll know shortly.'

'Did he threaten you?' Ayesha asked, she was in the passenger seat, leant forward.

'He's just a prick, quite pathetic really. He has a companion. A *Leanhaun* Shee. She keeps herself invisible. Most of the time she hides herself even from him.' Saskia very briefly described her two meetings with Broacha, while they waited.

A few minutes later Tadgh Byrne reappeared, interrupting the exchange; he came out of the cave house and assumed a stance at the centre of the enclosure; his hands were thrust into the pockets of his corduroys, lifting his shoulders. He kept his face down and his mouth set in a hard line. He lifted his burning gaze only to stare resentfully at Saskia, as she came back through the gate and walked towards him, stopping a few feet away. He could see figures inside the Mercedes. He could feel their eyes on him. Saskia stared at him inquiringly; the lute string tension inside her was so taut that it was almost painful.

'You can have what you came for,' he said bitterly. 'Regarding the blood, I hope you've brought your own fucking container.'

\*

Saskia sensed atmosphere as soon as she climbed into the back seat of Amelias Mercedes. There was division between these two and it intrigued her; additionally, they had just spent several hours in each other's company and the air between them smouldered dangerously.

'Whew! tonight is the longest I've driven. From and back to Leeds. Those little tracks in the forest are a bit hairy aren't they. I'm shattered now,' she announced disarmingly. She had left her jeep in the underground carpark next to Ayesha's BMW. She rested her hands on the seat backs in front of her and gazed from Amelia to Ayesha with inquisitive eyes. When they had set off again from Tadgh Byrne's house, she had almost expected Ayesha to choose to travel in her jeep.

'Are you sure that you don't want a comfort break before we set off?' she asked innocently.

'We'll break halfway at services. 'I'd rather get this stuff off our hands as quickly as possible, Saskia,' Amelia responded. The Alchemical material connected to Saskia's fetter, was currently locked in a samsonite briefcase on the seat next to Saskia.

'Okay, let's get off then.'

'Seat belt,' said Ayesha, coolly.

Ayesha gazed over her shoulder as Amelia drove onto the M62 in the direction of the A1, to peer at Saskia who was curled into a corner of the back seat. She looked relaxed, at ease, her beautiful dark lids were half closed. She met Ayesha's gaze, her eyes charmingly drowsy, and formed her lips into a delicate little kiss.

'You look shattered,' Ayesha told her, barely vocalising, unable to prevent a little appreciative smile from curving into her lips. She lifted her chin as she pleasured in Saskia's gesture of affection; her response was not lost on Amelia. *These two were made for one another,* she thought.

'I thought it was a mistake letting you play a lone hand, I was wrong,' Amelia commented.

Ayesha's eyes studied Saskia's face, watching for the establishment of conceit; nothing was on offer.

'You know I expected to have to use force and that I would be coercing Tadgh Byrne for hours,' Amelia said.

'You mean torture him?' Saskia yawned.

'Yes, that. I wouldn't have left a mark on his body though. Does that bother you?'

'No. He was a nasty little prick. He doesn't deserve his Fae mistress. At least she made him see reason.'

'But you had to convince her, little mantis.'

'I think she had a poke about inside my world. It convinced her how hopeless their situation was. She said I had powerful friends. You frightened her Amelia.'

Ayesha's shoulders moved into tension; Saskia saw her knuckles whiten; she searched Ayesha's expression; allowing a little frown to delve between her brows, it questioned, but Ayesha gave only a tiny, disappointed shake of her head in reply and turned to face forward.

'I'm in such awe.' Ayesha spoke between her teeth, unable to stop herself. 'It's obvious that I wasn't capable of doing even this part, on my own.'

'I suggest you take that up with Claire and Hal. They asked me to stay in play to ensure the Alchemy, if obtained, got safely into the possession of Theodor Bacchus. Given what happened at Claire's party, don't you consider it a sensible call?'

'What do you mean by that?' Ayesha's voice had fallen to a growl.

'Whatever you want it to mean.' Amelia's eyes flashed coldly.

'Amelia only meant that the threat level is really high; though I'm quite sure that you both agreed that it probably no longer existed after the attack failed, I recall.' Saskia was tempted to unfasten her seat belt and sit forward.

'Are you being deliberately divisive?' Amelia looked surprised.

'Yes of course she is. We fascinate her. She needs to know why there's bad blood between us; Saskia, Amelia was not referring to a level of threat when she made that statement, she was levelling a criticism at my actions.'

'Why? What did you do?'

'What did I do Amelia?' Ayesha asked discordantly.

'You want it? you went looking for Saskia and when she came back you weren't there, and despite the fact we specifically told her to go to the Place, she went looking for you instead. But you made the bad call, ultimately, your behaviour put her at risk.'

'I needed to make sure Ayesha was safe; I'd seen what was out there,' Saskia said, but Ayesha's raised voice drowned her out and Amelia was not listening to her anyway, her hostile gaze was shared between Ayesha and the road ahead.

'I wanted to know where she was, because I should have been with her,' Ayesha was defensive.

'No. you were irresponsible,' Amelia insisted. 'You can't stand to be away from each other. You both have the same issue, you are cunt-struck!'

For the next half hour Saskia avoided looking towards the rear-view mirror or towards Ayesha; she did not want a repeat of the icy stare that she had received from Ayesha, after Amelia's outburst. The atmosphere was uncomfortable, charged with negativity. She eased off one ankle boot with the other and drew her foot up onto the seat and squeezed her toes through her sock whilst she absorbed some of the atmosphere and fed off a little of the vibe. Eventually she stopped squeezing and put her foot back to the floor and spoke.

'Why don't you like each other?' she asked; she had reached the decision that the direct route might be the best way forward. 'Because I think that you used to.'

'Saskia please don't,' Ayesha begged.

'I'm going to have my say. I love you and I like her; and I know she snipes at you, and you take it. Yet at the quayside when Nathan and the Kadman order came for me, Amelia you said to that guy Jed: You have no idea how brave that was.'

'It was brave, I meant that.'

'I wasn't brave I was terrified.'

'But you still defied them, and that took real courage,' Amelia glanced at Saskia in her mirror. 'I admire courage in anyone.'

'You give and then you take away. I heard what you said, I have exceptionally good hearing. You said that young woman is worth any number of you, and you meant it!'

'You can be very annoying,' Amelia sighed.

'I know. What has she done to you?'

'Saskia stop,'

'No, keep your eyes on the road and slow down please Amelia. Ayesha, I like her, I want to be her friend. But friendship doesn't have to be a choice.'

'Oh, for goodness sake! Alright, I'm a disappointment to her. When Hal crashed my former life, she thought I would seek her out as my mentor, then she could mould me into Amelia mark two; bit short for that I'm afraid, but hey ho! Amelia has a strong personality, I opted for Claire's lighter touch.'

'Oh, for fucks sake Ayesha! It wasn't as simple as that. And look where Claire's soft touch got you! Silver fucking thorns in your body to wrack you to pieces with pain!'

Ayesha shrugged, her face was set, her mouth tight and curved down, the knuckles of both hands were white in her lap. 'You felt rejected. It was not my problem; you made no overtures.'

'I felt let down, like you had thrown everything back in our faces. You know what we are referring to don't you Saskia?'

'Yes, I know about Ayesha's compliance of thorns. I know about her liking for pain. I'm cool with it. We are both strange Amelia.'

'Yes, you are, aren't you?' Amelia eyes searched for hers again in the mirror, Saskia could see the tears of emotion in them. Amelia's mouth set determinedly.

'Do you know about Khalid Taharqa?'

'Yes, I know about him.'

'Amelia, this is going nowhere good,' Ayesha reasoned.

Amelia ignored the plea; went ahead. 'And that Ayesha has been involved with him since she was fourteen years old. Is still involved. She's still seeing him you know that?'

'You bitch!'

'Yes, I know she is. Did you suppose that I had no knowledge of it?' Saskia's voice had become cold. 'She laid it on the line to me from the start when I made it clear that I wanted her, that he was a presence in her life. I'm not naïve Amelia. I knew what I was getting into, it's Ayesha I feel sorry for, because she didn't.'

'I must have really put your nose out Amelia for you to be this vindictive,' Ayesha snapped. At the same time, she threw Saskia an enigmatic look.

'I am not vindictive, I just thought that Saskia had a right to know. But it appears that I got it very wrong. And when I heard you were in a relationship, I thought that you would walk away from Khalid Taharqa. When you didn't, I became angry with you all over again.'

'You couldn't just be our friend then? Like you couldn't just be Ayesha's friend? If you dislike him so much you should have kept her close. I, would.'

'I'm genuinely happy that you've found each other. And believe me I am a friend whatever you think of me.' Amelia concentrated on the road and the vehicles they were overtaking; she was aware of her own reflection though and she did not feel wonderfully comfortable with it. She gripped the steering wheel less firmly and dropped her speed, leaving the fast lane.

Ayesha breathed deeply, and allowed herself to relax, she had no desire to create division between Amelia and themselves. She unclenched her fists decisively.

'I suggest that we leave it there and move on,' she said, unexpectedly taking pity on Amelia. 'Saskia, there are bottles of sparkling water in a bag on the floor and bars of chocolate; get them out, will you? I'm thirsty and I'm sure Amelia is, and I know that she never says no to chocolate. And I want to know more about this *Leanhaun shee*.'

\*

'Poor Amelia, she feels rejected,' Saskia sighed, as she watched the black Mercedes exit the underground garage; its tyres squealed, echoing as they fought for traction on the epoxy resin surface layer. Amelia had insisted on dropping them right at the door of the lift. 'And in a strange way I don't blame her. I wonder what she would have said, if she knew that I am going to meet Khalid.'

'Don't be too sympathetic, she likes her own way. When she doesn't get it, she gets rattled. You've decided then? You will meet him?' Ayesha slipped her arm through Saskia's, she smiled at her; charmingly weary. She was dead on her feet, but sleep had eluded her and that was down to Amelia's presence in the car, even though they had completed the rest of the trip on relatively cordial terms. They had arrived at Bacchus House as first light crept through a hanging mist that was still diffusing the street lighting. Selene had met them, dressed to go out for a run; she looked very fit. She had made them coffee while they went for a much needed freshen up and a pee. She had taken possession of the Bran's alchemy and his blood. And finally waved them off again, never once having smiled.

'I suppose so. I need a distraction to get me through to my unfettering. Are you hungry?'

'I am my little mantis.'

'I think there's a frozen pizza left.'

'We do love pizza. Pizza for breakfast; is that what you are offering me?'

'Unless you fancy a yoghurt.'

'Pizza is sublime.' She appeared pensive and became serious. Saskia studied her expression waiting for her to voice her thoughts.

'I was scared for you little Mantis. But I'm so proud of you, you carried it off so well!'

'But don't get cocky yeah? I knew you were close by and that gave me confidence, but I think I was on a bit of a high.'

'It could have gone very wrong. And it would have been so much more difficult and unpleasant, if it hadn't been for the Fae.'

'I know. I'm not certain that he wouldn't have harmed me. I was scared too. Thank you for letting me play a lone hand. You know in a funny way; I regret not seeing Amelia doing her stuff.'

'I don't. The revelation in all of this is Selene Bacchus.'

'I know. What is she, seventeen? And with contacts like Max Angus.'

'He was an animal, wasn't he? Was he okay with you?'

'Very professional. God knows what else he does, he hinted at other stuff.'

'We'll probably never find out thankfully. Come on, Pizza, showers, and then bed.'

# Six

Khalid Taharqa was a man of considerable sexual appetite, and certain deviant preferences. He saw himself as a man to be reckoned with; wealthy, and with few, if any, qualms. He enjoyed success in business. He owned nightclubs and restaurants and hotels; a casino; he shared a thriving property portfolio with Ayesha Shah; it cemented the connection between them; it pleased him that she had refused an offer from him for her half, when she had originally inherited it. Khalid socialised with a prominent type of individual, politicians, and business types, who showed him respect; occasionally, he fucked their wives and daughters. He moved in criminal circles too, because it gave him satisfaction and opened channels that he occasionally exploited. These were types who ruled by fear, though Khalid found them amusing. In his personal world he feared nothing, he was the dominant beast. He claimed descent from Pharaohs, and he had the magical power of an adept.

He enjoyed control, though it was more of an imposition of his will, particularly when he was having sex, which he loved above everything else, apart from himself. He had a preferred type; young, under thirty; with slender nymphlike bodies, small breasts, slim hips, beauty; occasionally a waif, for variety; one of those who emitted an ethereal quality. For some reason he assumed that Saskia Challoner would fall into that category. Undernourished, so slender, she would give the impression that she would break.

He was proud of his magnificent gleaming body too. Of the starkness of his dark skin, every inch of which rippled with underlying muscle; he was exceedingly proud of his long, circumcised penis; of his consummate skill in bed, and of his endurance. He had just answered his mobile phone, he tossed it back across the bed from where he had claimed it, his mouth drew back in a contented smile that did not separate his lips. He exited the bed in a single fluid movement, cat like. As always, he felt self-assured; in control; he sustained a physical high that few men could. Khalid Taharqa had fire in the blood.

He glanced down at the other occupant of the bed, a new host at his casino, Allie, a tall young woman with noticeably short white hair, shaved at the sides and back; she lay face down on the bed, breathing hard; recovering. Her narrow hips made tiny pulsing movements. her naked body was toned, defined, sweating. She had an educated accent which he liked, and a filthy mind. They were in his expensively appointed apartment at his casino; one he kept for entertaining guests and girlfriends.

He padded across the polished floor to sit naked at his desk and stared at the computer screen; he opened his emails. He scanned down and found the one he had been anticipating; he opened the attached picture file. It held several images of Saskia Challoner, walking and eating out with Ayesha Shah. *My oh fucking my*, he thought. He leaned back in his leather swivel chair; his eyes widened, and his mouth transited into petulance, as reality superseded preconception. His lips drew back suddenly from his striking white teeth, and he smiled, allowing momentary self-deprecation. Then he grinned, his mood lifting instantly. Today was a good day. He had left his wife that very morning, for good. He had unexpectedly acquired a delightful new bed mate to add to his stable, after his manager had introduced him to the newly hired Allie Tasker. And just a few minutes ago Ayesha had phoned to inform him that Saskia Challoner had agreed to meet him the following evening.

He became aware of Allie watching him, she had turned her head, to rest the side of her face on the backs of her hands. She smiled, bending her knees, and crossing her ankles above her rear.

'You look very satisfied mister Taharqa.'

'I am Allie. Very satisfied.'

'Are you coming back to bed? Because I really do need to be satisfied some more myself.'

He laughed silently. It was good to be appreciated.

*

'Fucking hell! Saskia, what were you thinking?"

'You didn't object at the time.'

'I was caught up in the moment obviously.'

'So was I.'

'I'm not so sure. I don't doubt your passion but sometimes I think it never quite consumes you.'

Ayesha climbed back onto the bed; her dark eyes showed some resentment. She had returned from the on suite, where she had seen the love bites on her throat, made by Saskia during the previous night's sex. Saskia rose to a kneeling position to receive her; she pulled Ayesha to her and kissed her on the mouth. Ayesha resisted just a little, still feeling irritation. Then she yielded in anticipation of Saskia's slender fingers and beautiful probing tongue.

'No more biting for now,' she begged. She returned the pliant warmth of Saskia's lips, allowed her tongue possession of her mouth. Her eyes became lost in Saskia's beautiful green eyes; she wondered if it showed in her own dark eyes, how much she loved her. Her fingers caressed down over Saskia's firm breasts, teasing the hardening nipples for a time, then trailed over her abdomen, her hands separated at the flare of Saskia's slim hips, one stroked her taut rear, its fingertips lightly touching her anus, the other delved to her smooth mound; she pushed one finger into the tight mouth of her vulva, encountering the moistness of arousal; she retracted slightly to move its moistened tip over Saskia's clitoral hood.

Ayesha was correct; there was always some part of Saskia that remained detached. But it certainly did not lack desire and in fact was probably driven by it. Saskia drew a sharp breath followed by a little breathy sob. She was sensitive, her body often flinched in pleasure to Ayesha's touch during sex; her orgasms were intense, sometimes quickly achieved, sometimes not. The tip of her clitoris was incredibly sensitive when she was aroused, Ayesha brought her to her most intense orgasms by retracting its hood and stimulating it most often with her tongue, occasionally with a fingertip or a toy, though she always exercised care. In the ancient world the Achaeans referred to the clitoris as the Kleis, this meant key. She enjoyed stimulating the hood and the vaginal walls into which the organ of the clitoris extended. Saskia's heightened breathing matched the even rhythm of Ayesha's fingertips for some time, whilst she kissed Ayesha's mouth and face, neck, and shoulder with gentle sensuality; one hand with fingers locked into her hair at the back of her head; her other caressed, nails occasionally flexed as she pressed them into smooth skin. She followed the thorns of Ayesha's tattoo along her back, as she enjoyed doing, rotating a fingertip upon the tiny mounds, beneath which were implanted the silver thorns. Eventually she reached behind her, for their heavy pillow and manoeuvred it, to support her back and raise up her hips as they lay down. They were lovers who were mutually absorbed in exploring each other's sexuality. Neither had previously met any sex partner who could even modestly echo the excitement or the level of sexual pleasure they derived from each other, and this was a source of fascination to them. Saskia drew up her legs, parted them and enjoyed the delicious ride.

 Saskia genuinely wanted to make an impression on Khalid on so many levels, and she wanted so much to gain a knowledge of him, a feel for him; to distil his vibe. Part of that was her reason for marking Ayesha, though she had regretted the action the instant she had executed it; her other purpose and by no means the lesser one, had been to tell him unambiguously, that this belongs to me; she knew that he would not dare attempt to reciprocate if he valued his connection to Ayesha. She considered Khalid not as a rival, though he was that too, but to be her sworn enemy, though she would never tell Ayesha that.

 Orgasm consumed her, expanding in blissful pleasure. She listened to the sound of her own voice, yelping, and making little plaintive cries. Eventually Ayesha sat back on her heels and smiled down at the pleasured, whimpering wreck of her lover.

'My turn?'

Saskia panted and chuckled. 'I'm going to make you squeal like a murdered bunny.' Ayesha laughed as Saskia pulled her down onto her, then wrestled her over onto her back. Her sensitivity exceeded Saskia's, and her orgasms were velvet clawed pleasure that went on and on. She could not bear the sensitivity of her clitoris for long with its hood withdrawn, it was too much for her and she often stopped Saskia as she pushed the hood back; she could tolerate the delicate touch of Saskia's tongue for only a couple of moments at most. Though Saskia intended to address the issue, one night. Ayesha forgot about love bites, as her thoughts focused on the pleasures of Saskia's fingers and more particularly her tongue.

'You look gorgeous as usual. Just remember that you are coming home with me.'

'I know that. Saskia this is for you, not for him.'

'How will he know that?'

'He'll know, I promise. But I should cover this.' She pointed to the bruise on her throat where Saskia had marked her.

'You must. I apologise. It was a bad choice.'

'You admit you chose to mark me?'

'I wouldn't embarrass you for the world, Ayesha.' Saskia looked suitably ashamed, even a little distressed.

Ayesha rolled her eyes. 'I'm disappointed more than anything but I'll wear your brand.'

'Please wear your carnelian choker it will cover it perfectly and you are beautiful in it.'

'No. I promised I'd take you off the leash; let you show your pointy little horns I believe I said. This is your night after all; even if I must suffer an element of embarrassment.'

'Please. Ayesha. Wear your choker; for me.'

Ayesha's lips flexed into the tiniest of smiles making her look almost cruel; she lifted Saskia's chin with the tip of an extended finger to study the beautiful glum face. She felt a sudden tiny pulse of satisfaction at Saskia's contrition.

'Fetch it then.'

Saskia had opted to wear a stylish fitted black dress, it was sleeveless and fell to mid-calf, with a split to her knee; it had a sweetheart neckline, exposing her fetter. It revealed her toned arms and shoulders, the lissomness of her figure. She opted for patent killer heels in black, that flexed her calves beautifully. Ayesha had opted for a stunning red velvet wrap over dress, exquisitely detailed with silver embroidery and sequins contained in a diamond pattern, it was long sleeved and was quite brief at mid-thigh. She had selected red Prada stilettos and opted not to paint her fingernails and toenails.

The phone rang and Saskia answered. Startled, Ayesha felt a sense of rising panic. God this was going to be stressful. Saskia replaced the phone on its hub.

'The car's here,' she told Ayesha. She watched dispassionately as Ayesha drew a deep breath and smoothed her close-fitting dress with her fingers.

'Okay. Let's go.'

*Like a cat on hot bricks*, Saskia thought; amused.

*

'My Ayesha; beautiful, as always.' At first Saskia thought the words were a clumsy attempt to claim ownership, but she realised instantly that he was stating the absolute reality as he perceived it; her lover was his possession.

'Hello Khalid; let me introduce you; this is my beautiful girlfriend, Saskia Challoner. Saskia; Khalid Taharqa.'

'The fettered girl. Good evening, Saskia, I've so been looking forward to meeting you,' he glanced at her briefly, eyes for Ayesha alone.

'The man who claims descent from Pharoah's. Good evening, Khalid. I've been looking forward to meeting you too.' His eyes barely flickered over her in reply, almost dismissively, she decided; she smiled inwardly; so, he wanted to dent her self-esteem at the outset; she had not missed his fleeting search for mockery in her expression either, when she referred to his claim.

'That is a beautiful choker, I've never seen it before.'

'It's my favourite piece of antique jewellery; Saskia adores me in it. I'm wearing it for her. And on this occasion, it hides my love bites.' She evoked a long, fathomless look from Khalid at her statement, an unforgiving smirk from Saskia.

Khalid had met them in the foyer, immaculate in grey; his mouth expansive in a smile; his dark eyes had scanned them with zeal as approached them. He must have been watching for the car or been buzzed by his driver as they arrived, Saskia decided. They were holding hands as they entered, he tried not to show it unsettled him, failed; the micromovement of his muscles at the corners of his eyes had betrayed him as he saw their interlaced fingers. He was tall, very; lean, arrogant. Good looking? Arrogant. Saskia flexed, her fingers prepared to separate, Ayesha compressed, disallowed.

The fetter girl made Khalid uneasy, immediately; this close, her green eyes seemed to set about him, they had a lambency that he found disquieting; they inquired too deeply. She was exceptionally beautiful. She disturbed him on more than one level.

'This is a beautiful place Khalid. I've never been here until now. A new acquisition?' Ayesha praised, gazing about appreciatively. It was a hotel restaurant in a rural setting; it was called the Red Ox. It had its own mere. They had caught sight of its dark surface, sheened in lamplight, from the road. In the daylight, there were expanses of bullrushes to be seen along its edges and waterfowl on its breeze rippled surface. The Red Ox was stone built and rambled. Inside the restaurant it was warm and ambient, lit by wall lamps and a blazing fire. It was beamed, with a flagged floor and stone walls. A spacious, glazed extension afforded views of a well illuminated part of the mere for guests who wanted to be closer to the water. Khalid's master table was in a secluded area of the restaurant, set in an alcove to one side of the fire, behind a section of original supporting beams; the massive timbers were mellow with age and held together with wooden pegs.

'I'm incredibly pleased with it; I acquired it a few months ago,' he responded to Ayesha's question. 'I came by it as a debt, with a little money the previous owners way. Ayesha, will you sit on my left; Saskia on my right.'

The table was an antique, of six highly polished, flame mahogany boards. Designed to accommodate ten; by Chippendale or one of his imitators; all the chairs were armed and exquisitely carved, with padded seats; it was set for them to occupy the end that was deepest inside the alcove.

'I prefer to sit next to Saskia.' Ayesha said. Khalid stared at her, nonplussed. Saskia watched his expression, enjoying his momentary confusion.

'I...'

'It's okay Ayesha. You'll have me all night after all,' she said reasonably and sat down where Khalid had indicated. Ayesha's eyelids flexed a miniscule amount at each corner as she regarded Khalid, then she smiled adoringly at Saskia and shrugged.

'Very well my darling.'

Ayesha glanced at the wine menu. She was tempted to order champagne. 'Chardonnay.'

'Saskia; for you?'

'Lyres. No alcohol for me presently.'

'Saskia undergoes Alchemical action in a few days,' Ayesha explained. 'The Alchemist is Theo Bacchus. Just putting it out there.'

'You have immensely powerful friends Saskia. I know all about your covenant. Eleven seals I hear. Even two south of the Lhoegyr. A third had they been old enough. I am impressed.'

'Did you know I had eleven Ayesha? Last I heard it was six.'

'It's news to me. But I'm not surprised after the Pandemonium incursion. Are you tempted Khalid?'

'You know that I don't get involved in things like that. I think your covenant has sufficient fire power, without my meagre resource being included.'

'It's unlike you to undersell yourself Khalid.'

'Come on Ayesha. I've no magical agenda. Those are frightening men and women!'

Saskia had rested her elbows on the edge of the table and pressed the joints of her fingers together in front of her mouth, her thumb nails pressed to her lips. She was fascinated as she listened to the conversation of the two magicians. For a few moments personality had been removed from the table.

Khalid shifted his gaze between them. 'Hal could desire me inside out. Four of me in fact. As for Theo Bacchus, he could do the same to Hal. If any man can remove your fetter, it's Theo Bacchus. I don't understand why it is so important to them. And I don't think I want to. I'm a man of simple pursuits, and pleasures.' He smiled appreciatively as their first course arrived, as if to prove his point. They ate and talked through a pleasing meal of nouvelle cuisine, which Saskia was surprised to find she enjoyed. Khalid was a good host and he ensured that no alcohol was part of the recipe of any of Saskia's food. Ayesha relaxed and Saskia allowed herself to enjoy the evening, if guardedly. They talked about Ayesha's and Khalid's business, and Saskia talked about her enjoyment of antiques and a growing love for antiquities. It was Khalid who brought the subject back to magic.

'It is not my first love by any means. To me it's an occasional resource. It is interesting though, your fetter. I couldn't help but look. Quite elegant. I understand that your mother had it imposed on you.'

Saskia nodded. 'When I was twelve.'

'A somewhat extreme measure. Was there a reason?'

'She was batshit crazy. Do you need another?'

Khalid laughed, feeling a little of his inner tension slip away. Both Ayesha and Saskia laughed with him.

'What were you like? Before you were fettered.'

'All over the place. I was scared because of my mother's reaction when I began to show intent. I was home schooled so there were no issues, and I had no friends of my own age. And I only had intent for a few weeks. I was lucky to have Ben...Bernadette.'

'Who was Bernadette?'

'My mother's partner. I've come to believe that she was quite a Sorceress in her own right; I know that she scared Nathan Xavier. She educated me in magic, even though I missed out on application. She was a shield against my mum, and the craziness that got into her head, which drove her to have herself fettered and then me.'

'Are you okay talking about this darling?' said Ayesha cautiously. She knew that Saskia mostly avoided the subject, but she wasn't sure if it was because it upset her, or simply annoyed her.

Khalid glanced at Ayesha, aware of a shift in her posture, an increase of tension down the entire extent of her body and in her attentiveness. He noted her expression as she regarded her beautiful consort, it was tender and concerned. He decided to tease more from the conversation than was his original intention. He realised with surprise that he was interested, but that was subsidiary to a sense of fascination in Saskia, which had sneaked up on him.

'I'm fine with it. What do you want to know Khalid? I don't know why you would want to know but ask away.'

'I suddenly want to know what lives inside you, and I think the key to that, at least in part, is your mother.'

'Ayesha didn't tell me you were a psychoanalyst.'

'Until now I had no desire to be one.'

'Are you coming onto me Khalid? Should I remind you who is sitting next to you and opposite me?'

'I am extremely aware.'

'Hot, isn't she?'

'Yes, she is,' occasionally there were times when only candour had relevance.

'Do you think I'm hot?'

'Yes, I do.' He spread his hands helplessly.

'Which of us is hottest?'

'I was not this charred when I sat down,' he replied, which he decided was quite a good response on the spur of the moment.

Ayesha stared at Saskia, not amused; she had not even the excuse of having had alcohol. Saskia regarded Khalid; her green eyes had darkened with mischief.

'My mother was quite the Adept, I realise now, if I go by anything Bernadette told me. She could thoughtform, she had energised intent and elemental intent, and something else, which I saw on the night of Claire's party; the thing that Hal became. She could summon the Wurm, Wyrm, I've heard both. Am I saying it right?'

'That is a rare talent.' Khalid remarked.

'Are you sure Saskia?' Ayesha asked quietly, her face had assumed a solemn expression.

'Nathan said that she could. They practised sex magic to evoke it, he failed, she succeeded. I dismissed it when he told me because I didn't understand what he meant. He also said her behaviour became strange after that, though she had always been erratic. Getting to know more about what exists inside me mister Taharqa? And what about you?' She directed to Ayesha, more harshly than she had intended.

'I already know you,' Ayesha responded, a hurt look in her eyes.

'Do you?'

Khalid thought that he sensed division. He watched. Sensing the sudden tension between them, but not understanding its nature.

'Yes. The rest is detail, little mantis.'

Saskia's look softened and her eyes swam with unexpected tears. 'You are enchanting. I love you,' she told Ayesha, her voice had become tender.

'I know you do. I don't deserve you.'

Khalid had the sudden sensation of not being present. He found it uncomfortable. Unfamiliar. He played himself back into the game.

'It is also called the dragon in the deep. You understand it more deeply now from first-hand experience it would seem,' he remarked, gaining their attention. 'It's an atavistic force from the very beginning, when all the realities seen, and unseen divided. A reflection of it is supposed to exist inside all of us; few can connect with it. The dragon is a misnomer. It's something that came out of the chaos abyss; it undulates, its millions of miles long. The wannabes sometimes confuse it, with the extremely basic mechanism of the kundalini serpent.'

'You're surprising me Khalid,' said Ayesha, he had the uncomfortable impression that now she was laughing at him.

'I enjoy magical lore; I simply don't make it popular knowledge that I do,' he responded defensively. He directed his conversation at Saskia.

'I don't love magic. I don't fear it either. It has my respect. In my opinion there are areas that are best left well alone by most practitioners; there are pleasurable things too, harmless. I stay within my comfort zone. If your mother evoked the Wurm, it would be impossible for it not to change her in some way. If we go down the rabbit hole we are confronted with a labyrinth and by choosing to enter it, we find ourselves or lose ourselves. Perhaps your mother never quite found the way back out.'

'I will never forgive her.'

'You might, when you no longer have your fetter.' He frowned, he had never seen himself occupying the role of mitigator, appeasement was not in his nature, if he could avoid it. Except as means to an end game, though he was not sure that he wanted to placate the girl. He suspected that she was not sexually attracted to generosity or compassion.

'Ungenerous sorts, refer to you as fetter girl,' he said, amused.

'I have been called fetter bitch to my face.'

'Really?' He chortled.

'Amber and Pearl Shalako,' Ayesha informed. 'Not the most generous of spirits.'

'Yet, their seals now reside on Saskia's covenant.'

'You surprise me!'

'I wouldn't like them on my case. So, when is your transaction set for, Saskia?'

'In four days, sooner than was originally planned. Apparently, I will be very unwell.' Saskia felt odd, suddenly at the edge of panic. As if the reality of the impending alchemical action had hit her for the first time. She spooned ice cream automatically into her mouth for the next few minutes and watched Ayesha and Khalid converse, without really listening to what was being said; gradually controlling her sense of panic. By the time Ayesha announced she was off to 'freshen up,' she was once again cool and contained.

'You are much more than I expected.' Khalid told her directly. He had decided by then, that he very much wanted to fuck her.

'Did Ayesha undersell me?' Saskia laughed.

'No. I didn't believe her. She claimed that you were exceptional. I won't doubt her judgement again.'

'I don't know about being exceptional. I know that I'm not ordinary.'

'Will you meet me without Ayesha?'

'Why should I?' Saskia was coy.

'So that we can talk.'

'So that you can talk more freely, is what I suspect you mean.'

'I believe that applies to both of us. I've seen you looking at me, not without interest, and occasionally with hostility.'

'You're fucking my girlfriend; how should I look.'

'Yet you are here because you are curious about me.'

'I wanted to see what attracted her. How she responded to you.'

'And your conclusion?'

'I believe the connection is fragile and there is no energy between you. Ayesha is an addict; I envy you the goad. It's all you have. If you care anything about her, you will get out of her life.'

'Surely I am the incumbent,' he professed, rather lamely he realised.

'Hardly, she has sado-masochistic sex with you occasionally. That in my book is not incumbency. It is gratification. And I've seen you looking at me, I've seen what's in your eyes, and I'm sure that it hasn't escaped Ayesha.'

'I adore beautiful women. I simply must fuck them,' he admitted, grinning.

'At least that's honest. I can be honest too; I don't like men; I see them as performing dildos, with blood.'

'That is scathing.'

'True though! I'm attracted to type, mean, arrogant. It's a sensual thing. Only a buzz. It has no meaning. Just sex.' She shrugged.

'My ethnicity?'

'That too. Very much.' It was an honest reply.

'Will you meet me then, one to one?'

'I don't know.' She stared straight into his eyes. He believed her.

'I'll be content with that answer, you didn't decline.' He took his phone from his pocket and opened the menu. He placed the phone on the table in front of her.

'Give me a little. Give me your number.'

Saskia regarded him for some moments without speaking; he found it difficult to read her expression; he thought that her smouldering green eyes might hold a hint of contempt, and again perhaps an element of mockery, and he found himself thinking that he very much desired to watch them as they expressed orgasm. At any moment he knew that Ayesha would come back.

The opportunity would be lost for the present. He almost exulted as Saskia reached for his phone and tapped in her number. She handed it back to him. Ayesha returned a few moments later.

*

'He came on, to you?'

'Yes. You'd probably only just pulled down your panties.'

'I wasn't wearing any. And please don't be crude.'

'I was making a point.'

'What did you say to him?'

'I told him to stop fucking my girlfriend.'

'Did you?' Ayesha's eyes widened in dismay.

'Yes, what did you expect me to say?'

'What did he say to that?'

'He said he was the incumbent.'

'He didn't? The cheeky bastard!'

'Then he asked for my phone number.'

'You told him to go and fuck himself?'

'No, I gave it to him.'

'Saskia!'

'He asked me to meet him. I said I would think about it.'

Ayesha took Saskia's face gently between her hands. She gazed into it with mild disbelief, and she shook her head, at the same time smiling, almost laughing.

'Little mantis,' she said indulgently. She kissed Saskia on her mouth, a warm forgiving kiss. She drew a deep breath through her nose, and enjoyed the pliant response of Saskia's lips, and her slim warm fingers on the back of her neck. She sustained it until the lift had ascended to the penthouse floor and the door slid open. She drew back to Saskia's disappointment and took her hand and led her from the lift into their little lobby.

'Saskia, tonight Khalid was on his best behaviour. He met us in his clothes and the skin he stood up in. He had no accessories; he was not augmented. He smelled nice, didn't he?'

'Almost as lovely as you,' Saskia sighed. 'What are you talking about?'

Ayesha keyed the code and opened the door to the apartment. Snuggles checked them out with a quick swoop.

'Hi snuggles. Go beddy-bye's,' Saskia called out gently. They hung their coats and bags and passed into the spacious main room; Saskia watched as Snuggles dipped and merged into his book on the shelf. Ayesha took Saskia's hands in hers and stared directly into her amused eyes.

'Khalid employs the services of a very skilful sensorial alchemist. A woman: she makes his sex lotions for him. He applies an aphrodisiac oil to his body when he intends to have sex. Don't look at me like that, please,' she begged clutching at Saskia's wrists. 'He's addicted to sex. He accumulates beautiful women. He is attractive, but not that attractive. He uses a very potent sexual lure; very few women would be capable of resisting it. He had not applied it for his date with us; I would have recognised it! If you meet him, he will be augmented. I'm putting it out there. It will come for you like a storm. I'm used to it, I'm used to his oil too, I find it still turns me on, but I can get past it's effect if I really want to.'

'Fuck's sake Ayesha! I don't want to know this.'

'I'm trying to make you aware. Stop grinning. You'll see it as a challenge; I know you. Anyway, I don't want to talk about Khalid anymore tonight. Ask me whatever you like tomorrow.'

Saskia nodded in amused acquiescence, she trapped her lower lip between her teeth and regarded Ayesha speculatively.

'Just the dress?' she asked.

'What?'

'You're wearing just the dress.'

'Yes. Why?'

'Take it off.'

Ayesha assumed a little crooked stance and smiled a little crooked smile. Without hesitation her fingers went to the fastening of her dress, and she shrugged it from her body allowing its fall around her Prada clad feet.

'There. Nothing else. Just me.'

Saskia stepped closer to her, until only a few inches separated them. She could almost feel Ayesha's nakedness travelling to the inside of her skin. The air became charged with Ayesha's captivating scent, more strongly than she had ever experienced it. What was she wearing tonight? Vanilla, amber, musk, other things in some expensive concoction, possibly even more expensive than her own. It was delicious; possibly their conversation had heightened her awareness of smell, stimulated her cortex to respond, or maybe the sensuality of the moment, or her freedom from alcohol made some other part of her more attentive. Or maybe she was just incredibly turned on.

She kissed Ayesha's ripe lips very tenderly, her fingers caressed her cheek and slid beneath her hair. She withdrew her mouth, leaving Ayesha's lips still searching for hers, unsatisfied, and heard her gasp. She took her by the hand and led her into the bedroom, aware of the click of their heels on the laminated floors. She stopped on the large fleece rug on the floor on Ayesha's side of the bed. She explored her lover's dark searching eyes, saw the arousal in them, the excitement in them. She stroked Ayesha's nipples with the backs of her fingers until they suffused, coned. She maintained the gaze between their eyes, meanwhile. She kissed her again and pushed her gently but firmly down to sit on the edge of the bed. She withdrew again drawing Ayesha's ripe lower lip between her teeth, slowly and sensually, until released. She smiled into her lovers incredibly sexy eyes as she kicked off her killer heels and dropped to her knees at her feet. She removed one of Ayesha's shoes with a very studied purpose and let it fall, keeping the slim nude foot between her fingers, where it rested for her to study. It was a beautifully maintained foot, pedicured and cared for; slim and exceptionally beautiful. Saskia kissed the tips of the exquisitely formed toes. She slid her tongue between each of them, she took them into her mouth. Ayesha gasped in pleasure, watching her with fascination. She kissed and licked every centimetre of smooth skin, taking her time. When she had finished, she looked up at Ayesha and smiled knowingly, as she lifted the other foot and discarded the shoe, she caressed the foot in her fingers, pressing and spreading Ayesha's toes, watching the pleasure in Ayesha's eyes; only when she was ready to begin the process of sucking and licking, did she break away from their locked gaze. For the next few minutes, she was totally absorbed by her pursuit. When she finished, she set Ayesha's foot down next to the other so that they were both opposite her knees. She looked up at Ayesha with querying eyes; they held a tiny trace of defiance. They said: I enjoyed every intimate moment of that, shouldn't I have? She separated Ayesha's knees, until they were pushed against the side of the bed. She leaned forward and planted a demure delicate kiss at the top of the mouth of Ayesha's vulva. She sat back on her heels and extended her hands towards Ayesha, who accepted them and tightened her grip, supporting Saskia as she got to her feet. She released Ayesha's hands and reached behind for her zip, drew it down and slid the dress from her nude body. 'There; only me too, nothing else,' Saskia said.

'I didn't need an exotic alchemical lure to catch you. What did it for you?'

They had paused their lovemaking, to allow flushed damp skin to cool and to rest their bodies. And take time to enjoy each other. They lay side by side, facing, gazing at one another's bodies. Touching occasionally; breathing one another's breath, considering one another's eyes.

'Your eyes,' Ayesha breathed. 'Your mouth; your straight nose. You're eyebrows.' She chortled gently then.

'What about them?' Saskia half smiled; half frowned, at Ayesha's amusement.

'They're so intense.'

'Are they? And what won you, really?'

'It was all of those of course. But what enslaved me was your strange charm. You're magical Saskia! I knew I loved you when you played the lute for me that first time. And you caressed my feet then too.'

'They are very pretty feet.'

'They must be incredibly special feet after what you did with them earlier. What made you love me little mantis because I wasn't the most giving?'

'The fact that you did not want to be loved...'

'I see, I was a challenge.'

'...by anyone else.'

'Oh!'

'In the carpark at the Matelot when you drew my energy; then you kissed me. It was the most special thing that had ever happened to me.'

'I so did not mean to do that.'

'Yet you did.'

'I shouted at you and called you a praying mantis; little mantis.'

'You were defending your way of life.'

'I was scared and angry with you for rocking my world.'

'It only made me determined to burrow more deeply under your skin.' Her voice softened, almost hushed. 'I'm not comfortable with the word love you know. I've always found it a bit pathetic,'

'What do you prefer?'

'Enchanted. I believe that I'm enchanted. I hope that you are enchanted too, and it's an enchantment that I don't want to break. My unfettering worries me. I'm afraid that it might change me.'

'Stop you being enchanted with me, you mean?' Ayesha frowned suddenly concerned, Saskia saw her body tense a little.

'Maybe. I don't believe it could do that. But you might stop being absorbed in me.'

Ayesha studied Saskia's body, her eyes moving over her frame, quite a cool appraisal, Saskia decided. Eventually though, she squirmed her supple body across the narrow gap like a lissom serpent; she turned her back to Saskia and pressed her rear into her middle.

'Hold me,' she instructed. 'I've something to say.'

Saskia enclosed her in her arms and nuzzled her hair, enjoying the sensation of her nakedness.

'Tonight, I felt that I belonged to you. I think that Khalid felt that I belonged to you also. Not that he's bothered about fucking someone who belongs to somebody else. But that isn't my point! My point is that when you told me to take off my dress and I stood in front of you naked. And when you kissed my feet and sucked my toes. And when we began to make love. I felt just a little shy, and it was rather beautiful. I'll not change towards you.'

'I'll hold you to that.'

'I hope that you do.'

\*

'You look very smug.' Saskia remarked.

'You came. I'm bound to be smug.' Khalid had not risen when she arrived. He remained in his seat, watching her. He sipped black coffee, holding the white porcelain can between his long fingers.

For some moments Saskia did not look at him. She leaned on a teak handrail which capped a plate glass barrier; this circuited the epoxy resin floor of the open-air section of Khalid's rooftop restaurant. She enjoyed the breeze from the river in her face; it was a cold bright but sunless day, and she was wearing aviator sunglasses. It was ten a.m. the restaurant did not open until eleven. She wore a silk, Hermes scarf, a v neck cashmere jumper in tart red and a black wool, half-length coat with broad lapels. Her outfit was completed with black jeans and brushed suede ankle boots. She had a designer bag over one shoulder. It was a style she had begun to adopt more often.

'It's nice up here, in the open air,' she commented.

'Come inside and sit down with me. The coffee's for two.'

'I might have wanted tea.'

'I decided we would have coffee.'

'I see.' She turned her head to regard him, a half-smile playing around the corners of her mouth; she raised her dark brows behind her ray-bans. She shrugged and followed him into the awning, she sat down at the selected table. She felt just a little bit shaken. A little vulnerable. 'You like your own way, don't you?'

'Remove your glasses.'

'Okay!' she drew the word out, tilting her head at him inquisitively. He felt self-satisfied. He had her attention. She removed her bronze aviators.

His scent was not at all what she had expected. It had subtlety; its strength lay in the abstract, it appeared where she least expected it, at the gallery of her self-perception. It had reached out to her, almost deliberately, whilst she had stood several feet away. Now, when she sat, it enclosed her like a cage. It caused her to ask questions of herself. It made her feel naked inside and it reached inwards to seek out truths. She shivered as though someone had walked on her grave.

'What urged you to come in the end?'

'The fact that you make me curious enough to want to. And certain thoughts keep going through my head.'

'What thoughts?' He nodded towards the cafetière. Saskia compressed her mouth a little sullenly. She shrugged again, then poured coffee into a white can, she ignored the milk and sugar. She tasted it and pushed the tip of her tongue between her lips to remove its trace. It was strong. She had no idea of the bean. She wanted to ask but she did not do so. She sipped more of the coffee, feeling the strength of it merge with Khalid's scent. She hoped she appeared relaxed when she replied to his question, because she certainly was not feeling relaxed.

'Do I want to see you naked? Do I want to share a stained bed with you?'

'And your conclusion?'

'Probably. But that doesn't mean that I will.'

'I had you down as a creature of instinct.'

'I'm not! I assure you.'

'What would be so wrong with us sharing a bed?' He said reasonably; nonchalant.

'It might be bad for me,' she stared at his long fingers; they were strong fingers; the nails manicured; his skin was very black.

'Why might it be bad for you?'

'I might want to do it again. Then you would be fucking me, and you would be fucking Ayesha.'

'Don't you find that idea seductive. I know that I do.'

'A part of me wants it,' she replied candidly. 'You intend it don't you?'

'I didn't, until I met you. I considered you an annoyance.'

'I am annoying. I know that. You will find me annoying!'

'I will?'

'While you are in Ayesha's life, yes.'

He studied her while he sipped his coffee. She looked relaxed, confident. He knew that his alchemical scent would be claiming her, disturbing the continuity of her thoughts, dismantling any defences she had prepared against him in her mind; raising her level of sexual awareness; she was hiding the effects well. He placed his empty coffee can on its saucer and pushed it across the table towards her.

'Pour me more coffee Saskia.'

Without thinking Saskia took up the cafetière; carefully she filled Khalid's coffee can; it felt heavier than it should, and she felt clumsy all of a sudden.

'Two sugars.' A white porcelain bowl held cubes of brown sugar; there were sugar nips, with which to pick them up. She reached for them, but they appeared to slip from between her fingers. Saskia huffed and swore softly under her breath, as they bounced across the table and dropped onto the floor. She wondered if Khalid had used a mild form of intent to dislodge them from her grip, she could not put it past the man.

'Fingers will do,' he told her. Very deliberately, one at a time, she extracted two cubes of sugar from the bowl, between her fingertips and dropped each one into Khalid's coffee with a tiny plop. 'Now stir it for me. I stir it eight times.' Saskia became aware that she was bent low over the table, concentrating on the coffee can; she saw the spoon resting in the saucer beside it and picked it up. She squinted at Khalid resentfully, and paused with the spoon raised, bowl down over the coffee, like a dowsing pendulum.

'Ayesha warned me, about the scent.'

'I thought that she might. It's difficult to prepare for, though I'm impressed; you are resisting remarkably well. Stir my coffee for me, eight times; there's a good girl.'

Saskia lowered the spoon into the coffee. It was not that she felt that she could not resist doing as Khalid told her, it was that she did not want to resist; she knew that she could decide not to if she wanted to. Carefully, almost purposefully, she stirred the spoon round in the coffee, eight times.

'It's a very odd sensation,' she told him conversationally. 'It makes one feel willing.'

'In a sense, it changes the decisions of others in my favour. Initially it's overpowering, but after a short time it subsides and becomes much more subtle in nature.'

Saskia lay the spoon down in the saucer and slid Khalids' coffee towards him. She watched him take it up and sip it, as he studied her. She straightened in her chair and returned his stare; she felt slightly confused, unable to decide how to return his searching stare; she decided in the end to return a blank gaze.

'I'm leaving now,' she stated, though she remained in her chair. She drew a long breath, it felt shaky. Her mind felt as if it was un-focusing and refocusing from a new perspective. She felt like she was tripping.

'You've barely touched your coffee.'

Reactively, Saskia almost reached for her coffee, but managed not to, 'I'm not a fan.' She shrugged.

'As you please,' he replied casually. 'You know, I keep an apartment on the floor above this restaurant. The sheets are white and not yet stained.'

'Is that where you fuck your mistresses, your girlfriends?'

'Some of them. I have other places too.'

'I'm leaving now.' She did not want to trip.

'Yet you're still here.'

Saskia felt hot, sweat like a fine mist had risen on the surface of her skin. Her heart rate had risen. She felt that she required sex.

'I've an appointment in London tonight, with Theo Bacchus.' It was deflection, otherwise she had no reason to tell him. He appeared not to have heard her anyway. He stared straight into her. He leaned forward in his conspiratorial way, 'I think you and I would very much enjoy staining a bed together,' he told her.

Saskia persisted. 'For the removal of my fetter.'

He peered long and hard, his eyes looked deep inside her, still unsure of the measure of this unusual, beautiful girl. He drew a deep breath; he smiled dismissively, an element of contempt in it; suddenly decided.

'Thanks for the coffee. Maybe next time, tea?'

Saskia realised with surprise that she was addressing the door of the lift she had come up in, as it sealed her within its restricted space. She experienced a sense of claustrophobia and an odd detachment. She suppressed it. Khalid's scent was still with her; inside her. She could not recall getting up from her chair, she had no memory of leaving the restaurant. She could taste coffee in her mouth. She wondered what Khalid's skin would taste like in her mouth. She really did want sex.

*

'I thought you would be longer,' Ayesha remarked when she got back; she was in bare feet, on the couch and dressed in black leggings and a baggy red top off one shoulder. She was flicking casually through some glossy magazines. She had only been occupied in this way for a few moments, since she had seen Saskia climb out of her taxi, but it appeared as though it might have been for an hour.

'How did it go, little mantis?'

'It went okay,' Saskia lied.

'You look flushed.'

'Do you often read magazines upside down?'

'What! ... it isn't!'

'When I came away, I felt like I was tripping. I have blanks in my memory. I didn't fuck him. I wanted to. I've never felt anything like it. MI5 should have that stuff.'

'You sound okay. In control. I was out of it for a full day when I first experienced it. But I was only fourteen.'

Saskia had been about to slide onto her favourite end of the couch, but she changed her mind unable to think of anything but sex.

She took Ayesha by the hand and drew her to her feet.

'I need sex,' she told her.

'I thought that you would.'

## Seven

'Saskia's freaked out!' Selene was intense.

'What have you done?' Theo Bacchus turned to Saskia; he searched her frantic expression.

'It only occurred to me on the way down!'

Ayesha recognised that Saskia was close to tears. She tried to slip her arm around Saskia's waist, but she pulled away.

'I've kept away from alcohol and drugs just like you said. But this morning I was exposed to an alchemical scent. An enormously powerful one.'

'A sexual lure,' Ayesha supplied.

'A sex potion! Anything to do with you?'

'No, not Ayesha's. It's not her fault. It's my fault because I'm a cocky fucking idiot. I think I'm so bloody clever.'

'Saskia don't,' said Selene softly.

'I wasn't accusing her,' Bacchus protested. 'Saskia come with me. Selene, you too and stop goggling. Ayesha and Amelia remain in the study; make free of the guest room. Anything that you want, please ring the bell. Connie will be up soon with tea and coffee. Nothing for you I'm afraid Saskia.'

'I don't goggle by the way,' Selene said stiffly to her father as they ascended the staircase.

'I really do owe you Selene, your dad and you,' Saskia said to her as they walked side by side.

'You don't. I simply know the right people. Fate dealt you a cruel hand. We're both glad help.'

They turned into the corridor at the head of the stairs on the third level. A pair of imposing doors faced them, they were covered in black baize and embedded with large bronze studs. Bacchus pushed the doors inwards and held them apart as they passed between, then allowed them to swing smoothly back into position. A wide red corridor continued beyond; the walls decorated with stunning high-end modern art. Bacchus nodded towards a single black baize door to their left.

'Go in there. Selene will take care of you, and Saskia calm down. I am more than certain that a sexual lure will not harm your chances. It might even improve them!' He smiled with cynical humour.

'Now. You must prepare and I must prepare. You're in Selene's hands.' Saskia watched him as he walked away. Panther like, she decided.

'I find your father rather intimidating,' she remarked.

Selene shrugged. 'He's just dad.' She turned the door handle and pushed it inward. She stood with her back against the open door; studying Saskia as she walked into the room on the other side. Saskia gazed about curiously. The room was a bathroom or wet room, it was spacious, with an open shower at one end, it was lined in malachite, a stone Sakia loved; it covered the floor, walls, and ceiling. The room was illuminated by inset downlights. A huge copper bath occupied the centre of the floor. It was two thirds full; a large quantity of ice floated in the water. A few feet to its right stood a square table with a white acrylic top; two chairs were drawn under the table, on opposite sides; they were iconic series sevens by Arne Jacobsen, in teak with chrome legs. On the table were arranged some new white towels and several flasks, and a stainless-steel kidney basin next to a stainless-steel tray, on which were a small selection of instruments, including two Flays. Saskia shivered. She felt cold and nauseous.

'God, Selene I'm terrified.'

'Well, you aren't backing out now I spent the best part of two days purifying the water and ice in that bath, and mixing god knows what alchemical shit that my dad kept distilling, into it.'

'I won't back out! I've wanted this for too long! The effort won't be in vain I promise!' Saskia protested.

'I am joking,' Selene said unexpectedly, though she remained deadpan. 'It's water and ice. Give me all your clothes! I'll take care of them.'

'It looks freezing.'

'We're going to cook you before we freeze you; don't ask me why. The Sauna's through that door.' She pointed at a wooden door set into the wall on the opposite side of the room. Saskia undressed; she had arrived in plimsolls, jeans, T-shirt, and panties. She handed everything to Selene, who folded them for her and placed them on another series seven, placed next to the doorway. Selene examined Saskia's nakedness with cool detachment.

'You do know that you are going to be scarred?' she remarked.

'Do I look like a bimbo Selene?'

Selene almost broke into a smile.

'You know that you don't. All I'm meaning is, be prepared.'

'Oh god, that steam is smelly Selene!'

'Yes, those are alchemical vapours, they are important to this process, so breathe them in. They might make you throw up. Don't worry about it, just keep scooping the water onto the rocks. I'm not coming in with you. I'll be just here if you need me though. Thirty minutes, yes?'

As soon as she was alone in the Sauna, Saskia sat down on one of the benches and stared at her bare toes. She suddenly felt deeply sorry for herself, and tears began to stream down her face. At first, she palmed them away, but then she reached for one of the towels and folded it over her knees, she buried her face in conditioned fabric and began to sob bitterly, unaware that Selene Bacchus could hear every one of them.

'Ready?' Bacchus asked.

Saskia had towelled herself dry and the warmth of the room penetrated her body after her immersion in the ice bath. It had only been for a few minutes, but she shook, and the thick white robe Selene had handed her felt cosily comforting. She was as ready as she was ever going to be. Saskia nodded determinedly; she sat down.

'There will be the initial discomfort during the flaying.' Bacchus told her. 'Then I will apply the venom and then the veil. After a few moments the pain will begin, I hope that you have prepared your mind for this.'

'I'm assisting dad,' Selene told her, 'Ayesha is going to be with you; she has volunteered her hands, because you will need to grip something when the venom and the veil meld and enter your body to dispel the fetter. We need to pull the robe down from your shoulders.' She stooped helping Saskia to draw her arms out of her sleeves. She could feel her shaking.

'You're braver than me,' she told Saskia.

'I think that I'm simply determined.'

'I'm ready!' Saskia nodded, a single fierce nod. It began.

'Are you okay!' Ayesha whispered. She felt foolish asking the question, but she also felt utterly helpless. She was opposite Saskia, seated in the other series seven at the table. She had leant across to take Saskia's hands in hers. Her face appeared small; her eyes were big with worry. Saskia's knuckles had gone white, and Ayesha gritted her teeth against the tightness of her grip. She watched the sweat bead onto Saskia's skin and the silent tears as they flowed down her cheeks, to fall from her jaw, where they splashed onto the tabletop. Ayesha was unaware that she was crying too and that her tears were fascinating Saskia and in an odd way distracting her. She had gasped once, as Theodor Bacchus had begun to flay the fetter tattoo from her back, but after that she was silent; she concentrated on breathing evenly and slowly through her finely parted lips, trying to sustain calm. This was the easy part. But it was also the scariest part. Selene stood at the side of Saskia, pressing the kidney dish to her bare back to catch blood and detached skin. Her face looked as if it could be made from stone, but her jaws were locked hard, and her shoulders were tight.

'It does hurt,' Saskia responded to Ayesha in a small voice.

'The cutting is nearly finished,' Bacchus said. And a few moments later. 'There. Do you wish to see your removed tattoo?'

'Noh! What will happen to it?'

'I'll destroy it in a chemical salt. It's not simply skin and ink. I'm about to apply the venom. It will feel more than icily cold.'

Saskia gasped as Bacchus drizzled tiny amounts of the alchemical venom onto raw exposed tissue.

'Watch!' Bacchus snapped at Ayesha whose eyes were focused on Saskia's. She glared up at him; resentful.

'Watch; this is called the venom; you will need to repeat this on three more occasions over the next thirty-six hours,' he said less acerbically. 'Drizzle over the entirety of the wound. The venom will be absorbed, don't be disturbed by the trails of vapour it merely means that it's working.' He felt Saskia grow tense at his words and draw a shuddering breath.

'I'm sorry for this!' He told her. He took a tiny antique silver pepper pot and shook it lightly over Saskia's wound, sprinkling a fine dust over the raw flesh. 'The dust is called the veil.' He said directing his gaze to Ayesha. 'This all rests on your shoulders because Saskia will be incapable of anything. Selene has printed out instructions. Follow them to the letter.' As Bacchus ended his sentence, Saskia screamed in agony.

*

Saskia contorted in Ayesha's arms. Amelia drove them, her face was white, drawn by Saskia's distress; Saskia and Ayesha occupied the back seat. Ayesha did not know if she could cope with the next forty-six hours; they were only two hours into the venom and the veil, and she was distraught at seeing Saskia suffer unrelenting agony. She stroked Saskia's hair and neck and leaned over her, attempting to soothe her, knowing that it was pointless.

'Ayesha.'

'Yes.'

'I don't want you to do this alone.' Amelia searched the rear-view mirror for Ayesha, eventually her head raised into view, and she stared straight back at Amelia, her eyes like black onyx.

'What do you suggest?'

'That I stay with you. We do this together.'

'Not happening.'

Amelia's lips tightened. She tried again.

'Okay. What if I visit? A few hours each day until this is done. Give you a rest. You know that it makes sense.'

Ayesha's eyes lifted, looked up and to the side, tears welling out of them. Amelia knew that Ayesha was not cut out for this sort of thing; the fact that she was prepared to undertake it was impressive. She willed her to say yes. Ayesha's voice responded after a few moments hesitation; her voice subdued.

'Okay. Thank you.'

Amelia nodded; she did not dare to smile, not even in relief; even that might be misconstrued. Small victories. Saskia sobbed to herself; her face buried in Ayesha's lap; she released her breath in long shudders. Her pain was excruciating, it was her entire world at present. They had re-dressed her except for her T-shirt. Her body was wracked by shivering and cold sweats, and they had wrapped her in the towelling robe. An hour along the A1 she had struggled out of the robe; muttering about being 'too hot mum, I'm suffocating.' Ayesha had touched her skin; it was febrile.

In the carpark they got Saskia out of the car between them. Ayesha was thankful that no one was about, though the likelihood was, that anyone would assume Saskia was drunk, which was far from ideal. She shook them off angrily as they started to walk her to the lift.

'I can manage!' she hissed between her gritted teeth.

Amelia caught her as she pitched over, and they walked her the rest of the way to the lift.

'See, I told you,' She sobbed. She vomited on the floor of the lift on the way up.

'I'll come out and clean it up,' Amelia volunteered. Ayesha nodded; deciding that it would be good for her.

Saskia's pain grew worse; it blitzed her entire body. It contorted her and bent her like a drawn bow. It scooped out her eyes with white hot spoons and pushed needles down into her ears. It painted her skin with acid and drove nails into the roots of her teeth with a hammer. It tortured her joints and seared the inside of her bones with furnace like fire. Eventually Saskia's screams made her voiceless. Amelia and Ayesha had undressed her; they lay her on her bed naked; they could not soothe her; they could do nothing to ease her pain; they could only watch her agonies through tears of their own and ensure that she did not contort herself off the bed or damage herself against the wall or furnishings.

At three-thirty a.m. her eyelids flickered, and her green eyes disappeared up into her head. She went unexpectedly limp. Ayesha panicked, she felt desperately for a heartbeat and sobbed in relief when she found it, beating like a drum. Saskia appeared to be comatose. Her mind no longer aware of pain hammering every inch of her body. Ayesha began to sob softly in relief, she had no idea how long this state of calm would last, she thought, but she would take whatever was given.

'I must go to the loo,' she whispered at last.

'I'll wait for you to come back, and I'll go too,' said Amelia. 'Then shall I make us something to drink?'

'I'd like that. I'd like tea but I think we should have coffee.'

Amelia smiled. 'Do you really think that we're going to need anything to keep us awake sweetie?'

'No! Probably not. Tea then. Nice and strong. I'll be back in a minute.' She slid carefully from the bed and disappeared into Saskia's on suite.

Twenty minutes later Ayesha jerked out of reverie as Saskia emerged from her comatose state and began to writhe in pain. Ayesha was propped against the fabric of the headboard, sitting on a pillow; she quickly writhed down the bed and clutched Saskia's hand. She peered into the beautiful, pain contorted face and engaged with her eyes. To her surprise Saskia spoke to her.

'The pain's less; but still bloody awful,' she said in a hoarse voice. Her body shook with sobs. 'I need the loo, but I can't get there myself.'

Amelia appeared on the other side of Saskia's twisting body; she had been kneeling at the foot of the bed, chin resting on the back of her hands, silently watching both younger women. She had decided not to disturb Ayesha when she returned from the on suite; as yet, Ayesha had not questioned the length of her stay,

'Come on,' she said. 'Let's get her there.'

Saskia unable to walk on her own and she had to be almost carried; when they got her into the on suite, she was not able to control her bowel and she experienced diarrhoea, and then she vomited. She sobbed with pain and a very real sense of the indignity.

'I'm so sorry!' she told them, through chattering teeth.

Ayesha kissed her flushed face. 'Let's get you cleaned up little mantis,' she told her tenderly.

They cleansed her and got her back to bed, where she lay curled in a foetal position. Her body shook and she kept making little whimpers of pain. Amelia and Ayesha exchanged looks.

'Go now if you want to,' Ayesha told her.

'I'll go and clean the on suite. Then I'll phone Hal. Get him to bring me some changes of clothes. And Saskia needs to drink.'

'I know. But not yet; I think she's gone again. You're staying?'

'You know I am.'

*

'Stop snivelling.'

'Sometimes you go too far.'

'Do I?' he inquired, there was no menace in his words or demeanour; it remained unexpressed; intangible. Yet it was, as ever, present.

Saskia wiped semen from her chin and mouth with the back of her hand; there was blood there too, from her nose. It was not that she had no liking for her submissive role in their relationship; she enjoyed the sadistic streak in him; but there was a time and place after all.

'We're at the Bosola's party in a couple of hours.'

'I hadn't forgotten.'

'You want to show your property off at its best, don't you? We can always have fun afterwards.'

He grinned his usual sneering contempt.

'Make sure you cover the thorns; they are still unsightly.' She nodded. She regarded him cautiously and spoke.

'Will you introduce me to Holly Penn the artist? You have several prints by her. Remember you told me about her.'

'Why?'

'I might ask her to paint me. I've plenty of money.'

Nathan frowned at her; but it was a frown that expressed interest rather than annoyance. The thought appeared to chime with him. He nodded. 'If she's there.'

He picked up his discarded clothes and walked from her room; dispassionately she watched him leave; she got off her knees. She went into her on suite, without turning on the stark illumination from the downlights; she pulled the on cord of the single light above her long mirror and studied her reflection; the comforting darkness clumped behind her. The green eyes that regarded her were a little harrowed, the lids hooded. Her skin was pale; she had bruising around her left eye; she would cover it partially for the party, but mostly wear it with pride. She ignored the semen across her lower face and regarded the thin streams of blood from her nostrils; it had dripped from her chin and run down over her breasts. She tilted back her head and compressed with her thumbs, the section of her nose below the bridge, until the blood flow had all but stopped. Her ribs were bruised, when were they not? She turned her lower body, to gaze at the red strikes across her rear; added to fading bruising; Nathan enjoyed using his leather belt on her. Her legs were okay, her arms and shoulders. For some reason he liked them pale, flawless; he liked them to be seen. He did not mind injuring her face; he did not mind that being seen. She twisted her torso round then to examine the blackthorns of compliance. It was a week since they had been hammered into her back, there was still bruising and scabbing; they were still painful, but that was their purpose after all, though the pain they would eventually deliver would be exquisite. Two had been hammered into her fetter, two more between her shoulder blades, the remaining two were driven in half-way along her spine, either side of her vertebrae. She returned her gaze to the mirror and smiled with cold disdain. The darkness shifted behind and to her left; a face appeared in the mirror about fifteen inches above her left shoulder; it was sinister and eerie in the absorbed light and its body below the neck was lost in the shadows. It was the creature from the Frankenstein movie, the Karloff monster. There were anodes in its neck and its mouth was clamped shut like the jaws of an old animal trap. It regarded her with sullen dispassion, through gleaming eyes, from beneath heavy eyelids.

'Huh! hello you,' she greeted it ruefully. It had started to appear a couple of weeks ago, not that she had much recollection of event, and its appearances had become more frequent. It was in the habit of manifesting after Nathan had shown her brutality. She had wondered if it was an entity, maybe Nathan's house guardian, but she had dismissed that idea. It appeared to be personal to her, and she had seen it observing Nathan with genuine malevolence.

'Stick around!' she said to it, 'talk to me while I'm in the shower.'

Slowly and with minimal movement, it shook its head, surprising her. It receded, and became one with the darkness, but she had the oddest sensation that it was still present. She showered, enjoying the jets of water as they drenched every inch of her skin. Her body shifted uneasily as the water began to grow uncomfortably hot; she reached for the control; by then it was scalding. She was unable to move, then she remembered the pain.

*

'Hals gone. He heard that scream, out in the lobby.'

'I hadn't thought her capable of that at present, she woke up and gave it everything,' Ayesha replied, she had pinned up her long hair, a thing she rarely did. 'Thank you for staying. In my pride I thought I'd be able to manage. But I really don't think that I could have.'

'Yes, you could if you had to,' Amelia said gently. 'I can see that.'

'She's settled down again, I think she's just in severe pain now.'

'Bacchus said she would trip. But that was like a mini coma!'

'Do you think we should phone Bacchus, ask him?'

'It's almost seven. Selene will probably be up and about.'

'I'd lost track of time. Will you phone her?'

'Of course.' She had almost turned to leave but she paused. She took a deep breath.

'I am your friend Ayesha. And I have managed it badly.'

'You have!' Ayesha sniffed; her eyes had been made very red with crying and more tears were grouping.

'Any friendship between us, you almost ruined it.'

'Almost?' Amelia felt her own hot tears well up.

'I think that you heard what I said, bring a bottle of water back with you, so we can give Saskia a drink. Then some more tea wouldn't go amiss.'

Smiling through her tears Amelia went on her way to phone Bacchus house. She came back with water and the phone from the main living room, on speaker.

'I've got Selene. She's gone to speak to Theo Bacchus. Apparently, they are both up by six every morning.'

'Hi Amelia,' Selene's voice spoke from the phone. 'Dad says that's good! His opinion is that she's in a very deep hallucinogenic state. Anything else happens, call us.'

'Thank you, Selene. You do know you're a treasure.'

'No, I'm not. We'll talk later. Bye.'

'Short and sweet.'

Ayesha shrugged. 'It's only her manner. She's been a friend to us.'

'Let's get some water into Saskia.'

'Okay. Then we had best look at her fetter. It's only a couple of hours to her next application.'

'You should get a couple of hours sleep, you look wrecked, and we are no good to her totally exhausted.'

Ayesha nodded. She did not think that she would sleep, but she did sleep, and she jerked awake on her bed to Amelia's touch on her hand.

'Twenty minutes. You shower then I will.'

'Okay.' Ayesha squeezed Amelia's hand. 'I'll be five minutes.'

'Saskia's almost pain free,' Amelia remarked.

Ayesha showered quickly and changed into loose clothing, her skin was still partially damp. She went into Saskia's room. Saskia was sitting up, her knees drawn up and encircled by her arms. She looked dreadful, but she smiled with wan affection.

'Saskia.' Ayesha whispered; she caressed her face and hair with her fingers.

'I must be mad. Ten minutes and I go back into that nightmare. I'm terrified.'

'I'm sorry I slept.'

'I'm not. I want you strong. I'm pleased you let Amelia stay.'

A few minutes later Amelia appeared, showered, and changed. Her face was tense with strain.

'It's time,' she said.

Saskia screamed. She begged them to end the pain. When at last her screams stopped, she sobbed bitterly, and her body twisted in a lonely agony.

'I suggest we give her oblivion for a couple of hours; she didn't go into one of those little comas for hours after the first venom and the veil,' Ayesha said.

'I agree.'

'Saskia. Saskia! Listen to me.'

'Mmmghh.'

'We're going to send you to sleep. We are going to give you the sleeping draught. A few drops in your mouth.'

Saskia's eyes fluttered, she nodded, understanding. Despite her agony she tasted the bitter drops as they fell into her dry mouth. Within a few moments she had fallen into a deep sleep.

*

Saskia stood alone at the party. Everyone there was ignoring her. She expected nothing more. Most people there regarded her simply as Nathan's property. His beautiful, sulky slave. Everyone knew that he mistreated her, and because she appeared to embrace her role, no one had any sympathy for her. Many of the guests were puzzled that Hal and a few others within his social group, with real credibility, were countenancing Nathan by accepting him into their society. Only a very few people there had a true grasp of the reality of things. That the idiot girl in the black sequinned mini dress and strappy heels, had handed herself and her powerful magical legacy, into the hands of a man who was certain to abuse both.

'I liked you,' Ayesha told her approaching her. She was stunning in a long red tapering dress; it had a low neckline and a long slit, and she was wearing strappy red stilettos. Her ivory skin was jewelled, her fingers, ears and throat adorned with gold and carnelian. She was holding a cocktail glass filled with something red and alcoholic. Saskia had seen her consume several in the hour she had been there. She was in the company of a very tall Black man, with gleaming skin, who was currently in conversation with Amelia, Hal's wife.

'I liked you too,' Saskia told her.

'When you made the choice to go with Nathan, you really fucked up everything; you know that?'

'I think I do.' She drank neat vodka from her square glass. It was her third. 'Don't be seen talking to me; it will send your credibility through the floor.'

'I don't really care. This is partly my fault. I should have grabbed you and shoved you into Claire's office. Chanced myself against Nathan. I like to think it would have been my day. He's abusing you badly, isn't he?'

'Most days. It's what I signed up to though. Did he abuse you when you were with him?'

'It was only for a brief period, and mine was consenting.'

'So is mine.'

'Mine, limited him to my taste.'

'Your compliance.'

'He told you about that.'

'From what I can see of it, it's exceptionally beautiful. I'd like to see all of it.'

'That won't be happening,' Ayesha smiled thinly, which made Saskia feel suddenly incredibly sad.

'Nathan complied me. With blackthorns,' Saskia confided.

'Then you really are fucked,' Ayesha replied. She drew away, peering about for Hal, so that she could relate her news to him.

*

'I'm so pleased she's stopped throwing up, and we got water into her, and its stayed down.'

'This is dreadful Ayesha. I wish I could take some of the pain for her.'

'Do you think that I wouldn't?'

'Oh, I know you would. I believe that you would take it all for her.'

'I truly hope this is worth it for her.'

'It must be. The back of your hand and your wrist are a mess where she's clawed you.'

'I don't care!' Ayesha shrugged. Saskia knelt beside her, her arms stretched out before her, fingers spread and pressed hard against the wall. Her head hung forward between her arms. Sweat dripped from her face and her body shook with tears of pain that had become just shuddering breaths.

'You need to eat something Ayesha,' Amelia said.

'As do you.'

'I want coffee.'

'Me too. Can I have some toast, with honey?'

'I'll only be minutes.'

By the time Amelia returned Saskia had fallen into one of her mini comas. Ayesha looked at Amelia in utter relief. They drank coffee and munched toast, in mutual silence.

\*

'When I'm of no use to you anymore, are you going to get rid of me?'

'Get rid of you! Why would I get rid of you?' Nathan grinned. 'You provide me with too much entertainment.'

They were on her bed. Saskia had drawn up her knees and sat propped against pillows, she was breathing fast and hard, her body glistened with sweat. Nathan lay on his side breathing heavily; his skin was also sheened in sweat. He studied her bruised face, her bottom lip which he had split open; and the blood that coursed down her chin; his eyes barely touched on the bruising around her throat.

'Open your mouth.' She did as he told her at once, she knew better than to hesitate. He peered at her perfectly formed teeth; there was blood on them and in her spit.

'Any loose teeth?'

She shook her head. It was the first thing she had checked for with her tongue after he had struck her. She had not yet worked out why he had hit her. Some imagined disobedience or slight? probably on a whim?

'Good, you avoided a trip to the dentist.'

'You might kill me one night. I almost passed out. I did the other night.' He didn't answer. Merely gazed at her with his ever-present sneer.

'May I go and clean myself up?'

'You can do what you like! I'm going to my own bed.'

He swung himself off the bed. He had no clothes to gather up; he had come to her naked that evening. The Karloff monster stood in the shadows by the door, dimly seen, almost beyond the range of the subdued lighting around the bed. Dispassionately it had watched everything they had done on the bed, through hooded, sullen eyes. A scene of gothic voyeurism that Saskia was sure Holly Penn, deviant artist that she was, would feel actuated to paint. Nathan did not see it, he could not. It glowered at him, even hunched it towered over him as he passed it on his way to the door. It growled at him and extended its long fingers and hands at the end of long scarred wrists; wanting to seize and strangle. It turned its squared head and questioned Saskia with dystopic eyes.

She shook her head. 'I can't end it yet,' she responded quietly when Nathan was beyond hearing.

*

'What the fuck are you playing at?'

Samantha Challoner was furious. She arrived at the café in a two-piece red suit and red stilettos, clutching a designer bag. The suit jacket was fastened by a single large button, and she was obviously wearing nothing under it. Her short skirt was mid-thigh, and she was probably wearing nothing under that too. She was limber like her daughter and exceptionally beautiful but lacked Saskia's frisson of dark spirit. She was not the Samantha Challoner that Saskia remembered, this was an earlier version of her mother, recalled in photographs, stylish and chic. Her hair was edgily short.

'I'm having an espresso, in the lovely spring sunshine, at this relaxing pavement café. I'm definitely not playing at anything.'

'You know what I mean! Cappuccino!' Samantha snapped her order to the waiter and slammed her designer bag down onto the circular metal tabletop.

'No what do you mean?' Saskia peered at her inquisitively from behind a pair of large sunglasses; they hid some of her bruising, but not all. Her mother she noted, had arrived in the company of a young woman, she had left her at the corner. She was tall and lean in a fawn suit; she had dark blonde, collar length hair; she had that Italian look.

'You are fucking Nathan! He is a cunt! Look what he's doing to you!'

'I didn't know you cared.'

'I do care. I express it badly.'

'I'm enjoying the abuse. And the sex is amazing. You should know.'

'We all like a bit of pain, but don't say I didn't warn you.'

'I can handle it!' Saskia regarded her mother with contempt, though it was lost on her, concealed as it was behind the large sunglasses; only the curl of her mouth revealed anything she was expressing.

'Are we in France by the way?'

'Of course, we are in fucking France. In Nice where else?' Saskia recalled her mother's often proclaimed love for France.

'It's lovely! I must come again, preferably when I'm not meeting my dead mother.'

'I'm not dead.'

'Excuse me mum but I recall waving you off into the fire.'

'Flesh and bone! Since when has that decided life or death?' She was scathing. 'How often did I tell you the body is your enemy. Most of humanity doesn't understand that.'

'Where is this really?'

'Nice. A version of it. My reality exists within it.'

'I suppose you had to do something all those times you kept falling asleep.'

'I suppose I did.'

'Giving no thought to me.'

'That was never so and isn't now.'

'So, what have you been up to in your version of reality?'

'Shopping and fucking mostly.'

'Is that it, the height of your ambition? Shopping and fucking!'

'For the present. Yours isn't too far off that. I can feel the thorns in you. You allowed him to comply you, you silly little cow! That affects me!'

'We are trying them out for the first time tonight.' Saskia said gleefully. 'How does it affect you?'

'Because I'm still attached to you.'

'That's not a good thought. What do you really want mum?' Saskia was suspicious, this was news to her. Something was wrong, but she only sensed an undetermined vibe.

'I want you to stop!'

*

Ayesha had a brutal, thudding headache. It hammered at the back of her eyes and made her feel sick. She took painkillers, though at first, she had been reluctant. She asked herself why she should not suffer some pain when Saskia was writhing in agony. But she knew that was illogical; she needed to be there for Saskia, pain distracted her from what mattered. The painkillers barely touched the pain and she almost sobbed in frustration. There was a remedy but for some reason she was reluctant to go there. Amelia made the decision for her; she had seen her take tablets; she had watched her massage her temples and bury her face in her hands.

She knelt next to Ayesha on the rug; Ayesha had her body propped against the bed; her legs curled under her. She was watching Saskia's sweat-soaked body, misery in her eyes, as it jerked in pain.

'You're tired, but that's not it. You're in pain,' Amelia said softly.

'I have a terrible headache, and I can't decline my pain.'

'I did wonder; why do you think that is?'

'I don't know. Maybe I deserve it, and I do, don't I?'

'No, you don't. I think you're too stressed, it's as simple as that. I'll take it away for you.' Amelia's long, cool fingers felt incalculably soothing as they rested on the back of her neck; they appeared to extend cool tendrils that pushed inside her neck and head; they wrapped around the pain and tenderly prised it out of her.

'Lay down on the rug, sleep.'

'Just for an hour.'

'Just for an hour. I promise I'll wake you.'

*

'Do you think that I'm a hard-faced little bitch Roger?'

They were standing at the end of the pier at Whitby, eating fish and chips out of a polystyrene tray. At the spot where Saskia had poured Roger's ashes into the sea, accompanied by a solemn Ayesha. It was blustery and the dark waters were lifting against the stonework of the pier extension. Roger was in a suit and coat and looked quite well. Saskia was in a flimsy dress, an open leather biker style jacket, and Doc Martens; the strong breeze lifted her dress showing her thighs. She shivered in the cold, off sea wind.

'I think you can be uncompromising.'

'Are you paying me a compliment?'

'Not intentionally. I think that you use people.'

'Really?' Saskia was a little shocked.

'Yes. You find their weakness which is usually you, and you exploit it.'

'No, I meant do you really think I use people?'

'Yes of course you do. Half the time you intend to. The other half you do, but you aren't conscious of doing it. It's second nature to you.'

'I sound awful.'

'Not really. Why did you ask? About being a hard-faced little bitch?'

'Because it occurred to me that I might be one. I needed someone I trust, to tell me the truth.'

'You are quite cunning, occasionally sly, probably unprincipled with an emphasis on unscrupulousness. But I don't think that you are a hard-faced little bitch.'

Saskia felt tears pricking her eyes as the home truths registered in her brain.

'You do have morals that an alley cat would be ashamed of.'

'I just happen to like sex.'

'And you're just a bit twisted. Maybe more than a bit.'

'I have a dark side!'

'Very dark! you're still the daughter I never had. You did right by me Saskia. And I want the best for you. That young woman's good for you; a bit odd, but good for you.'

'Ayesha.'

'The one you brought to my house. I could see she was falling for you even then. Don't hurt her too much, she's in love with you, you know.'

'I can't believe I'm having this conversation with you.'

'Mmh! Look I know she's weird too but cut her some slack for heaven's sake. Or you'll end up losing her. Do you want that?'

'It's the last thing in the world I want.'

'Now! This Nathan character. He's a proper cunt. If I were you, I'd let Frankie here break his fucking neck!'

With a jerk of his tray, he indicated the Karloff creature who leaned on the metal railing a few yards away and gazed down into the slopping water with fascination. Saskia considered the novelty of experiencing two realities concurrently.

'Fancy a chip, Frankie?' Roger called out.

\*

'I don't know if I can do it!'

Saskia was crying like a baby. She was trembling and her skin was damp with icy sweat. When it was not damp with icy sweat it was damp with hot sweat.

'I think it's killing me.'

'Bacchus said no. Your heartbeat is mostly good. You will not go into shock or sepsis. The alchemy is too strong, Saskia.' Ayesha wiped at her tears and stroked her cheeks and hair. They were kneeling knee to knee on Saskia's bed. The third venom was due within minutes.

'What would you say if I told you I wanted to stop?'

'I would say: then we stop. It is your choice, and I'll support your decision whatever it is,' Ayesha told her staunchly.

'Truly?'

'Yes, little mantis, truly.'

Saskia compressed her mouth. She drew a shaky breath. She leaned toward Ayesha and kissed her on the mouth; little shudders passed through her frame.

'Good, then I'm ready.'

\*

'Stop! Nathan please! I've had enough I really have.'

The pain withdrew. It had thin, hard fingers; they had penetrated to the core of her body. They had gripped and twisted; they had drawn the breath from her in gasps; then they had wrenched it out in cries.

Initially they had enjoyed sex. Unusually Nathan had not been brutal with her; he had not been gentle, far from it, that was not in him, but he had not hit her or inflicted damage in other ways. Then he had decided that it was time to try out her compliance. He had taken her into the wet room. It had black polished walls and a dark resin floor; he decided to illuminate it with the single down light from above the mirror, highlighting her pale nudity in the semi dark. He said it was best that he complied her in there, in the event she was sick. He had been right to do so. He made her kneel at the centre of the floor, then touching where the blackthorns had been driven into her back, he desired intent into them.

In conversation, Nathan had told her about Ayesha Shah's compliance. He had commented from experience, that it could induce more pain than the traditional method. It came with a goad, which could be charged; it directed and concentrated intent. Saskia wondered if Ayesha could endure more pain than herself; how interesting.

'Maybe a little more!' Nathan grinned. 'Then sex.'

Saskia was aware of the effect it was having on him. It quite obviously excited and aroused him.

The Karloff monster had watched them for most of the hour that they had spent in the wet room; maybe drawn by Saskia's cries of pain. It towered behind Nathan; its hunched shoulders lifted and fell evenly; it loomed. The only emotion it expressed was the aggression it felt for Nathan; it was indifferent to the abuse and the sex. It was not an autonomous entity though, somehow it was linked to her, she understood that; she felt connection. It was waiting for something. It was waiting for her.

\*

'Why did you have me fettered?'

They had met by the Royal Armouries Museum. Next to the Aire. The sun was out but it was coolish. Samantha Challoner appeared much more in keeping with how Saskia remembered her. She was in trainers and blue jeans, with lots of horizontal tear-like splits across the front of the legs. She was wearing a roped, cream, hand knitted jumper and a long dark grey coat, unfastened. Her hair was unchanged from their meeting in Nice. Her green eyes smouldered, registered annoyance, the thin line of her mouth even more. Saskia's green eyes smouldered back.

'I hate Leeds!' she informed Saskia.

'I don't mind it.'

'I don't leave my home without cause.'

'I didn't ask you to. I didn't want to see you. What do you want?'

'I want you to stop what you are doing. Don't fuck everything up!'

'This is about you, isn't it?'

'It's about both of us!'

'I'll ask again, why ...?'

'To protect you darling.'

'Crap! You are fucking mental. A fucking control freak!'

'I only ever wanted to protect you.'

'By choosing my future for me. Denying me what belonged to me! How dare you?'

'It was for your own good.'

'I prefer the version of you in Nice.'

'So do I!'

'Don't you think that you were being presumptuous and a shit bitch too? I know you were batshit crazy. But what prompted you to decide on matching fetters?'

'It's simple sweetheart.'

'Don't sweetheart me!'

'I did it to protect me from what I already had and the Wild, which was destined to become mine. I didn't know that I was going to die before I inherited it. I had you fettered to protect you from it too. The Wild.'

'I didn't want protection. I wanted my magic.'

'I knew that it would draw me in. It would be simply too dark and delicious to deny. And you were a strange child, you had an element of dark fae in you, I realised it would seduce you even more than me! I had to act when your intent started to appear. So, I prevented it.'

'But what's there in the Wild that can be so bad? So dangerous!'

'The Wurm! the dark heart of it! what else? I've seen it! It terrified me! It messes with you like nothing else, believe me! Saskia stay away from the Wild, don't fuck things up!'

'I don't know what you mean by 'fuck things up' but Nathan's taking me there in a couple of days to look around my legacy. He has plans.'

'He was always an ambitious bastard. Don't give him what he wants. He's too dangerous.' Samantha Challoner gave her daughter a final glare, turned and stalked away.

*

'I don't know if I can take the pain anymore Ayesha. But I must.' Saskia's voice was barely audible, her shoulders began to shake with tears. Her nude body was propped in Ayesha's arms her head resting under her chin. She appeared drawn and white; her eyes looked out of dark hollows; she had been drained of everything she had. Saskia raised her head; weakly she shifted her position, drawing herself up next to Ayesha. With an effort she controlled her sobbing.

'I'm pathetic.'

'No, you aren't.'

'How long?'

'About five minutes. Then in a couple of hours, we'll administer the remaining sleeping draught, just like we discussed; the venom makes you sick about then; so, after we've got you clean. Thank goodness the effects relent for a bit when you have your little comas.'

'I wonder if I still have the pain during them, it's just that my mind isn't aware of it.'

'Don't think about it. Let's get this over with.'

'You look shattered. I've never seen you look so weary.'

'It doesn't matter about me. Come on, have some more water. Let be bathe your face again.'

Saskia nodded; she kissed Ayesha's shoulder, then closed her eyes, enjoying the small luxury of having Ayesha apply a cool, damp face cloth to her febrile skin.

Amelia watched them, seated in a chair by the door to the on suite, a tray on her knee. She pitied Saskia, she hoped that all of this was worthwhile, and she would regain her magic; more than anything, she hoped the obvious bond between these two young women, would endure and evolve. She had a feeling that they had a chance. She got to her feet and brought over the tray which held the last venom and veil. Looking totally miserable, Saskia eased herself down the bed and into position, burying her face between the pillows.

'The wound is definitely smaller,' Amelia remarked.

Ayesha nodded. 'It's healing very rapidly Saskia, just like Bacchus said it would.'

'Hooray.' Saskia's voice was muffled in the pillows but the sardonic note it held was unmistakable. A few moments later agony gripped her, and her body contorted like it was going to break in two. Ayesha and Amelia held her between them.

A couple of hours later, almost to order, Saskia moaned that she was going to be sick. They got her to her on suite barely in time and she vomited though there was little to come out except bile. Then she had diarrhoea with comparable results. They cleaned her pain wracked body in the shower and took her back to the bed. They positioned her twisting trembling body between them; they held her head as still as they could.

'Open your mouth Saskia, let me take the pain away.'

Saskia moaned and parted her dry lips. Ayesha emptied the tiny phial of liquid into her mouth. A few drops, quickly absorbed, and in just a few moments Saskia was still.

'Right!' said Amelia determinedly. 'Let's get her comfortable. You have a shower. Then I'll have one. Then I suggest we have tea and something to eat.'


Amelia brought in more tea in porcelain mugs. She handed one to Ayesha.

'Beans on toast never tasted so good!'

'I know.'

'When you are both ready, you're coming to dinner with us. Intimate, just the four of us.'

Ayesha swallowed; she gave her a weary smile.

'Okay, we can do that. Have you phoned Hal?'

'Yes. He sounded tired.'

Ayesha caught herself nodding. She was perched on a corner of the bed, one leg folded beneath her; the mug of tea rested between her fingers, cold, half consumed. She had watched Saskia's sleeping figure in a sort of daydream, now she was wide awake. She glanced at the time, then at Amelia, who was stirring in her chair. Amelia gave a little gasp and massaged her eyes with her fingers.

'I've been asleep, I'm sorry,' she admitted guiltily.

'Don't be. I think that I've been asleep sitting up. Amelia it's been nearly three hours and Saskia's still asleep! I think that she's lapsed into one of her mini comas.'

'That's good, isn't it?'

An hour later and Saskia was still asleep. Her breathing was shallow but evenly spaced. Ayesha took her pulse.

'It's about seventy. I think she's still comatose.'

'I think that we should phone Bacchus.'

Ayesha nodded. 'I'll get the phone.'

Selene told them that Bacchus was out but should return soon. She listened to Ayesha's concerns and told her she would phone her back, as soon as she had talked to her father. She was about to hang up.

'Hang on, here's dad now.'

Ayesha had the phone on speaker, and they listened to the exchange at the other end. Selene gave a concise, exact description of what was happening with Saskia. They could hear Bacchus's reply, but he was not close enough for his words to be distinctive. He was brief.

'I don't know if you got any of that,' Selene said coming back onto them. 'But dad believes it's a positive thing and there shouldn't be anything to worry about. She might even sleep through or beyond, don't worry if she does. Fingers crossed eh. I hope she does because I can't imagine the sort of pain, she's been in. How are you two?' She surprised them by inquiring.

'Stressed, tired and worried. But maybe not quite as worried now,' Ayesha replied.

'Phone us if you need to. Dad's going to call you himself in a few hours. I suggest you both get some sleep if you can.'

'That's the nicest she has been,' said Amelia.

'I think she is nice, but for some reason she just prefers to present that cold mask. She's on my Christmas card list now anyway; that'll shock her.'

'Mine too.' They laughed, surprising themselves.

*

'I was sick again this morning.'

'We're you?' Nathan was disinterested.

'I don't want to be pregnant! I've told you to be more careful! I don't want a fucking child!'

'If you are, it can be aborted.'

Saskia nodded, satisfied for the moment; she was not a child person. She had never understood the imperative in people to breed. She looked down at her arms and studied the bruises; he never bruised her arms, she thought. Her eye hurt, again. She glanced into the vanity mirror at her damaged socket; the eye looked a bit inflamed too and she hated anything that diminished the beauty of her green irises. Being violently abused, she decided was becoming very boring. When she had originally made the decision to go with Nathan, it had been made in anticipation of him being a little more creative than he had proved to be. Life was full of disappointments.


Nathan brought the Shogun to a halt a yard short of a grazing sheep. There were several others in the vicinity of the nearby ruin. Her ruin. They had come up in the Shogun because Nathan considered it more suitable for their purpose. He had conceived the notion of driving the vehicle into the Wild. As it was a location, he saw no reason it could not be done. There was reference in one of the journals to a Challoner riding a horse into the Wild, after all.

She had never seen Hoardale, yet she recalled it; same with the Wild; she wondered how that worked. She decided not to tell Nathan. Life was decidedly strange at present. Lots of blanks. Maybe it was caused by the number of times Nathan struck her.

Nathan grinned, feeling immensely pleased with himself. He set the Shogun in motion again.

*'It is not down on any map, true places never are,'* he said.

'Just drive over the sheep why don't you?' said Saskia, but the sheep was no longer there. Hoardale had changed. There was no ruin, no farm on the hillside. The trees of the dense woodland ranged halfway around the edge of the mere. There were more trees behind them but growing further back; there were swathes of dense bullrushes along the low bank.

They climbed out of the Shogun. It was pleasantly warm; sunshine glimmered on the waters of the mere; it flashed on the wings and bodies of giant dragonflies. Saskia could hear frogs and grasshoppers and the hum of insect wings; she relished the warmth of the sun on her. But she recalled snow and ice. Heavy snow and a penetrating cold. Her experience of the last time she had been there. Yet she had never been there before.

Nathan laughed. He spread his arms wide; his palms upturned.

'Ah this is magnificent!' he said. His strange eyes mocked her. 'Can you feel the magic beating inside this place? It's primal.'

Saskia shook her head; her eyes were distant. She was recalling malevolent red eyes and bared fangs.

'And I'll be the one to unlock it. Nathan Xavier. I'll be more powerful than any of them!'

'Will you?' she said, offhand.

'Where the fuck is your head today?' He exclaimed, suddenly angry with her.

She shrugged. 'I'm sorry. I don't know. I'm just not with it.'

'Trust you to spoil my moment!'

She felt a sudden surge of resentment. 'It is mine you know, this Place.'

'You think so? it belongs to me. It's mine because you belong to me. I own you.' His eyes were gleaming, his face was raging. 'I can do whatever I want with you. To you. With impunity.' As if to emphasize the point, he struck her across the face; a violent blow with the back of his hand that threw her head to one side and sent blood flying from her mouth over the bonnet of the shogun. She voiced a pathetic little cry, and her hand flew up to her mouth, but she realised blood was pouring from her nose also. Nathan hit her again on the other side of her face, equally hard. She blacked out for just a second, she heard herself moan. There was more pain and more blood.

'You bastard!' she said, her voice barely present.

He responded by punching her between her ribs, winding her. She would have doubled over but he caught her by the throat as she fought for air. He waited until she had stopped struggling for breath.

'Take off your dress!' He snapped.

She was in a sleeveless red figure-hugging dress, the hem not even mid-thigh, and patent black ankle boots with four-inch heels. Nathan decided how she dressed. Mostly she approved. She had thought the style inappropriate for their trip today, though she passed no comment.

'Nathan, no, please!' her mouth and nose were full of blood, the taste was intense; ugly. She wanted to be sick, but she fought it away. She was shaking, crying, falling apart. Nathan's eyes were vicious, his expression cold, despising her.

Nathan reached into the collar of her dress with his fingers and yanked it apart, she felt the zip go and the dress come apart. He dragged it down over her arms and body, left it on the grass around her feet. She was naked underneath. He forced her against the side of the Shogun with his forearm against her throat. He tugged at his flies with his free hand, guided himself out. He pushed open the mouth of her vulva with uncompromising fingers and thrust up hard into her with his penis, hurting her. This would not last long she told herself.

Saskia had seen it among the trees; watching. Its long fingers worked spasmodically; she could see the hatred in its strange unforgiving eyes, even from there. But it was a figment of her imagination, wasn't it? Something from her psyche, what could it do? She leaned on the car for support. Nathan had penetrated her quite brutally; she could barely put her legs together. She felt faint from the blows to her head. She knew that she did not want this anymore. What had Roger Lavery said to her on Whitby Pier: *That Nathan character, he's a proper cunt!* She should let Frankie break his fucking neck!

'Go on then!' she yelled. 'Break his fucking neck.'

Nathan did not immediately look up. To him Saskia's shout was that of a stupid girl venting her spleen. But as the heavy footfalls came nearer, he heard them and looked up; his eyes widened in disbelief, and Saskia realised that he was now able to see it. He would know what it was, Saskia thought, a fictional creature. The RKO version of Mary Shelley's Frankenstein's monster. It would shock him, send cold fingers clutching up into his abdomen, but he existed in a magical world, where strange things were possible, where the boundaries between imagination and reality often blurred. He would recover his equilibrium quickly. Saskia frowned, puzzled by thoughts. Curiosity everywhere. She tried to remember something, what was it? Why was it suddenly so relevant?

Saskia saw the sneer take over Nathan's mouth; it genuinely loved to exist there. He released vis ultima; then again. She saw the beginning of fear when his intent had no effect. The creature loomed; reaching; pleased. He declined time and struck it three times with vis ultima to the head. Time reclaimed its tenure. There was no loss of glee on the Frankenstein creatures face. Saskia saw real fear fall across Nathan's features. He yelled in terror and tried to escape, but his hand made shoes slipped on the grass; he tried to writhe away but by then it had him by the ankle and it drew him to it. It ignored all his efforts to break free and all the intent he lashed out at it with. He shrieked as it broke his bones, and it shrieked too in an unholy sort of copycat, mocking joy; she could hear his bones cracking. It went on for some time. Eventually Nathan stopped shrieking and could only moan pathetically and struggle feebly. Then it broke his neck, and he was still.

She remembered suddenly what she had been trying to recall. Her location when she had watched the movie. It had been in Ayesha's apartment, after the storm. Before she played her Lute for her. She had dedicated a piece she had composed to her, Ayesha's dark eyes. How could that be? How was it possible? Yet she recalled it with total clarity. She never played her Lute for Nathan; he never asked her.

The Frankenstein creature picked up Nathan's broken body and lifted it above its head. It carried it to the edge of the mere. Perhaps it intended to discover if it would float like the little girl in the movie, she thought. Saskia followed. Oddly, she no longer had pain in her groin. Or in her eye, or across her face. Her tongue was stinging though, and she could still taste blood.

The Frankenstein creature threw Nathan's body into the mere, Saskia was not aware of a splash. She reached out to touch the Karloff creatures back, to brush it with her fingers because it suddenly appeared tenuous; it disappeared, like a spectre in headlights. She crossed her body with her arms; seeing that they no longer had bruising. She looked down into the water expecting to see Nathan's body or a part of it before it sank out of sight, but there was nothing, not even agitation on the surface. She felt disorientation. She was horizontal not vertical. Her eyes were closed, not open. So, she opened them, and found herself gazing into Ayesha's worried eyes.

'Ayesha's dark eyes,' she breathed. 'Ow my tongue hurts!' she could taste blood in her mouth.

'Hello my little mantis,' Ayesha smiled. 'You've bitten your tongue. but you're okay. We were worried about you. You've been asleep for almost twenty hours.'


Amelia went out to buy provisions. She left a few hours later, she appeared tired but relaxed. Ayesha saw her to the lift. They exchanged easy smiles, even, to Ayesha's surprise, a goodbye kiss on the cheek.

'Are you sure you're okay with me going home?'

'I can manage. I want to.'

'I'll come back tomorrow evening.'

Ayesha nodded. She reached out and touched Amelia's arm. 'Thankyou.' It was solemn, meant.

'Clean slate?'

'Oh yes!'

Ayesha returned to the bedroom. She curled on the bed next to Saskia, who was propped up on pillows, sipping spring water from a bottle. She had been awake for a couple of hours; long enough for a bath, though appetite eluded her; the thought of food made her feel nauseous. Ayesha kissed her on the arm. Then on the lips.

'You're breath smells of alchemy. Your skin too, I can smell the oils from your bath, but the alchemy is reasserting itself.'

'Does that mean you won't be sleeping with me?'

'It means that I might not be licking you.' As if to prove the point she licked Saskia's arm and wrinkled her nose in mild disgust.

Saskia smiled indulgently, it turned into a yawn. Ayesha snuggled into her.

# Eight

Ayesha emerged from the shower feeling vaguely numb. She had been on the edge of an emotional precipice for several days and she realised that it was time to withdraw and let herself recharge. She was in love with Saskia, but she was not a natural carer; now that Saskia was no longer in pain, she wanted time to herself, for just a little while. She considered phoning Amelia; the offer was on the table, but she decided against it. Amelia had brought shopping the previous evening, so they had everything they needed. She could manage, she decided; Saskia would sleep for a few more hours; she could chill, read perhaps, or watch Tv. Saskia was still swimming in alchemical toxins. Bacchus said another forty-eight hours and they would be gone from her system; her strength would return then. Ayesha would have liked to have taken the lift down to the gym for an hour, but she was reluctant to leave Saskia alone in the apartment. She had practised some Pilates and callanetics before her shower, instead. Afterwards she addressed neglected maintenance; her feet, hands, and skin, tidying her nails, moisturising. She brushed her hair; she did not bother with makeup. She dressed in black leggings and a strappy close fitted red top; she let her feet stay bare. She studied her reflection; she looked drained; hollow eyed, so lacking sleep; nothing like Saskia though who looked an utter wreck and was still unable to stand without help. She frowned when the doorbell rang. Someone else in the block, the apartment was soundproofed, but just maybe they had heard Saskia's screams. She checked the monitor and compressed her mouth, irritated, but not she felt, as irritated as she should be. Khalid stood in their entrance. She opened the door to him. He was dressed in a dark blue suit, white shirt, and handmade black shoes.

'You shouldn't be here.' He knew the key code to the main door unfortunately. Her mouth tightened; she was too tired for this.

'I hadn't heard anything from you. You would have put me off if I'd phoned. Are you going to let me in?'

She gave him a sullen look, then a begrudged half smile. Ayesha heaved a sigh; although she knew that she did not love him, she was still attached to him by bonds of compliance, and they were not easily broken. They were not even friends. They were familiars in a sense. They had a history going back ten years. Sex and her enjoyment of pleasure-pain forged a dominant link between them; she was aware that nothing else could, though she was uncertain if Khalid understood that. He wielded a powerful influence over her and when she had denied that he was the sexual incumbent in her life, it was not altogether true. She wanted him to go away; but she needed a distraction too. She allowed the threshold; as he entered, she caught his scent, a trace no more in the air. '*You bastard*' she thought.

He bent to kiss her mouth in greeting, taking possession.

'Saskia's asleep, talk quietly.'

He nodded. 'How is she?'

'It's done. We believe that the fetter's gone. We are travelling down to see Theodor Bacchus when Saskia feels well enough. It was disturbing Khalid.'

She led him through into the kitchen and he lifted a long haunch onto a tall stool. He watched her as she made them coffee, eyeing the curve of her rear inside her tight black leggings and the firm shape of her trim body. He stared at her nude feet, aware of their prettiness.

'I'm certain it was. You look drained but beautiful. Did you manage Saskia on your own?'

'No Amelia was with me until Tuesday night. I hadn't reckoned her as someone who would get down on their hands and knees and clean up vomit, or shit for that matter.' Khalid stared at her, partly amused.

'Really? The great Amelia Bosola?'

'I believe we've buried our differences.'

'I see.'

'But I don't think we'll ever see eye to eye about you.'

He shrugged. 'I won't lose any sleep.'

'Have your coffee, and then you really have to go.'

He exhaled heavily through his nostrils. 'I've missed you.'

'Have you?' her lip curled.

'Of course, I have. I care about you Ayesha.'

'Bullshit! You want what you see as yours. I know what you're like; it's part of your attraction.'

'I asked you to marry me when my divorce comes through.'

'No, you assumed that you would marry me when you got your divorce. A not-so-subtle difference. You are pushing boundaries, please stop. You must have known that there would come a day when I might no longer be a completely free agent. A time when you could no longer assume that I would come running to your bed or let you into mine, whenever you felt like it.'

'I'm the one who has had their nose pushed out of joint.'

'The logic behind that statement is fundamentally flawed and you know it.'

'You have always said that you have never met anyone as good in bed as me,' Khalid reasoned. He looked so smug, she thought. 'And that I gave you your most intense orgasms, these were details you confided in me, in intimacy.' Ayesha felt close to tears. She did not want this conversation.

'Khalid, I enjoy compliance. I do love the pain. I enjoy the sex with you, you're a very skilful lover. You give me intense pleasure. Why are we having this conversation?'

'We don't need to have a conversation at all.'

Khalid stared at Ayesha without ambiguity; he was as much aware of her nature as she was herself. He knew that she was brave; she would take on the world, but when the battle was over, she became fragile, win, or lose she needed a place to hide away in for a time, and that place was usually sex.

She had not occupied one of the bar stools; she had remained standing; arms crossed defensively; her coffee untouched. Khalid very deliberately picked up his own coffee can and took a mouthful of the contents; he licked his lips, enjoying. He watched her, holding her emotional gaze. He had the instincts of a predator. He sensed her vulnerability. Ayesha needed solace, and often it was the familiar that provided it. He finished his coffee. Stood.

'I'll leave then,' he announced.

Ayesha uncrossed her arms, her hands falling to her sides in tight fists. She shifted her stance. Her dark eyes looked ashamed as tears filled them and rolled down her cheeks.

'I don't want you to, but you must be quiet.' Before that moment she had never hated herself with such intensity. She felt shame, but shame had the ability to be a dark pleasure.

She led him to her bedroom, silently closing the door behind them; she undressed in front of him; he regarded her appreciatively; he looked satisfied, smug. She began to undress him, because she knew that he expected it, that he enjoyed her doing it. She kissed and licked his skin; she dropped to her knees, the tip of her tongue intimate. He caught her by the wrists and pulled her hands away from his erect penis. He drew her to her feet, enjoying the sensation of her body as it pressed and moved against his erection. He turned her about guiding her towards the bed, she gazed over her shoulder at him, her dark eyes burning. She knelt on hands and knees to receive him and voiced a tiny gasp of pleasure as he penetrated her. She allowed the sex to dominate, allowed Khalid to dominate the sex, she pushed away the clamouring thoughts of everything else. Orgasm eluded her though, mocking her beyond the barrier thrown up by her guilt. She repositioned. Eventually she achieved climax, velvet talons clawing inside her. She had mounted Khalid, her back to his gaze, she pushed down hard on his penis, lifted, pushed down, establishing a rhythm, and stimulated herself. She arched as she climaxed; raised her head and opened her eyes. She gazed directly into Saskia's moody stare, took in the slight sway of her figure, dressed in an oversized black T-shirt, which Ayesha had helped her into; she was framed in the open doorway, supporting herself against the jamb, with one outstretched hand.

'Having fun?' She inquired as she slid to the floor, her slide ending in a jarring bump.

Ayesha was agile, she dismounted with the skill of a gymnast and twisted away from Khalid. Her body was still expressing orgasm, but it felt numbed and somehow ugly.

'Get out!' she hissed at Khalid.

She vaulted off the bed and approached Saskia, her thoughts jarred; they felt suddenly like nails being tossed around inside a bucket; she felt utter devastation. She felt about to unravel. She only had one clear thought. How could she save what could not be saved? Tears of abject misery started to flow down her cheeks.

Saskia held up her hand to fend her off; she looked as if she was shielding herself from the sun.

'Don't touch me!' she growled; her voice sounded hoarse.

'Let me help you please.'

'I said don't touch me.'

'Saskia you're still poisoned. Let me help you.'

'Yeah, tell me about it! You could try telling me that I hallucinated this later I suppose. Try it!'

'I wouldn't do anything like that. Khalid please will you go?' She was aware that Khalid had left the bed and was watching them; his expression held an element of calculation, the beginning of a smirk lurked on his mouth.

'Yes, fuck off Khalid before I call Snuggles!' Saskia rasped, she looked at him very darkly.

'What the hell is Snuggles?' he frowned.

'My Guardian!' replied Ayesha suddenly looking concerned. 'Saskia treats it like a pet. She can see it permanently and it follows her around.'

'But it recognises me!' he protested.

'She knows how to rescind!'

'What!' Khalid showed the beginnings of disquiet. He reached for his trousers ignoring his boxers.

'Snuggles!' Saskia tried to yell; her voice almost gave out.

'Saskia!' Ayesha reached for her, but Saskia knocked her hand away.

They heard the thud of 'Alice's Adventures in Wonderland' as it fell to the floor from the shelf in the living room.

'I'm leaving for fuck's sake!' Khalid snarled. Ayesha could see that he was unnerved; he was shaking. Her Guardian was probably on a parr with Claire's father's, extremely dangerous; in her present state she was uncertain that Saskia would use discretion; she did not want the problem of disposing of what would be left of Khalid's body once Snuggles had finished with him, and she was not sure that she would be able to call the Guardian off; now that it had almost become Saskia's familiar. Khalid was an Adept, but the Guardian would brush away even his energised intent like feathers.

Snuggles appeared in full physicality in the doorway, grinning fiendishly. It dropped to a level just above Saskia's head, a position that appeared almost protective, Ayesha thought. She edged back just a little, erring on caution.

'Let me dress!' Khalid snapped, almost panicked.

'Take your clothes into the entrance Khalid; let him through, please Saskia, for heaven's sake!'

Saskia nodded begrudgingly, she pushed herself backwards across the corridor, on her rear, pushing with her feet and steadying herself on her palms, until she felt the opposite wall at her back. Then she braced her bare feet and straightened her legs, as she forced her body to edge slowly up the wall. Ayesha tried to help her, but Saskia angrily shook her off. Her skin glistened with sweat, and she was white with effort, by the time she was upright. Snuggles remained on station and visible, above her head.

Ayesha followed Khalid along the corridor, ensuring that she was between him and her Guardian, in the event Saskia suddenly lost it and set it on Khalid. She exchanged no more words with him and turned her head away from him when he spoke to her; his clothes were bundled in his arms.

Saskia grinned evilly. 'Funny yeah,' she panted to the Guardian. 'Bed-byes.'

Ayesha closed the door on Khalid, leaning her nude body back against it. She turned and made her way back along the corridor; her face looked stricken. Snuggles passed above her head making its way back to 'Alice's Adventures in Wonderland' now Saskia had dismissed it. Saskia shook her head as Ayesha stopped a couple of feet from her.

'Fuck you!' she said, she breathed rapidly with the effort of sliding across the corridor and gaining her feet. Staggering from her bedroom to Ayesha's, had already about done her in.

'What got you out of bed? Did you hear us?'

'I woke up, I felt awake, not groggy like I've been, I felt hungry.'

'I'll get you something darling. I'm so sorry.'

'I'm not hungry anymore. I'm going back to bed, and I need the loo.'

'Let me help you, please!'

'I don't want any help from you. You reek of him.'

'I'll shower. Give me five minutes, just five minutes.'

'I'll manage.' Saskia turned away from her, using the wall for support. She made her way along the corridor hand over hand. Ayesha realised that the only thing keeping her on her feet was bloody-mindedness.

'Fuck! Fuck! Fuck!' She shot to the shower. She cried in misery under the water jets; she wanted everything of Khalid's scent gone from her body. She washed her hair. She spat mouth wash; brushed her teeth savagely. She sobbed as she drew on a towel robe. She didn't try to dry her hair, leaving it wringing wet. Then she flowed at a run from the on suite to find Saskia, dreading what was to come.

She found her crawling on her hands and knees, from her on suite, towards the bed. Ayesha crouched beside her. She placed her arms around her and with surprising strength lifted her onto her feet. Arms still locked around her she walked her to the bed and lowered her onto it; she propped her on pillows and joined her; she kneeled next to her. She took Saskia's hand in hers.

'Please, don't hate me.'

Saskia looked ill, her efforts had exhausted her, but her eyes peered into Ayesha's frightened face with dislike.

'You're trembling,' she remarked.

'Yes, I am. I'm scared.'

'Right now, I do hate you.'

'Okay. I understand.'

'I wish that I didn't feel like this. I'm weak as a kitten.'

'Bacchus says it will be a couple more days before the alchemy leaves your body. And what was in you from the Bran.'

'So, my body's swimming in dead Bran too?'

'Something like that.'

'I feel dreadful. But it's nothing compared to the pain I experienced.'

'I'll look after you!'

'Is that what you were doing?'

'Saskia don't!'

'You promised never to invite him to the apartment.'

'I know. He came unannounced. I was vulnerable. Weak. I hate myself.'

'Sometimes I wish that I didn't feel what I do for you!' Saskia said bitterly.

Ayesha withdrew her hands; she hugged herself; her eyes had enlarged with misery. The shadows of tiredness that circled them were not lost on Saskia. Now she looked on the point of breaking down. She felt conflicted, because she felt like she wanted to hurt her, but she also wanted to cuddle her. She was alone with Ayesha and her fetter was gone. It was something to celebrate, but she felt too hurt. She gazed curiously at the young woman on the bed with her. She wanted to know her inside out, though she knew that she was still far from achieving that; but she knew her sufficiently to realise that inside she would be distraught.

'Right now, I just want to be alone with you. Pathetic isn't it.' Saskia's voice was almost a whisper and it faded almost to nothing, as her words became tearful.

'No, it isn't. I'm ashamed of myself.'

Tears leapt into Ayesha's eyes, and she threw herself on her lover caressing and cuddling; she kissed her drawn face with hot dry kisses.

'Don't for one moment think you're forgiven. Don't dare to think that I have forgiven you,' Saskia cautioned her; she returned her embrace; needing to give Ayesha solace.

'I know.' Ayesha responded, and she did; there would be a reckoning.

'I hate him, Ayesha; right now, I think I hate you.'

Khalid's visit had damaged them; something in Saskia had been knocked askew. She considered it a cynical act; it would not go unanswered, she decided. She gazed at Ayesha's dark hair spilled over the pillows next to her, the sleeping face, so incredibly beautiful. She found even the sound of her breathing beautiful. *I am so angry with you,* she told her silently.

'I'm so angry with you!' Samantha Challoner exclaimed. Her voice disembodied.

'You think that I give a damn!' Saskia replied aloud, waking herself. She shivered; goose bumped. She looked at Ayesha's sleeping face, her hair spilled over the pillows, exactly like in the dream. She waited for her mother's voice, but it didn't come.

It was two days since Khalid's visit; they had slept for much of that time; it appeared that Ayesha needed sleep, as much as she did. Saskia realised that she felt awake, cleansed; hungry. She carefully swung her legs out of bed and pushed herself cautiously to her feet. Standing, she tested out her legs. She was shaky but okay. She had a long cardigan behind her door, she put it on over her T-shirt, leaving it open. She left Ayesha sleeping.

She was sweating by the time she reached the kitchen, but it felt strangely good. She wanted bacon and eggs but decided that she should not risk having bacon. She decided to make scrambled egg on toast. Black coffee. She relished every mouthful. She habitually preferred tea to coffee, but right then she wanted coffee and she had started on her second cup when Ayesha turned up; she looked pale and still half asleep; concerned.

'You should have wakened me.'

'Why?'

'I would have made it for you.'

'I'm perfectly capable. Would you like some coffee?'

'I'll get it. You go back to bed.'

'I don't want to go back to bed,' Saskia told her firmly; she poured Ayesha a cup of coffee. She stared at her, mildly defiant.

'Sit down, have your coffee. It's nice just sitting here.'

'You mean you'd have been happier if I hadn't joined you.'

'I didn't say that. It's nice not being in bed.'

'I understand. I'm being a pain.'

'I'm being rebellious. But yes, you are being a pain.'

It was a mild rebuke; there was more of an edge to it than that, Ayesha could hear it in Saskia's tone. She felt it permeating the space between them. In the days to come she presumed that she would be challenged, called out; tested. She was not let off the hook. She had not expected to be.

'It's time to change your dressing. The skin has been healing remarkably quickly. Stay still.' For a moment she sounded like the Ayesha of their first acquaintance Saskia thought, amused. Ayesha stood up. If Saskia did not want to be friends, they could at least deal with practicalities. She pulled down the collars of Saskia's cardigan and T-shirt, holding them together. She removed the square dressing. Peered hard. She was silent for a time.

'Come with me.' She stalked out of the kitchen.

Saskia frowned and followed her. She eyed the stiff shoulders, the straight back, the luxurious hair. She was being haughty; it was a ridiculously cute look. She followed Ayesha into her on suite.

'Stand in front of the mirror wall.' Ayesha instructed; she had got a large vintage hand mirror from the shelf. She drew down Saskia's collars again; she held the mirror up directing it over Saskia's shoulder.

'It looks as if I won't need to change your dressing after all.'

The skin was unblemished where there had been originally a raw wound. Saskia saw a band of bone white skin, its edge slightly uneven, maybe seven inches long, no more than an inch in width.

'It's completely healed.'

Ayesha pressed a cautious fingertip to the surface of the skin. It felt smooth, cool?

'What do you feel?'

'Nothing. It feels numb.'

'The sensation may return.'

'I don't care if it doesn't. Now I just want to own magic again!' Saskia was excited; eight years the bastard thing had tormented her; now it was gone! her green eyes flashed, became lambent. She was flushed, and a film of perspiration had broken out on her skin. She threw off her cardigan and T-shirt and walked into the open shower.

'Nothing else matters!' she grinned and turned on the water jets. 'All I give a damn about in the entire world is my magic!' To Ayesha's surprise, she added: 'And you!'

After her shower Saskia was distant for the rest of the day. Her coolness to Ayesha returning. Ayesha felt on edge. She tried to engage in conversation, but it proved bitty and a little unforgiving; until the evening and Saskia became enthusiastic, when Ayesha suggested an Indian takeaway; she insisted on going with her to collect it; she looked quite shattered when they came back in and laughed about it. They ate off their knees. Saskia savoured her food and watched Ayesha whilst they ate. Ayesha felt as if she was being checked out by a wolf, as Saskia's eyes played over her; they transited into their darkest green. They became quite baleful, and she glanced hard at them a few times seeking out any sign of dislike. There was none and Saskia smiled as though she had caught on. Ayesha had chilled a bottle of Chardonnay much to Saskia's pleasure. It was the first she had had to drink for weeks.

Amelia rang as Saskia loaded the dishes into the dishwasher. Ayesha put the phone on speaker. She and Amelia were amiable; Saskia wondered, with mild malice, just how amiable Amelia would have been had she known about the Khalid incident. She saw Ayesha glance at her with just a hint of concern in her eyes, as if she had caught some indication of her thought.

'You sound remarkably good Saskia,' Amelia remarked.

'I feel wrung out, but if I ask myself to do something ordinary, I can do it. I feel shattered for a bit afterwards, that's all. Ayesha's permanently on hot bricks.'

'Look after her Saskia, I saw what it did to her. I can almost see you giving me a look Ayesha, but it's true, you went through your own piece of hell.'

'Saskia's wound has completely healed,' Ayesha remarked moving attention away from herself.

'Really? It must be something in the alchemy.'

'It's just scar tissue,' Saskia said. 'Quite numb.'

'I've heard something on the grapevine about Nathan Xavier by the way.'

Saskia's ears pricked up; Ayesha appeared interested too.

'Do tell,' she said.

'He's gone into hiding. Apparently, he was followed by something for several days.'

'What sort of something?' Saskia and Ayesha asked together.

'Something unnatural, presumably. My source said it manifested in his house, and outside, only Nathan was able to see it. In daylight apparently. It scared him. He used intent and thoughtform unsuccessfully. It's all a bit vague and he's taken off; he's been incommunicado for a couple of days.'

'Perhaps he was taken,' Saskia suggested hopefully. They all laughed. Coincidence? Saskia wondered. Bacchus would know, she thought.

After Amelia's call Ayesha asked Saskia what she wanted to do. It occurred to her that the day might have drained her.

'I'd like to watch a film,' she announced.

'Okay. Do you want to choose?'

'I know which one. Bride of Frankenstein!'

\*

'You were flawless, until the very last moment. Then you went into self-destruct,' Saskia said.

They were walking by the Aire, in skinny jeans and ankle boots, hands thrust into the pockets of leather jackets. Saskia's was black, cinched by a belt at her waist. Ayesha's oxblood and biker style. It was a pleasant late morning, the sky half and half. Saskia's vitality had returned, Ayesha was surprised at how rapidly she had become herself again.

'I'm not perfect. And neither are you!' an edge of resentment crept into Ayesha's voice. She had started the conversation; another attempted apology that Saskia appeared to want to derail. There was still distance between them, Ayesha simply wanted it to go away. Guilt felt uncomfortable.

'I know that. But I wouldn't have let Khalid through the door.'

'You aren't me. It's not that easy.'

'I understand that; ultimately, he is to blame. I believe that it was very deliberate on his part. But you let him in when you promised me that you wouldn't?'

'I needed you, but you weren't there.'

'You're saying that the blame lies with me.'

'I'm not saying that. That's ridiculous.'

'It's subjective. Answer me this: Would you have told me about it. Would you have owned up? If I hadn't caught you at it.'

Ayesha winced. Put that way it sounded sordid.

'I honestly don't know. You are pushing me right to the edge there.'

'Isn't that where I'm pushing myself, right to the edge?'

'I don't have an answer Saskia.'

'Was he wearing an alchemical scent.'

'He was. But it wasn't that.'

'You were vulnerable. You had been through an ordeal; it wouldn't take much to blow your resistance to pieces,' Saskia reasoned.

'Don't make excuses for me little Mantis.'

'I am making excuses for you. Take me up on them.'

'I knew what I was doing.'

'Take me up on them.'

'Saskia I've so much to say, but not about this. I just want things to go back to how they were.'

'Big ask.'

'Please don't be so cold towards me.'

'I haven't forgiven you.'

'Will you forgive me?'

'I really don't know; Does it matter if I don't forgive you?'

Ayesha felt herself go cold inside.

'Don't look like that. We'll work it out. Let's go back.' Saskia took her hand, surprising her.


Saskia withdrew her mouth; Ayesha watched her beautiful face recede and descend to her breast. She felt her coned nipple taken into Saskia's mouth and gently teased by her tongue. She sighed softly, barely audibly. Their lovemaking had lasted for most of the afternoon; they were rarely frantic lovers and there were many moments of genuine tenderness and sensuality between them. But that afternoon it had been beautiful; she felt almost chaste, and it had made her want to cry. She felt Saskia move her mouth tenderly down the length of her abdomen, eventually her tongue pressed between the lips of her vulva; she tensed, as Saskia pushed back the taut hood of her clitoris with cautious fingertips. She felt the tip of Saskia's tongue explore with infinite care. She shifted her hips, uncertain, the sensation intense, too much. She allowed. Too much, she almost stopped her. She could hear her own breath in short little gasps, and tiny cries that were hardly more than breaths. She extended a hand with the intention of pushing Saskia's head away; for some reason, her mind thought of the intensity of the pain delivered by her thorns, was it so different. Pleasure in another form. She paused her hand. She responded to the intensity of the sensation in her clitoris, in the same fashion she responded to the pain of her compliance; she invited it in. Pleasure clawed at her, then bliss followed.

'No more. I can't take any more just now.' Minutes later and she had writhed down the bed, to take Saskia's face between her hands. She stared into those beautiful green eyes longer than she had ever dared. Tears spilled from her own eyes, and she began to sob. She felt Saskia cradle her.

'I'm in love with you! You were in so much pain! You screamed for hours. I think I slept for five hours in four days, I got into a routine of not sleeping. I was a wreck. I had nothing left when he came. Just for a little while I couldn't…didn't need, for just a little time to give you anything more. I was going to read for a few hours or watch some rubbish on Tv, then he came. I hate him for it. I hate myself because I was so fucking easy.'

They had gone to bed on their return from their walk to the apartment; The moment they were through the door Ayesha had led Saskia by the hand to her bedroom; she had initiated sex, removing her clothes with an assuredness that she did not feel. Gambling with her pride that Saskia would not reject intimacy on the bed on which she had surprised her with Khalid. She had given a little joyful laugh when Saskia returned her kiss; making Saskia pull back, and peer curiously at her; after that Saskia laughed softly, amused at her joy.

Hunger drove them from the bed. Ayesha suggested Pasta Bolognese. Saskia made an expected phone call to Bacchus House; to her surprise it was Theodor Bacchus who answered. As usual it was a brief conversation. Afterwards she went into the kitchen; she appeared quite excited. Ayesha was stirring ingredients into bubbling pasta sauce, she paused and set her head on one side, her expression curious.

'We have been invited to dinner,' Saskia announced. 'With the Bacchus's; tomorrow at Seven. And we've been invited to stay overnight. I said yes.' She grinned.

# Nine

Bacchus house was huge and oozed mystery; Saskia would have liked nothing better than to explore. But the invitation did not extend to that, and Selene did not offer a tour. The Bacchus's were used to entertaining and having guests stay over, and Selene was a good, if unenthusiastic host for her father. They were given a stylish room with a cool on suite. Selene came for them at seven. She was in a white above the knee camisole dress that showed off a toned figure. Connie, Bacchus's housekeeper, proved to be a superb chef. Selene and Ayesha discovered a mutual liking for antiquities and design, Bacchus, and Saskia shared their enthusiasm for antiques. After the meal Bacchus said they should have drinks in the study where there were comfortable chairs and an open fire. They could talk 'shop' for an hour, he said. He had already briefly examined Saskia's scar.

'Do you feel that your fetter has gone from inside you? Only you'll know.'

'I can't feel its pressure anymore. The hotness inside my head has disappeared. I simply know that it's gone!'

'Then tell me everything you experienced,' Bacchus invited.

Saskia found herself under sustained scrutiny from three pairs of attentive eyes. She began by describing her agonies in a very matter of fact manner. Then after a short hesitation she moved onto the very real events she had experienced during her lapses into the mini comas; a revelation to Ayesha; it was the first mention Saskia had made of her hallucinatory states; it caused her concern. It must have shown on her face she realised, because Saskia laid a reassuring hand on hers.

'I didn't want to dissect them before now, I think once is enough. I knew that we were going to talk. To be honest they aren't healthy, as you'll find. I'm a bit concerned about Selene listening in.'

'I'm old enough!' Selene said coolly. Saskia thought she detected a hint of scorn in Selene's expression.

'It's not nice stuff.'

'Don't worry about me, I've seen plenty of 'not nice stuff' I can assure you.'

Saskia glanced at Bacchus.

'Don't concern yourself about Selene,' he told her.

'Okay.' Saskia gave a little shrug, then a little cough. 'You must understand, that to me, what I'm about to tell you, was all very real. It happened. I experienced it. It was so much more than dreaming, I have memories from that other life, they are fading, but they were tangible.'

Saskia related the events she had experienced during her mini comas. Occasionally her voice faltered because it was genuine memory; mostly she was very much in control, only occasionally faltering. Ayesha watched her in silence.

'At first I thought that the abusive sexual content was a product of your psyche,' Selene remarked, when Saskia had finished. She sat forward in her chair leaning on one broad leather arm. 'Until I realised that you had tapped into an alternative reality. There were other indications, including an elevated level of lucidity, but mostly there was continuity. There were hints of mixed memory, which is interesting.'

'Why would I tap into the experiences of another me?'

'For that explanation you might need a highly experienced Psychoanalyst, familiar with magic and the boundless edge; not someone you come across every day, I might add. And I am certainly not one of those. I suggest that the alchemy accessed deep levels of your psyche and gave you access to the Boundless Edge. You went down a very deep rabbit hole. And found a version of yourself, this Nathan Xavier, and Frankenstein's monster, at the bottom.' Selene got her wine from a side table and sank back into her club chair.

'It's probable the Karloff monster became totemic,' Bacchus suggested. 'It represented the animus in your personality. In an esoteric sense the animus and the anima are where magic manifests as it transitions into the physical. I believe your psyche selected your animus to represent your magical self; it selected the Frankenstein creation in the vintage movie, which obviously left a deep impression on you, to represent the manifestation of your power, waiting and biding its time. Probably it unintentionally created a thoughtform in the alternative Saskia's reality; this eventually killed Nathan in a manner that reflected his own brutality. Your psyche selected Nathan to stand for the tyrannical nature of your fetter. It is all alchemy, of a kind.'

'You mean Nathan became my fetter?'

'It was always about your fetter. Nathan Xavier was an almost perfect manifestation of it.'

'Why not the Bran? he made it after all, Part of him existed in it; in me!'

'Although he made it and his essence chained it, it was never about him. You regarded him as pathetic; I recall; your psyche regarded him as contemptible. Nathan wanted to rule over the Wild. He was a far more suitable candidate. You set him up to be destroyed. The alternative Saskia was in rebellion. In the end it was you that killed the other Nathan. Saskia, I do believe that it was you who manifested as the Frankenstein monster that the other Saskia saw.'

'What about my mother? How did she fit in?'

'She tried to stop you, simply that,' Selene explained. 'She could only ask you. She had no power to stop you. She was fettered even after physical death.'

'Do you think it was her.'

'I'm inclined to believe so.'

Bacchus spoke at this point. 'You were making shockwaves in her personal world. If anything of her was in your fetter, or had taken residence in you, it's possible you were threatening to damage her reality beyond repair, with the action you were taking.'

'Serves her right. Are you telling me that she might still be hanging about? it won't mean I'll see more of her, will it?'

'Maybe in your dreams or perhaps your nightmares,' replied Selene, who seemed to find the possibility amusing. Saskia gave her a frosty look.

'Why did you think that I would be shocked, by what amounted to severe domestic abuse?' Selene inquired, a little frown of puzzlement delving between her ice blonde eyebrows. 'I'm sure there's much worse within a few hundred metres of us all.'

'That was my error. I underestimated you; the sexual aspect was not good, it concerned me,' Saskia replied. 'I'm sorry I rattled your cage.'

'You didn't really. I suppose it was thoughtful of you.' Selene shrugged. 'There's nothing wrong with a bit of consensual depravity. Or even pain. But Nathan was truly violent. Is your Nathan as violent? Presumably so. Did he hit you?'

'He's not my Nathan. Yes, he did hit me. And it did attract me.'

'But she attracted you more.' Selene indicated Ayesha with a little sideways glance; at which Ayesha's eyes widened in surprise.

'Selene, that's enough. Bacchus spoke softly but firmly. 'Will you pour some more wine for our guests?'

Saskia laughed, quite amused. 'It's okay.' She tapped the back of Selene's hand with a finger as she poured wine into her glass.

'I'll have to re-think you.'

'I told you that I wasn't a treasure. More Southern comfort dad?'

'We've something to add,' said Ayesha. 'Something interesting to tell you about Nathan Xavier.' She described what Amelia Bosola had told them about Nathan's recent encounters with an eldritch entity. How it followed him. That his magic had had no effect on it; that he had disappeared, according to a couple of mutual connections, and gone into hiding.

'Perhaps taken sanctuary with one of the orders,' Bacchus mused.

'That's really quite odd, considering your experiences,' Selene remarked.

'Metaphysical.' Bacchus said. 'I've always affirmed that magic is metaphysics in the raw.'

'If we are to equate the events, I think he'll re-emerge soon, if he's alive. Because whatever it was, I believe it will have stopped following him now,' Selene suggested.

'Oddly cool,' remarked Saskia. She turned her attention meaningfully on Theodor Bacchus.

'Bacchus what is in this for you? There must be some sort of quid pro quo. I've nothing to offer. You have everything in abundance. Obviously, you are wealthy and enormously powerful. I don't know how I can repay you. Selene there must have been a financial cost.' She searched Selene's face, but it remained expressionless. She moved her gaze to Theo Bacchus; his ice flow eyes met her smouldering green eyes and held them. His face took on an intensity she had not seen before in him.

'Hal asked me to do this for you. I said I would attempt it. It's been successful. I hope that your magical ability is restored. But I can't do anything about that. I believe it will be, I simply don't know when. What I do ask of you, both of you, is amity. The Lhoegyr is an ancient division between northern and southern practitioners of magic. Only the orders keep it relevant. In my opinion it is obsolete. It has artificially divided a society for centuries. I would like to see it gone. Hal Bosola and others are of the same mind. You, Saskia Challoner, own the Wild, which is a powerful magical asset, if you can access its secrets. Eventually you may become a force to be reckoned with. In the name of common sense, please do not actively perpetuate the Lhoegyr. Talk to Hal. Holly Penn. There are others. Your covenant now has fourteen seals. From both sides of the Lhoegyr. And others will add theirs. I'm not asking you for a decision, I am asking you for good will.'

'Then down with the Lhoegyr,' replied Saskia, instantly.

*

'I'm going to spend some time in Thirsk,' Saskia announced unexpectedly. It was during their homeward journey the next morning.

'I want to get to know Mocking-beck house and I want to go through the contents.' They were the first words she had spoken since leaving greater London; they had just passed the sign for Grantham. She had appeared introspective all morning, and Ayesha had wondered if she had become cool towards her again. It seemed to come and go. Now she had the answer.

'I see! Am I invited?'

Saskia remained silent, as though unsure how to reply. Ayesha glanced at her and saw that she was observing her, very much in the praying mantis persona that had earned her Ayesha's pet name for her. Saskia's expression was obscure, her eyes impassive.

'I take it that I'm not. You don't want me there.' Ayesha's mouth had gone dry, she felt suddenly vulnerable. She decided to tread very cautiously.

'I want to do it on my own. In fact, I want some time on my own, I did mention it at the party.' Saskia explained.

'Yes, I recall you announced something about it, before you had even run it by me first!' Time on her own, Ayesha did not like the sound of that.

'I'm sorry, it was insensitive of me.'

'I get it! you want some space after everything that's happened. The Khalid thing! You need to get away from me.'

'I wouldn't put it like that. Are you okay with it?'

'I'll have to be. How long?'

'I don't know.'

'Days?'

'Yes.'

'Weeks?'

'Maybe. I'm sorry.'

'So am I.' Ayesha blinked at tears. It was a hammer blow to her; it had come out of nowhere and she felt sick. She wondered if she should put up more of a fight. Maybe not right then.

'Did Diz Cardray-Adams make an inventory? I presume she did.'

*God that was cold blooded*! Ayesha thought. Here she was, falling to bits over Saskia's announcement, and all Saskia was interested in, was inventories.

Ayesha's lips felt numb as she replied. The words did not feel as though they belonged to her. 'There is an inventory, a list of the higher value items. And the larger items and furniture. The rest was classified as sundries, and she gave them an overall value. I'll get you a copy.'

'Good. I liked the feel of the place when you took me there. I liked its atmosphere. I thought at the time it would be a lovely place to live.'

They finished the rest of the journey almost in silence. The rest of the day passed similarly. They ate together quietly and went to bed together. Saskia surprised Ayesha by initiating lovemaking, kissing her shoulders and neck tenderly from behind her; she had thought that they would not be intimate that night, after Saskia's distance towards her. Ayesha responded eagerly; she experienced a heightened sense of Saskia as she searched for indications and subliminal meanings within her caresses and kisses and intimacies. She discovered nothing that had not existed before or anything that no longer existed. It was beautiful again and she became lost in its magic. Shortly after two a.m. Saskia woke up and found that Ayesha was no longer beside her. She was not in the on suite and she went to look for her. She found her naked in the darkness, knelt in the vast window in the living room; she appeared small as she gazed out over the lights; her hands were clasped in her lap; She was crying softly.

'You're going to break up with me, aren't you?' Ayesha said as Saskia dropped to her knees beside her; her voice had fallen almost to a whisper.

'Is that what you think?'

'It's what I believe.' Ayesha felt a mixture of dismay and resentment.

'I promise you; I am not breaking up with you.'

Ayesha's voice faltered when she responded, she reached out for her lover's hand and rested the side of her head against her shoulder.

'I don't know if I believe you.'

## Addendum

The Bran cried out in his sleep, making a plaintive sound, and woke himself. He lay panting, and shaking, soaked in sweat, with misery tears streaming from his eyes. He felt overwhelming panic, overwhelming dread. He climbed to the edge of the bed on trembling legs, frightened by the hammer blows of his own heart. This was the fourth consecutive night he had woken like this, the fourth night he'd experienced nightmares and dreamed of his own horrific death. Because he was the man he was, he wondered if the dreams were prophetic and forewarned of his own real death, though he knew instinctively that part of him had already died. He knew the Alchemist had been successful in removing the fetter from Saskia Challoner, that all the threads of himself that he had woven within her had been poisoned to death, and the essence of himself that resided within them, had returned to haunt him. He wiped the sweat from his face with his fingers and palms and reached for the half bottle of whisky that stood next to the bed, his only solace. Broacha was distancing herself, she had allowed him no sense of her in recent days. Broacha did not begrudge him the relief contained in the bottle of spirit, she watched over him as she had always done, though her displeasure with him was very real, and for the present she allowed him no sense of her; it would pass however and then she would take away his nightmares, and give herself to him again, and wait patiently for the darker things that would eventually come for him, to take their place.

I make no excuse for being inspired by the Triptych: 'The garden of earthly delights' by Hieronymus Bosch, in the creating of the Pandemonium scene, in Claire's Garden,

Printed in Dunstable, United Kingdom